KU-003-828

LIBRARIES NI
WITHDRAWN FROM STOCK

# THE

# FLIGHT

# JULIE CLARK

HODDER &
STOUGHTON

First published in Great Britain in 2020 by Hodder & Stoughton
An Hachette UK company

3

Copyright © Julie Clark 2020

The right of Julie Clark to be identified as the Author of
the Work has been asserted by her in accordance with
the Copyright, Designs and Patents Act 1988.

All rights reserved. No part of this publication may be reproduced, stored
in a retrieval system, or transmitted, in any form or by any means without
the prior written permission of the publisher, nor be otherwise circulated
in any form of binding or cover other than that in which it is published and
without a similar condition being imposed on the subsequent purchaser.

All characters in this publication are fictitious and any resemblance
to real persons, living or dead, is purely coincidental.

A CIP catalogue record for this title is available from the British Library

Hardback ISBN 978 1 529 38475 8
Trade Paperback ISBN 978 1 529 38476 5
eBook ISBN 978 1 529 38473 4

Printed and bound in Great Britain by Clays Ltd, Elcograf S.p.A.

Hodder & Stoughton policy is to use papers that are natural, renewable
and recyclable products and made from wood grown in sustainable
forests. The logging and manufacturing processes are expected to
conform to the environmental regulations of the country of origin.

Hodder & Stoughton Ltd
Carmelite House
50 Victoria Embankment
London EC4Y 0DZ

www.hodder.co.uk

*Dedicated to all the women who have come forward with their stories. Whether it be in front of a congressional panel on live television or alone in a windowless human resources office—we hear you. We believe you.*

Tell me about despair, yours, and I will tell you mine.
Meanwhile the world goes on.

—Mary Oliver, *Wild Geese*

# PROLOGUE

John F. Kennedy Airport, New York
Tuesday, February 22
**The Day of the Crash**

*Terminal 4 swarms with people, the smell of wet wool and jet fuel thick around me. I wait for her, just inside the sliding glass doors, the frigid winter wind slamming into me whenever they open, and instead force myself to visualize a balmy Puerto Rican breeze, laced with the scent of hibiscus and sea salt. The soft, accented Spanish swirling around me like a warm bath, blotting out the person I was before.*

*The air outside rumbles as planes lift into the sky, while inside garbled announcements blare over the loudspeaker. Somewhere behind me, an older woman speaks in sharp, staccato Italian. But I don't look away from the curb, my eyes trained on the crowded sidewalk outside the terminal, searching for her, anchoring my belief—and my entire future—on the fact that she will come.*

*I know only three things about her: her name, what she looks like, and that her flight departs this morning. My advantage—she doesn't know anything about me. I fight down panic that I might have missed her somehow. That she might already be gone, and with her, the opportunity for me to slip out of this life and into a new one.*

*People disappear every day. The man standing in line at Starbucks, buying his last cup of coffee before he gets into his car and drives into a new life, leaving behind a family who will always wonder what happened. Or the woman sitting in the last row of a Greyhound bus, staring out the window as the wind blows strands of hair across her face, wiping away a history too heavy to carry. You might be shoulder to shoulder with someone living their last moments as themselves and never know it.*

*But very few people actually stop to consider how difficult it is to truly vanish. The level of detail needed to eliminate even the tiniest trace. Because there's always something. A small thread, a seed of truth, a mistake. It only takes a tiny pinprick of circumstance to unravel it all. A phone call at the moment of departure. A fender bender three blocks before the freeway on-ramp. A canceled flight.*

*A last-minute change of itinerary.*

*Through the plate glass window, fogged with condensation, I see a black town car glide to the curb and I know it's her, even before the door opens and she steps out. When she does, she doesn't say goodbye to whoever is in the back seat with her. Instead, she scurries across the pavement and through the sliding doors, so close her pink cashmere sweater brushes against my arm, soft and inviting. Her shoulders are hunched, as if waiting for the next blow, the next attack. This is a woman who knows how easily a fifty-thousand-dollar rug can shred the skin from her cheek. I let her pass and take a deep breath, exhaling my tension. She's here. I can begin.*

*I lift the strap of my bag over my shoulder and follow, slipping into the security line directly in front of her, knowing that people on the run only look behind them, never ahead. I listen, and wait for my opening.*

*She doesn't know it yet, but soon, she will become one of the vanished. And I will fade, like a wisp of smoke into the sky, and disappear.*

# CLAIRE

Monday, February 21
**The Day before the Crash**

"Danielle," I say, entering the small office that sits adjacent to our living room. "Please let Mr. Cook know I'm going to the gym."

She looks up from her computer, and I see her gaze snag on the bruise along the base of my throat, concealed with a thin layer of makeup. I automatically adjust my scarf to cover it, knowing she won't mention it. She never does.

"We have a meeting at Center Street Literacy at four," she says. "You'll be late again." Danielle keeps track of my calendar and my missteps, and I've pegged her as the one most likely to report when I don't arrive on time to meetings, or when I cancel appointments that my husband, Rory, deems important. *If I'm going to run for Senate, we don't have the luxury of making mistakes, Claire.*

"Thank you, Danielle. I can read the calendar as well as you can.

Please have my notes from the last meeting uploaded and ready to go. I'll meet you there." As I leave the room, I hear her pick up the phone and my step falters, knowing this might draw attention at a time when I can't afford it.

People always ask what it's like being married into the Cook family, a political dynasty second only to the Kennedys. I deflect with information about our foundation, trained to keep my focus on the work instead of the rumors. On our third-world literacy and water initiatives, the inner-city mentoring programs, the cancer research.

What I can't tell them is that it's a constant battle to find any privacy. Even inside our home, people are there at all hours. Assistants. Household staff who cook and clean for us. I have to fight for every spare minute and every square inch to call my own. There is nowhere that's safe from the eyes of Rory's staff, all of them devoted Cook employees. Even after ten years of marriage, I'm still the interloper. The outsider who needs to be watched.

I've learned how to make sure there's nothing to see.

The gym is one of the few places Danielle doesn't follow, trailing after me with her lists and schedules. It's where I meet Petra, the only friend I have left from my life before Rory, and the only one Rory hasn't forced me to abandon.

Because as far as Rory knows, Petra doesn't exist.

---

When I arrive at the gym, Petra is already there. I change in the locker room, and when I climb the stairs to the rows of treadmills, she's on the landing, taking a clean towel from the stack. Our eyes meet for a moment, and then she looks away as I help myself to a towel.

"Are you nervous?" she whispers.

"Terrified," I say, turning and walking away.

I run for an hour, my eyes on the clock, and when I step into the sauna at exactly two thirty with a towel wrapped around my body, my muscles ache with exhaustion. The air is thick with steam, and I smile at Petra, who sits alone on the top row, her face red with heat.

"Do you remember Mrs. Morris?" she asks when I sit down next to her.

I smile, grateful to think of something from a simpler time. Mrs. Morris was our government teacher in the twelfth grade, and Petra almost failed the class.

"You studied with me every afternoon for a month," she continues. "When none of the other kids would come near me or Nico because of who our father was, you stepped up and made sure I graduated."

I turn on the wooden bench to face her. "You make it sound like you and Nico were pariahs. You had friends."

Petra shakes her head. "People being nice to you because your father is the Russian version of Al Capone doesn't make them friends." We'd attended an elite school in Pennsylvania, where the children and grand-children of old money viewed Petra and her brother, Nico, as a novelty, sliding up to them, as if on a dare, to see how close they could get, but never letting either of them all the way in.

And so we'd formed a trio of outcasts. Petra and Nico made sure no one made fun of my secondhand uniform or the beat-up Honda my mother used to pick me up in, rattling its way to the curb, belching exhaust in its wake. They made sure I didn't eat alone and dragged me to school events I'd have skipped otherwise. They put themselves between me and the other kids, the ones who made cruel, cutting remarks about how I was merely a day student on scholarship, too poor, too common to truly be one of them. Petra and Nico were friends to me at a time when I had none.

---

It felt like fate, the day I walked into the gym two years ago and saw Petra, an apparition from my past. But I wasn't the same person Petra would remember from high school. Too much had changed. Too much I'd have to explain about my life and what I'd lost along the way. And so I'd kept my gaze averted, while Petra's stare drilled into me, willing me to look up. To acknowledge her.

When my workout was over, I made my way to the locker room, hoping to hide out in the sauna until after Petra had left. But when I'd entered, she was there. As if that had been our plan all along.

"Claire Taylor," she said.

Hearing her say my old name made me smile despite myself. Memories came rushing back, found in the tone and cadence of Petra's voice that still carried a trace of the Russian she spoke at home. In an instant, I had felt like my old self, not the persona I'd cultivated over the years as Rory's wife, glossy and unknowable, burying her secrets beneath a hard surface.

We started slowly, making small talk that quickly turned personal as we caught up on the years since we'd last seen each other. Petra had never married. Instead, she drifted through life, supported by her brother, who now ran the family organization.

"And you," she said, gesturing toward my left hand. "You're married?"

I studied her through the steam, surprised she didn't know. "I married Rory Cook."

"Impressive," Petra said.

I looked away, waiting for her to ask what people always asked— what really happened to Maggie Moretti, the name that will forever be linked to my husband's, the girl who'd catapulted from anonymity to infamy simply because, long ago, she'd once loved Rory.

But Petra just leaned back on her bench and said, "I saw that interview he did with Kate Lane on CNN. The work he's done with the foundation is remarkable."

"Rory is very passionate." A response that conveyed truth, if anyone cared to dig deeper.

"How are your mom and sister? Violet must be done with college by now."

I'd been dreading that question. Even after so many years, the loss of them was still sharp. "They died in a car accident fourteen years ago. Violet had just turned eleven." I kept my explanation brief. A rainy Friday night. A drunk driver who ran a stop sign. A collision in which they both died instantly.

"Oh, Claire," Petra had said. She didn't offer platitudes or force me to rehash things. Instead she sat with me, letting the silence hold my grief, knowing there was nothing that could be said that would make it hurt less.

––––––––––––

It became our routine, to meet in the sauna every day after our workouts. Petra understood that because of who her family was, we couldn't be seen talking in public. Even before we knew what I was going to eventually do, we'd been cautious, rarely communicating by phone and never by email. But in the sauna, we resurrected our friendship, rebuilding the trust we used to share, remembering the alliance that had gotten us both through high school.

It didn't take long for Petra to also see what I was hiding. "You need to leave him, you know," she'd said one afternoon, several months after we'd first met. She was looking at a bruise on my upper left arm, the remnant of an argument Rory and I'd had two nights earlier. Despite my efforts to hide the evidence—a towel pulled higher around my chest, hung around my neck, or draped across my shoulders—Petra had silently watched the progression of Rory's rage across my skin. "That's not the first one of those I've seen on you."

I covered the bruise with my towel, not wanting her pity. "I tried to, once. About five years ago." I'd believed it was possible to leave my marriage. I'd prepared myself for a fight, knowing it would be messy and expensive, but I'd use his abuse as leverage. *Give me what I want and I'll stay silent about the kind of man you are.*

But it hadn't happened that way at all. "Turns out, the woman I'd confided in, who'd tried to help me, was married to an old fraternity brother of Rory's. And when Rory showed up, her husband opened the door and let him in, *old boy*-ing himself right alongside Rory, secret handshake and all. Rory told them I was struggling with depression, working with a psychiatrist, and that maybe it was time for something inpatient."

"He was going to have you committed?"

"He was letting me know that things could get a lot worse." I didn't tell Petra the rest. Like how, when we'd gotten home, he'd shoved me so hard into the marble counter in our kitchen, I'd cracked two ribs. *Your selfishness astonishes me. That you'd be willing to destroy all I've worked to build—my mother's legacy—because we argue. All couples argue, Claire.* He'd gestured around the room, to the high-end appliances, the expensive countertops, and said, *Look around you. What more could you possibly want? No one is going to feel sorry for you. No one will even believe you.*

Which was true. People wanted Rory to be who they thought he was—the charismatic son of the progressive and beloved Senator Marjorie Cook. I could never tell anyone what he did to me, because no matter what I'd say or how loudly I'd say it, my words would be buried beneath the love everyone felt for Marjorie Cook's only child.

"People will never see what I see," I finally said.

"You really believe that?"

"Do you think if Carolyn Bessette came forward accusing JFK Junior of hitting her, the country would have rushed to support her?"

Petra's eyes widened. "Are you kidding me? This is the #MeToo era. I think people would be falling all over themselves to believe her. They'd probably create new Fox and CNN shows just to talk about it."

I gave a hollow laugh. "In a perfect world, I'd hold Rory accountable. But I don't have it in me to take on a fight like that. One that would go on for years, that would seep into every corner of my life and tarnish anything good that might come afterward. I just want to be free of it. Of him."

To speak out against Rory would be like stepping into an abyss and trusting that I'd be caught by the generosity and kindness of others. And I'd lived too many years with people happily watching me free fall if it meant they could be close to Rory. In this world, money and power were equivalent to immunity.

I took a long breath and felt the steam reach down into my deepest corners. "If I left him, I'd have to do it in a way where he could never find me. Look what happened to Maggie Moretti."

The edges of Petra's face were blurry through the steam that billowed between us, but I could see her gaze sharpen. "Do you think he had something to do with that?"

"I don't know what to believe anymore," I answered.

---

Over the next year, Petra and I assembled a plan, choreographing my disappearance more carefully than a ballet. A sequence of events so perfectly timed, there could be no room for error, and now I sit, hours away from executing it. The hiss of steam clouds the air around us, Petra just a faint shadow on the cedar bench next to me. "Did you mail everything this morning?" I ask her.

"FedEx, addressed to you, labeled 'Personal.' It should arrive at the hotel first thing tomorrow."

I couldn't risk hiding all I'd gathered at my house, where anyone—the maids, or worse, Danielle—might find it. So Petra kept everything— forty thousand dollars of Rory's money and a brand new identity, thanks to Nico.

"The new government technology is making it harder to make these," he'd said, the afternoon I'd driven out to see him. We were sitting at his dining room table in his large home on Long Island. He'd grown into a handsome man, with a wife and three kids. And bodyguards— two posted at his gated driveway and another two at his front door. It occurred to me that Rory and Nico were not so different. Each of them the chosen son, pushed to carry the family into the twenty-first century, with new rules and regulations. Both expected to do more than the last generation—or at the very least, not lose everything.

Nico slid a fat envelope toward me, and I opened it, pulling out a pristine Michigan driver's license and a passport with my face and the name *Amanda Burns*. I flipped through the rest—a social security card, a birth certificate, and a credit card.

"You'll be able to do anything with these," Nico said, picking up the driver's license and tilting it under the light so I could see the hologram embossed on the surface. "Vote. Pay taxes. Fill out a W-2 form. This is high-level stuff, and my guy is the best. There's only one other person who can make a full package this good, and he lives in Miami." Nico handed me the credit card—a Citibank account with my new name on it. "Petra opened this last week, and the statements will be sent to her address. When you get settled, you can change it. Or toss this card and open a new one. Just be careful. You don't want someone to steal your identity."

He laughed at his joke, and I could see the boy he used to be flash across his face, sitting next to Petra and me at lunch, eating his sandwich while doing his math homework, the weight of who he was expected to become already bearing down on him.

"Thanks, Nico." I passed him the envelope containing ten thousand dollars, a small fraction of the money I'd managed to siphon off and squirrel away over the past six months. One hundred dollars here. Another two hundred there. Cash back whenever I could, slipping the money into Petra's gym locker every day so she could hold it until I was ready.

His expression grew serious. "I need you to know that if something goes wrong, I can't help you. Petra can't help you. Your husband has resources that would put me, my livelihood—and Petra's—at risk."

"I understand," I told him. "You've done more than enough, and I'm grateful."

"I'm serious. All it takes is one tiny thread connecting your new life to your old one and it'll all fall apart." His dark eyes latched onto mine and held. "You can never go back. Not once. Not in any way, ever."

———————

"Rory's scheduled the plane to leave around ten," I tell Petra now. "Did you remember to include my letter? I don't want to have to rewrite it on hotel stationery ten minutes before I leave."

She nods. "In with the rest of it. Addressed and stamped, ready to be mailed from Detroit. What did you say?"

I think about the hours I'd spent, the many versions I'd shredded, drafting a letter that would close the door on any possibility that Rory might try to follow me. "I told him I was leaving, and that this time, he would never find me. That he should announce our separation publicly, tell them it was amicable and that I was not going to be giving any public statements or media interviews about it."

"One week before he announces his run for Senate."

I give her a smirk. "Should I have waited until after?"

Once I'd saved enough money to carry me into a new life, I began to look for the perfect opening to leave. I studied our Google calendar of upcoming events, searching for a trip I'd be taking alone, focusing on cities near the Canadian or Mexican borders. I found it in the Detroit trip. I'm scheduled to visit Citizens of the World, a social justice charter school funded by the Cook Family Foundation. An afternoon school tour followed by an evening dinner with donors.

I lean back on the bench behind me and stare up at the ceiling, obscured by a layer of steam, and run through the rest of the plan. "We land around noon. The school event starts at two, so I'll make sure we go to the hotel first so I can get the package and put it somewhere safe."

"I called the car rental place. They're expecting a Ms. Amanda Burns to pick up a compact around midnight tonight. Will you be able to get a cab?"

"There's a Hilton just down the road from where I'm staying. I'll catch one from there."

"I worry about someone seeing you leave with a suitcase in the middle of the night. Following you. Calling Rory."

"I'm not taking it. I bought a backpack big enough for a couple changes of clothes and my money. I'm leaving everything else—including my purse and wallet—behind."

Petra nods. "If you need it, I booked a room with the credit card at the W in Toronto. They're expecting you."

I close my eyes, the heat making me woozy. Or perhaps it's the pressure of having to get every detail exactly right. There's no room for even the tiniest mistake.

I feel the minutes slipping away. Pushing me toward the moment when I'll take the first step in a series of steps that will be irrevocable. A part of me wants to forget it all. Go to Detroit, visit the school, and come home. Have more days in the sauna talking to Petra. But this is my chance to finally get out. Whatever options I have now will narrow to nothing once Rory announces his run for the Senate.

"Time to go." Petra's voice is soft, and my eyes open again.

"I don't know how to thank you," I tell her.

"You were my only friend all those years ago. You don't have to thank me. This is me, thanking you," she says. "It's your turn to be happy." She tightens her towel around her body, and I can see the flash of her smile through the steam.

I can't believe this is the last time we'll sit here. The last time we'll talk. This room has been like a sanctuary, dark and quiet, with just our whispered voices, plotting my escape. Who will sit here tomorrow with her? Or the day after that?

I feel the finality of my departure looming, how absolute that ending will be, and I wonder if it'll be worth it. If it'll be better. Soon, Claire Cook will cease to exist, the shiny pieces of her facade cracked and discarded. I have no idea what I'll find underneath it all.

*Thirty-three hours until I'm gone.*

# CLAIRE

**Monday, February 21**
**The Day before the Crash**

I meet Danielle outside the Center Street Literacy offices, fifteen minutes late. "Not a word," I warn her, though I know she's probably already texted Rory three times.

She trails me through the doors and into the large common area they use for book talks and writing workshops. The room is busy at this hour, filled with students and tutors. I imagine how different it would be if Rory were passing through, the wave of excited murmuring, starting at the front and rippling backward as he made his way into the space. But no one gives me a second look. Without Rory, I'm just another face, there and gone. Unremarkable. Which will be my advantage very soon.

I pass through and up a set of stairs to the second floor, which houses the Center Street administrative offices, and into the small conference room where everyone is already assembled.

"So nice to see you, Mrs. Cook," the director says with a warm smile.

"You too, Anita. Shall we get started?" I take my seat, Danielle directly behind me. The meeting begins with a discussion of the annual fundraiser coming up in eight months' time. I can barely bring myself to feign enthusiasm for an event that will occur long after my disappearance. I amuse myself by imagining what the next meeting will be like. Quiet talk about how I left Rory, how I never let on there was any trouble, that I smiled through this meeting and then vanished. *Where did she go? A person doesn't just walk out of her life and disappear. Why can't anyone find her?* Which one of them will be the first to bring up Maggie Moretti? To whisper the question that every single one of them will wonder, if only for a moment: *Do you think she really left him, or do you think something happened to her?*

―――――――――――

Rory had told me about Maggie Moretti on our third date.

"Everyone always asks me what happened," he'd said, leaning back in his chair and crossing his legs. "It was a tragedy, from beginning to end, and I still don't think I'm completely over it." He picked up his wine and swirled it in the glass before taking a sip. "We'd been fighting nonstop, and Maggie wanted us to get away for a quiet weekend. To reconnect and really talk without the distractions of the city. But nothing was different there; we were just rehashing the same old stuff, except in a new location." His voice had grown quieter, the sounds of the restaurant receding. The way he spoke—the emotion in his voice—felt so raw and real. It didn't occur to me at the time that he could possibly be lying. "Finally, I got fed up and left. I jumped into my car and drove back to Manhattan. Several hours later, our neighbors upstate called 911 and reported the house was on fire. They found her crumpled at the base of a staircase. I had no idea anything had happened until the police contacted me the following morning. It wasn't in the papers at the time, but the coroner found smoke in her lungs, which meant she was alive when the fire started. I'll never forgive myself for leaving when I did. I could have saved her."

"Why did they think you'd been involved?"

He'd shrugged. "It makes for a better story. I get it, and I don't begrudge the media, although my father never forgave the *New York Times*. It was a blessing my mother wasn't alive to see it, to worry about what it would do to her polling numbers." His bitterness surprised me, but he covered it quickly. "The real shame is what it did to Maggie's memory. Because of me, the whole world knows her name for all the wrong reasons. For how she died, not for who she was." He looked out the window next to us, lost in regret. Beyond it, the New York street sparkled in a soft drizzle, the lights glittering like jewels in the dark. Then he pulled himself back and drained his glass. "I don't resent the police for doing their job. I understand they did what they felt they had to do. I was lucky that justice prevailed, because it doesn't always. But the experience shook me."

The waiter had approached, clearly waiting for a break in the conversation to slip the black sleeve containing the bill in front of Rory, who'd smiled that warm, charming smile that cracked my heart in half, wanting more than anything for him to feel for me what he once felt for Maggie Moretti.

---

"Mrs. Cook, would you be willing to chair the silent auction again this year?" Anita Reynolds, the director of Center Street Literacy, looks down the long table at me.

"Absolutely," I say. "Let's meet on Friday and figure out who we can start approaching for donations. I've got a quick trip to Detroit, but I'll be back by then. Two o'clock?" She nods and I enter the appointment in the shared Google calendar, knowing it will pop up on Danielle's iPad right behind me and Rory's computer at home. These are the details I have to remember—scheduling appointments, ordering flowers, making plans for a future I won't be living. Details that will cover my tracks and keep everyone believing I'm a devoted wife, committed to the many important causes championed by the Cook Family Foundation.

*Thirty-one hours.*

———————————

When I return home, I head upstairs to change my clothes and see that Danielle has repacked my bag while I was at the gym. Gone are the trendy clothes that I prefer, replaced with the more conservative suits and three-inch heels Rory likes me to wear.

I lock the bedroom door and step into my closet, reaching into a tall pair of boots and pulling out the nylon backpack I paid cash for at a sporting goods store last week. Flattening it, I slip it beneath the zippered lining of my suitcase. One piece at a time, I remove the clothes I plan to take with me from their hiding places and pack them. A form-fitted down jacket, several long-sleeved T-shirts, and an NYU baseball cap I bought the other day to hide my face from hotel lobby security cameras. I pull my favorite pair of jeans from their place on the shelf and slide everything beneath what Danielle packed for the event. Just enough to get me through the next day or two. Not enough for anyone to notice items missing from my drawers or closet. I zip the bag closed and place it by the door and sit down on the bed, relishing the solitude of a locked room.

It still amazes me how I ended up here. So far from home, from the person I once thought I'd become. I have a summa cum laude from Vassar with a degree in art history. I landed a coveted job at Christie's.

But those years had been hard and lonely. I'd been numb, struggling to stay afloat since my mother and Violet had died, and falling in love with Rory felt like waking up. He understood what I'd lost, because he carried his own grief. He was someone who understood the way memories could creep up on you and squeeze until you had no breath. No words. When the only thing you could do was wait for the pain to subside, like a tide, allowing you to move again.

---

Outside my locked bedroom door, I hear people in the hallway, their voices a low murmur I can't make out. I tense, waiting to see if they'll try to enter, bracing myself for another lecture about locked doors. *They can't do their jobs, Claire, if you insist on locking yourself in every room.* Downstairs, the front door closes and Rory's voice floats up to me. I smooth my hair and count to ten, trying to wipe the anxiety and nerves from my face. I have one night left, and I have to play the part perfectly.

"Claire!" he calls from the hallway. "Are you home?"

I take a deep breath and open the bedroom door. "Yes," I call.

*Twenty-eight hours.*

---

"How is Joshua doing this semester?" Rory asks our chef, Norma, as she pours our wine at dinner.

Norma smiles and sets the bottle on the table next to Rory. "Very well, though I don't hear from him as much as I'd like to."

Rory laughs and takes a small sip, nodding his approval. "That's how it's supposed to be, I'm afraid. Tell him I'm hoping for another semester on the dean's list."

"I will, sir. Thank you. We're so grateful."

Rory waves her words away. "I'm happy to do it."

Many years ago, Rory decided to pay college tuition for every child or grandchild of his household staff. As a result, they are fiercely loyal to him. Willing to look the other way when our arguments grow loud, or when they hear me crying in the bathroom.

"Claire, try this wine. It's incredible."

I know better than to disagree with him. Once, early in our marriage, I'd said, "It tastes like fermented grapes to me."

Rory's expression had remained impassive, as if my words hadn't registered. But he'd lifted my glass from the table, held it in an outstretched hand, and then dropped it to the floor where it shattered, red wine puddling on the hardwood and rolling toward the expensive rug underneath the table. Norma had come running from the kitchen at the sound of breaking glass.

"Claire is so clumsy," he'd said, reaching across the table to squeeze my hand. "It's one of the things I love about her."

Norma, who was crouched down cleaning up the mess, looked up at me, confused about how my glass had ended up on the floor three feet away from the table. I'd been mute, unable to say anything as Rory calmly began eating his dinner.

Norma carried the soggy towels into the kitchen, then returned with another wineglass and poured me more. When she'd gone, Rory set down his fork and said, "This is a four-hundred-dollar bottle of wine. You need to try harder."

Now, as Rory stares at me, waiting, I take a tiny sip from my glass, trying and failing to find oak undertones or the hint of vanilla Rory claims are there. "Delicious," I say.

After tomorrow, I'm only drinking beer.

———

When we're done eating, we move into Rory's office to go over a few talking points for the speech I'm giving at tomorrow night's dinner. We sit, facing each other across his desk, me with my laptop balanced on my knees, my speech pulled up in a shared Google doc. This is Rory's preferred platform. He uses it for everything, since it allows him to access anything any of us is working on, at any moment. I'll be working on something and suddenly I'll see his icon pop up on my screen and I'll know he is there, watching me.

It's also how he and his long-time personal assistant, Bruce, communicate without documenting anything. In a shared doc, they can say things to each other that they might not want to put into an email or text message, or say over the phone. I've only seen and heard little snippets over the years. *I left you a note about that in the Doc.* Or *Check the Doc, I put an update in there you're going to want to read.* The Doc is where they'll discuss my disappearance, hypothesize about where I went, and perhaps outline their plan to track me down. It's like a private room that only Rory and Bruce can access, where they can speak freely about things that no one else can know about.

I bring my attention back, asking several questions about the group I'll be speaking to, focusing my energy on the success of the event. Bruce huddles in his corner of the office, taking notes on his laptop, adding our comments into the speech as we speak, and I watch him on my own screen, a cursor with his name attached to it, the words appearing as if by magic. As he types away, I wonder how much he knows about what Rory does to me. Bruce is the keeper of all Rory's secrets. I can't imagine he doesn't know this one as well.

When we're done, Rory says to me, "They're going to ask you about next week's press conference. Don't answer any questions. Just smile and bring the conversation back around to the foundation."

The buildup to announcing Rory's candidacy has been excruciating. Leaked rumors every few days, tons of media speculation about Rory picking up where his mother left off.

20

Marjorie Cook had been famous for her bipartisan negotiating skills, her ability to swing the most difficult and conservative senators toward more moderate policy. There had been quiet talk of a presidential run, long before Hillary or even Geraldine Ferraro. But Marjorie had died of colon cancer Rory's freshman year of college, forever leaving a mother-shaped hole that filled with a potent combination of insecurity and resentment that often bubbled over, burning those who dared to keep his mother in the foreground when discussing his political future.

"You haven't given me any details about the press conference to share," I tell them, watching Bruce pack up his desk for the night, tracking his movements from the corner of my eye. Pens in the top drawer. Laptop into its case, then into his bag to take home.

After Bruce leaves, Rory sits back and crosses his legs. "How was your day?"

"Good." My left foot jiggles, the only indication of my nerves. Rory's gaze lands on it, eyebrows raised, and I press my heel into the carpet, willing myself to be still.

"It was Center Street Literacy, right?" He steeples his fingers, his tie loose around his neck. I watch him, as if from a great distance, this man I once loved. The lines around his eyes are evidence of laughter, of happiness that we shared. But those same lines have been deepened by rage as well. A dark violence that has blotted out everything good I once saw in him.

"Yes. Their annual fundraiser is coming up in eight months. Danielle should be transcribing the notes and will get them to you tomorrow. I'll be taking on the silent auction again."

"Anything else?" he asks. His voice is neutral, but something in the set of his shoulders grabs my attention. My instincts—finely tuned after years of reading the subtext of Rory's tone and expressions—are screaming at me to be careful.

"Not that I can think of."

"I see," he says, and then takes a deep, meditative breath, as if he's trying to center himself. "Can you please close the door?"

I stand, my legs feeling weak beneath me as I walk slowly to the door, terrified he's somehow figured out what I'm about to do. I take my time, measuring my pace, trying not to panic yet. When I sit again, I've wiped the fear from my face, replacing it with neutral curiosity. When he doesn't speak right away, I prompt him. "Is everything okay?"

His gaze is cold. "You must think I'm stupid."

I'm unable to speak, or even blink. I've lost before I've even begun. My thoughts race, trying to find a foothold, trying to compose myself, to explain away whatever he's discovered—the clothes, the money I've been siphoning off, my meetings with Petra. I fight the urge to throw open the door and run, giving up whatever I've gained. I look toward the darkened windows, reflecting the room back to us, and manage to say, "What are you talking about?"

"I heard you were late again today. May I ask why?"

I let out a slow breath, all my nerves loosening. "I was at the gym."

"The gym is less than half a mile from the Center Street offices." Rory pulls his glasses off and leans back in his desk chair. His face slips out of the puddle of light cast from his desk lamp and into darkness. "What are you not telling me?"

I suffuse my voice with a warmth I don't feel, desperate to allay his fears before they take over. "Nothing," I insist. "I decided to stay for a spin class that started at two thirty."

"With whom?"

"What do you mean, like who was the instructor?"

"Don't be obtuse," he snaps. "You're constantly either heading off to the gym, or coming back from it. It's every day now. Is it your trainer? That would be a pathetic cliché."

"I don't have a trainer," I tell him, my mouth suddenly dry and sticky. "I lift weights. Run on the treadmill, or take spin classes. I was sore after my workout, so I spent some time in the sauna and lost track of time. That's all." I fight to keep my face blank, but my hands betray me, gripping the arms of the chair as if bracing for a blow. Rory's gaze catches on them, and I force myself to relax. He stands and walks around his desk and sits in the chair next to mine.

"We have a lot of hard work ahead, Claire," he says, taking another sip of whiskey. "Starting next week, all eyes will be on us. There cannot be a trace of scandal."

I have to dig deep to deliver my line convincingly, one last time. "You don't need to worry."

Rory leans over and brushes a soft kiss across my lips and whispers, "I'm glad to hear it."

---

When Rory finally climbs into bed around eleven, I pretend to be asleep, listening to the sound of his breathing settle and slow, waiting. When the clock reads one, I ease out of bed, eager to get the final piece I need before I leave, swiping Rory's cell phone from the charger on his nightstand before I slip into the darkened hall. I can't risk his phone buzzing with a call or text, waking him up.

Our townhouse reeks of old money. Dark wood, thick rugs plush beneath my bare feet. I'm no stranger to middle-of-the-night wandering. It's the only time our home feels like mine. I move through the rooms unobserved, and as I take my final late-night stroll, I feel a sense of sadness. Not for the townhouse, which has been nothing more than a luxurious prison, but for myself.

It's a complicated grief, not just the loss of my name and identity, but also the life I once hoped I'd have. The death of any dream deserves to be mourned, all its intricate facets touched one last time.

I pass through the living room with its large windows that look down onto Fifth Avenue, glancing at the door that leads to Danielle's office, and wonder what she'll think when I go. If she'll be blamed somehow, for failing to keep track of me. Or if she'll feel bad that she didn't do more to help me when she had the chance.

I head down the narrow hall that leads to my office, a small room dominated by a heavy mahogany desk and a Turkish rug that probably costs more than what my mother's Pennsylvania house was worth. I look forward to creating a home with furniture that isn't worth six figures. I want color on the walls and plants I have to remember to water. I want mismatched plates, and glasses that don't require a complicated reordering process to replace if they break.

I glance over my shoulder, as if I expect someone to catch me in my own office in the middle of the night, reading my thoughts, knowing what I'm about to do. I listen hard, the silence a loud rush in my ears, straining to hear the hint of footsteps two floors above me. But the doorway remains empty, and the only sound is the pounding of my heart.

From my top desk drawer, I pull out the small thumb drive I used before Rory insisted everyone work in shared docs. My gaze catches on a photograph of my mother and my sister, Violet, hanging on the wall. It was taken before I left for college, before I met Rory and changed the trajectory of my life.

"We're going on a picnic," my mother had announced from the doorway of the kitchen one Saturday afternoon. Violet and I had been on the couch, watching TV. Neither of us wanted to go. We were in the middle of a *Twilight Zone* marathon. But my mother had insisted. "We don't have too many weekends left before Claire leaves," she'd said. Violet had glared at me, still angry that I'd chosen to go to Vassar instead of the local state school. "I want to spend the day outside with my girls."

Three years later, they were gone.

I'd been on the phone with my mother less than an hour before it had happened. We'd only chatted briefly, but I can still hear her voice across

24

the line, telling me she couldn't talk, that she and Violet were headed out the door for pizza and she'd call me when they got home. In the years since it happened, I've often wondered if they'd still be alive if I had kept her on the phone longer. Or perhaps, if I hadn't called at all, they might have been through the intersection and gone by the time that drunk driver flew through it.

In my dreams, I find myself there with them, the *thump-thump* of the windshield wipers, the two of them laughing together in the car, my mother singing along with the radio and Violet begging her to stop. And then a sudden screech of tires, the sound of breaking glass, the crush of metal on metal, the hiss of steam. Then silence.

---

My eyes linger now on the image of Violet, caught mid-laugh, my mother just a blurred figure in the background, and I ache to take it off the wall, to slip it between the layers of clothes in my suitcase and bring it with me, like a talisman. But I can't. And it nearly destroys my resolve to have to leave it behind.

I tear my gaze from my sister's smiling face, forever frozen at age eight, with only a few more years ahead of her, and make my way to Rory's spacious office. Lined with wood paneling topped with book-shelves, his enormous desk dominates the room. His computer sits on top of it, dark and silent, and I walk past it to a section of the bookshelves behind. I pull the red book from its spot and set it down, reaching my hand into the empty space, feeling around for the small button hidden there and pressing it. The paneling that lines the wall below the shelves pops open with a tiny click.

Danielle isn't the only one who's been taking notes.

I pull it open and slip Rory's second laptop from its hiding place. Rory doesn't keep hard copies of anything. Not receipts. Not personal notes. Not even photographs. *Hard copies are too easy to lose track of. Too hard to control*, he'd once explained to me. This machine is where everything hides. I don't know exactly what's on it, but I don't need to. No one keeps a secret laptop unless he's hiding something big. Perhaps there are financial records that outline undoctored foundation accounts or money he's siphoned off and redirected offshore. If I can get a copy of the hard drive, I'll be able to leverage it if Rory ever gets too close.

Because despite what I've directed him to do in my letter, I have no doubt Rory will go to great lengths to find me. Petra and I discussed the possibility of faking my death. An accident where the body couldn't be recovered. But Nico had warned us off that plan. "It would be all over the national news, which would make your job harder. Better to make it look like you've left him. You'll get a little bit of attention in the tabloids, but it'll fade fast."

As expected, when I open the laptop, I'm asked for a password. And while Rory has all of mine, I don't know any of his. What I do know, however, is that Rory cannot be troubled by details such as maintaining passwords. That's a job for Bruce, who keeps them in a small notebook in his desk.

I've been watching Bruce for weeks now, my eyes tracking the green notebook as he'd riffle through it, punching in passwords whenever Rory needed them. I arranged flowers on the table just outside Rory's office or searched through my purse in the doorway, tracking where Bruce kept the notebook during the workday and where it went at night.

I cross the room to Bruce's desk and run my hand along the far side, engaging the lever that releases a small drawer, the notebook nestled inside. I flip through it quickly, past account numbers and passwords to various services—Netflix, HBO, Amazon—my fingers shaking, knowing every minute, every second counts.

Finally, I find what I'm looking for near the back. *MacBook.* I type the series of numbers and letters into the computer, and I'm in. The time at the top of the screen reads one thirty as I slip the thumb drive into the USB port and start dragging files onto it, the icon showing a number in the thousands, slowly counting down. I glance at the door again, imagining all my plans coming to a halt in Rory's office, copying his secret hard drive in my pajamas, and try not to picture what he would do if he caught me. The rage I'd see in his eyes, the four quick strides he'd take until he could grab me, shoving me or dragging me out of his office, up the stairs to the privacy of our bedroom. I swallow hard.

A creak from somewhere above me—a footstep or floorboard settling—sends my heart pounding against my chest and a thin sheen of sweat to break out on my forehead. I creep into the hall and listen, holding my breath, trying to hear past the rush of panic flooding through me. But all is silent. After a few minutes I return to the computer, staring at the screen, urging it to go faster.

But then my eyes fall on Bruce's notebook again, filled with passwords that would allow me to look into every corner of Rory's life. His calendars. His email. *The Doc.* If I had access to that, I'd be able to keep an eye on them. To know what they're saying about my disappearance, to know if they're looking for me, and where. I'd be able to stay one step ahead of them.

With another glance at the empty hallway, I flip through the notebook, back several pages, until I find Rory's email password, and grab a yellow Post-it Note off Bruce's desk, copying it just as the computer finishes with the files. The clock in the downstairs entry chimes two, and I pull the thumb drive from the port and slide his computer back into its hiding place. I close the drawer with a small click and replace the red book on the shelf, return Bruce's notebook to its hiding place, and check the room for any signs that I've been there.

When I'm satisfied, I make my way back to my office. There's only one thing left to do.

I slide onto my chair, the leather cold against the backs of my legs, and open my laptop, my Detroit speech still on the screen. I close the window, knowing my icon will disappear from the top of everyone else's version, and log out of my email. When I'm back to the Gmail home-page, I sit for a minute, letting the silence of the house and the faint ticking of the hall clock wash over me. I take a deep breath and let it out, and then another, trying to steady my nerves. Trying to think through every contingency, every little thing that might go wrong. I glance at the clock again, reminding myself that at two in the morning, no one will be awake. Not Bruce. Not Danielle. Definitely not Rory. For the millionth time, I wish for a smaller house. One where the walls weren't so solid. Where the carpets didn't absorb people's footsteps so well, where I could reassure myself with the sound of Rory's soft snoring. But he's two floors above me, and I need to get this done.

I enter his email address and squint at the Post-it, carefully entering the password. Then I press return. Immediately, Rory's phone buzzes on the desk next to me, an alert lighting up the screen. *Your account has been accessed by a new device.* I swipe left to clear it, then turn to my computer, Rory's inbox in front of me. At the top of a long string of unread messages is the alert. I delete it, quickly toggling over to his trash, and delete it from there too.

My eyes scan his homepage, looking at the various folders, before clicking over to the Doc. They've labeled it *Meeting Notes*. I open it, holding my breath, wondering what I might find, but it's empty. Waiting for tomorrow. I imagine myself holed up late at night somewhere in Canada, a silent observer as Rory and Bruce deconstruct my disappear-ance, trying to figure out what happened. But more than that, I'll be privy to everything Rory and Bruce say to each other, every conversa-tion they think is private.

At the top, it reads *Last edit made by Bruce Corcoran five hours ago.* I click on it, wondering what the edit history might show, and a long list pops up on the right-hand side of the screen. *3:53 Rory Cook added a comment. 3:55 Bruce Corcoran added a comment.* But no specifics. My eyes travel down the long list to the bottom of the window, where a box that says *Show Changes* is unchecked. I hover my cursor over it, tempted, but I leave it unchecked. I'm logged in, and that's all that matters.

I click over to my computer settings, where I change my own password, making sure I'm the only one who can access it.

When I'm done, I close it and head up the stairs and back into our bedroom, where Rory still sleeps. After returning his phone to the charger, I take the thumb drive and the Post-it with his password into the master bathroom. I pull the long plastic tube of my travel toothbrush from my packed toiletry bag and twist it open, tossing the cheap toothbrush into the trash and wrapping the Post-it around the thumb drive. Then I drop them both into the tube and twist it closed again, burying it underneath my face lotion and cosmetics. With the bag zipped, I look at myself in the mirror, surrounded by the luxury Rory's money has given me. The marble counters, the deep soaking tub and shower the size of a compact car. So different from the tiny bathroom I grew up using. Violet and I used to argue about who got to use it first in the mornings, until my mother disabled the lock. "We don't have time for privacy," she'd say. I used to dream about the day when I could lock the bathroom door and spend as much time in there as I wanted. I'd give anything to go back to how it used to be, the three of us in and out, squeezing past each other in the tight space, brushing teeth, putting on makeup, drying our hair.

I won't miss any of this.

I flip off the light and make my way back into the bedroom, where I slip into bed next to my husband for the very last time.

*Twenty-two hours.*

# CLAIRE

**Tuesday, February 22**
**The Day of the Crash**

I must have slept, because the next thing I know, my alarm is yanking me awake. I blink the sleep from my eyes, taking in the room around me. The sun is up, and Rory's side of the bed is empty. The clock reads seven thirty.

I sit up, letting my nerves settle and excitement take over, before moving into the bathroom where I turn on the shower, letting steam obscure my face in the mirror. On the counter, I check again for the thumb drive, reassured that it seems to be undisturbed.

Then I step into the shower, letting the hot water pound on my back, exhilaration flooding through me. After more than a year of careful planning, constant terror that the smallest error might lead to the discovery of what I'm about to do, the moment is finally here. I'm packed. I have everything I need. Rory is gone—to the office, to a meeting, it hardly matters. All I have to do is get dressed and walk out the door one last time.

I finish quickly and wrap myself in my favorite robe, my mind already hours ahead. A quiet flight to Detroit, a school tour, and a banquet to keep me busy until everyone is asleep. A series of boxes I can check off, one at a time, until I'm free.

But I pull up short when I enter my bedroom to find Constance, the upstairs maid, lifting my suitcase onto the bed and unzipping it. She begins to remove the heavy winter clothes that are packed on top of my undergarments.

I grip my robe tight around my neck. "What are you doing?" My eyes are glued on the suitcase, tracking her hands as she pulls things out, bracing myself for what she'll find at the bottom—a nylon backpack slipped under the lining. Blue jeans that don't belong anywhere near the Detroit event. Several long-sleeved shirts and a down jacket no one has ever seen before.

But she only carries the cold-weather items back to the closet, returning with lighter things—dresses and slacks in linen, setting my bright pink cashmere sweater on the bed, a flash of color that seems out of place and much too thin for this cold February morning. She smiles at me over her shoulder as she repacks everything and says, "Mr. Corcoran would like to speak with you."

He must have been lurking in the hall, because at the mention of his name, Bruce steps into the doorway and halts, clearly uncomfortable to find me just out of the shower. "Change of plans," he says. "Mr. Cook is going to do the Detroit event himself. He wants you to go to Puerto Rico. There's an organization down there—a humanitarian group that's working on the hurricane relief effort—and he thinks it's a cause the foundation should take on."

I feel as if my entire world has shifted on its axis, gravity yanking me hard toward the center of the earth. "What did you say?"

"Mr. Cook is going to Detroit. He and Danielle left early this morning," he repeats. "He didn't want to wake you."

Constance zips my bag closed again and slips past Bruce, disappearing into the hallway.

"Your flight leaves from JFK at eleven."

"JFK?" I whisper, unable to keep up.

"Mr. Cook has taken the plane, so we had to book you on Vista Air. There's some kind of weather event brewing over the Caribbean, and it's the last flight out before they close everything down. We were lucky to get you on it." He glances at his watch. "I'll wait out here while you get dressed. We'll need to get you to the airport by nine."

He closes the door, and I sit down hard on the bed, my thoughts careening. All my plans, vanished in the few hours I slept. Everything I'd assembled, the forty thousand dollars, the fake ID from Nico, my letter, and all of Petra's help. Waiting in Detroit, where Rory will open the package and know.

———————

Somehow, I manage to get dressed, and soon we're in the back of a hired town car, heading toward the airport. Bruce runs through the itinerary, his tone just a shade less respectful than when Rory's around, but I'm barely listening, trying to grab on to something that will somehow turn this around.

My phone buzzes with a text from Rory.

> Sorry about the last-minute change of plans. We're about five minutes from the hotel. Call me when you get there and enjoy the warm weather. It's 35 degrees here.

So he doesn't know yet. Maybe there's still time to fix this. I grip my phone tight in my hand and urge the car to go faster, to get me to the airport where I can figure out what to do next.

"You'll be staying in San Juan," Bruce says, reading off a document on his phone. "You're booked for two nights at the Caribe, but Danielle says it could be three, so she'll cancel the meeting you have on Friday."

He looks up at me, so I nod, not trusting my voice to respond. Every inch of me is frantic to call Petra, to figure out how to fix this, but I'll have to wait until I'm at the airport, until the only people who might overhear my conversation are strangers.

––––––––

They drop me at the curb, Bruce giving me final instructions. "Vista Air, Flight 477," he tells me as I exit the car. "The boarding pass is on your phone, and someone will be on the other end to meet you. Call Danielle if you have any questions."

I head toward the sliding glass doors that lead into the large departure terminal for Vista Airlines, aware of the car, still idling at the curb. *Keep walking*, I instruct myself. *Be normal*. I fall into the security line that winds through several rows of travelers, unlocking my phone and scrolling through my email, looking for the Detroit itinerary Danielle sent me the other day, and dial the hotel there.

"Excelsior Hotel," the woman on the other end answers.

"Good morning," I say, trying to keep my voice calm and warm. "I was scheduled to stay at your hotel this evening, but had a change of plans. Unfortunately, I was expecting a package to arrive for me this morning, and I'd love it if you could forward it."

"Of course," says the woman. "What's your name?"

Something loosens in my chest, and I take a deep breath. I can make this right. Have her send it to the Caribe and leave from there. "Claire Cook."

"Oh, right, Mrs. Cook! Yes, the package was delivered this morning. I gave it to your husband not ten minutes ago," she chirps, no doubt still thrilled by the encounter.

I grip my phone, my vision growing spotty, and I fight hard to stay upright. I picture Rory, arriving in a swirl of activity, making his way straight to the hotel room, where he'll catch up on emails, phone calls, and review his speech. At some point, he'll remember the FedEx package. It won't matter that it's addressed to me. I can see him opening it, peering inside at the tightly bound packets of cash. Reaching in and pulling out the plain envelope that holds my new driver's license, passport, credit cards, and other forged documents. His eyes scanning the name—*Amanda Burns*—then landing on the picture of me. And a letter, stamped and addressed to him in New York, explaining everything.

"Mrs. Cook?" The woman's voice jerks me back into the present. "Can I help you with anything else?"

"No," I say, my voice no more than a whisper. "That will be all." I disconnect, letting my mind sort through the other possibilities. I could go somewhere else. Simply walk up to the counter and purchase a ticket to Miami or Nashville. But that would leave an electronic trail. All the cash I'd planned on using to erase my tracks is in Detroit. With Rory.

I scroll through my contacts until I find it. Nina's Nail Salon on Park Avenue, with Petra's number linked to it.

She answers on the third ring.

"It's me. Claire." Suddenly aware of the people around me, I lower my voice and explain what happened. "Rory changed the plans. He's sending me to Puerto Rico. And, Petra." I can barely say the words. "He's in Detroit." I'm desperately trying—and failing—to control my mounting hysteria.

"Oh my god," Petra breathes.

"I called the hotel there. They already gave the package to Rory." I swallow hard. "What am I going to do?"

The security line inches forward, and I move with it. On the phone, Petra's quiet as she thinks. "Get back outside and catch a cab here. You can stay with me until we figure something else out."

I'm just a few people away from the front of the line, my options shrinking with every minute that passes. Once Rory discovers what I was planning, he will lock down all of our accounts until he has me home again. My thoughts fly back in time, to the last time I tried to leave. I imagine the two of us at home, the evidence of what I was about to do spread before me, and what will surely happen next. Perhaps he might even follow the instructions I gave him in my letter, releasing a statement announcing our split and requesting the world respect my privacy, flipping my own plan against me. It's possible I've written my own suicide note.

"It's too close," I tell her. "Someone will see me and tell him."

"I live at the fucking Dakota. No one comes up if I don't want them to."

"So do at least three of Rory's friends," I remind her. "He is going to pull my entire life apart and study it. My bank cards. Credit cards. And cell phone records, which will now lead him straight to you. To Nico. And me, if I try to hide there." My gaze slides over the uniformed TSA agents directing people left and right toward X-ray machines. There are only three people ahead of me in line. "I think my chances of disappearing are better in Puerto Rico," I say. "So much is still off the grid after the hurricane. People will be more receptive to cash and won't ask a lot of questions." But what I don't say is how hard that will be with almost no money, on an island with limited exit points. I can't do it without some kind of help. I know I promised I wouldn't, but I have to ask. "Does Nico know anyone down there?"

Petra blows out hard, thinking. "I think so," she finally says. "I don't know much. Nico keeps me pretty far removed from the guys he does business with. But they're not nice people, Claire. And once they have you, Nico might not be able to get you out right away. Are you sure you want to do that?"

A cold sliver of dread inserts itself beneath my ribs as I imagine a dark car. A nameless face. Perhaps a cold room full of women, bound and chained. Scattered mattresses, stained and lumpy, across a concrete floor. Then I think about what rage looks like when it slips across Rory's face, of what he will do to me once he gets me alone again. The level of humiliation and outrage he will feel about what almost happened. "Call him," I say.

"Where are you staying?"

I give her the details, and I can hear her digging around in a drawer for a pen.

"Okay. Someone will contact you there. Be ready to go as soon as you hear from us."

A tremor of fear passes through me as I wonder if Nico will be able to help me. And whether I want him to.

But Petra's still giving directions. "Find an ATM and take out as much cash as possible…just in case."

I've reached the front of the line, and people are waiting for me to end my call and put everything onto the conveyor belt. "I have to go," I tell her.

"Try to stay calm," she says. "I'll be in touch as soon as I can."

And then I end the call, doubt tumbling around inside of me, feeling as if I have just slipped into a nightmare—spinning, turning, three hundred sixty degrees of danger.

# EVA

John F. Kennedy Airport, New York
Tuesday, February 22
**The Day of the Crash**

The desperation in the woman's voice was unmistakable. *It's me. Claire.* The way the words cracked when she said them, as if she were fighting back tears. Eva stood, riveted, as she listened to the hysterical unraveling of a woman in danger. A woman on the run. A woman like herself.

Eva glanced around at the travelers that surrounded them, pressing in on all sides as they wound their way through security. The family with several large suitcases that surely would have to be gate-checked. The couple behind her, whisper-arguing about not leaving for the airport on time. Eva looked to see if anyone else was paying attention. If anyone might remember the distressed woman on the phone and the quiet stranger in front of her, listening.

*Claire.* Her name, a single syllable, seemed to echo in Eva's mind. Eva shuffled closer, pretending to be absorbed in her phone, the prepaid one she'd bought less than twenty-four hours earlier in a different airport, and took in the details of the woman. The expensive Birkin bag. Trendy sneakers paired with tailored slacks and a bright pink cashmere sweater draped elegantly over her narrow frame. Dark hair neatly brushing her shoulders.

"I think my chances of disappearing are better in Puerto Rico," Claire said. Eva leaned closer, so as not to miss anything. "So much is still off the grid. People will be more receptive to cash and won't ask a lot of questions."

Eva felt her pulse quicken at the phrase *off the grid*, because that's exactly what Eva needed. Puerto Rico was the answer, and Claire would be how she got there.

When they reached the front of the line, a TSA agent directed Eva to an X-ray machine on the left, while pointing Claire several rows over to the right. Eva tried to follow, but the TSA agent blocked her from hopping lines. She kept her eye on Claire, tracking the bright pink sweater as she passed through the X-ray machine, gathered her things on the other side, and disappeared into the crowd.

Eva fought the urge to push her way through. She hadn't waited all morning just to lose Claire now. But she was stuck behind an old man who needed several passes through the scanner. Each time the red light flashed, Eva felt pressure building inside of her, anxious to get to the other side.

Finally, the man removed a handful of change from his pocket, counting it carefully before dropping it into a tray, and successfully passed through.

Eva shoved her coat and shoes into a tray and tossed her bag onto the conveyor belt, holding her breath as she took her turn. On the other side, she scurried to put everything back together again and grabbed her phone and duffel bag, searching the concourse for the pink sweater. But Claire had vanished.

Eva felt the loss like a swift kick. Anything else she might try—buy another plane ticket, a bus ticket, a rental car—could be traced. It would lead the people tracking her straight to wherever she went.

Eva scanned the crowds, slowing down in front of every restaurant, looking into every corner of every newsstand. Up ahead was a bank of monitors. She'd find the departing flight to San Juan and locate Claire at her gate. She couldn't have gone far.

But as Eva passed a bar, she saw the pink sweater, sharp against the gray window behind her. Claire, seated alone, nursing a drink, her eyes scanning the crowded terminal, alert, the way an animal scans the horizon for predators.

Eva let her eyes slide past and kept walking. Claire wasn't going to open up to a stranger asking if she could help. Eva planned to come at this sideways. She wandered into a bookstore and grabbed a magazine, flipping through it until Claire had time to settle.

Across the way, she saw Claire lift the drink to her lips.

Eva replaced the magazine, exited the shop, and walked toward the large plate glass windows overlooking the tarmac before veering left and heading toward Claire. When she was close enough, she lifted her silent phone to her ear and infused her voice with a touch of panic and fear, making sure to let her duffel bump against Claire's stool as she sat.

"Why do they want to talk to me?" Eva asked, lowering herself next to Claire, who shifted sideways, irritation rolling off her in waves.

"But I only did what he asked me to," Eva continued. "As soon as we learned it was terminal, we discussed it." Eva covered her eyes with her hand and allowed the last six months to come crashing back. How much she'd risked. How much she'd lost. She needed all of that emotion now, to craft her story and pass it off as the truth. "He was my husband and I loved him," she said, grabbing a napkin across the bar and pressing it against her eyes before Claire could notice there were no tears. "He was suffering, and I did what anyone would have done." Eva paused, as if someone on the other end was talking, before finally saying, "Tell them I have nothing to say." She yanked the phone away from her ear and stabbed at it, disconnecting her fake call and taking a deep, shuddering breath.

Eva signaled the bartender and said, "Vodka tonic." Then, more to herself than to Claire, she said, "I knew this would catch up to me. I just had no idea how quickly." She took a sip of the drink the bartender deposited in front of her, while next to her, Claire shifted on her stool, away from Eva, the rigid set of her shoulders enough to silence most people. But Eva pinched her eyes closed and worked her hysteria a notch higher, letting her breath grow ragged and uneven. She tried to grab another napkin from a stack just beyond her reach, bumping her shoulder into Claire again, forcing Claire to hand her one.

"Thanks," Eva said. "I'm sorry I'm such a mess, bursting into your quiet corner. It's just..." She trailed off, as if gathering courage to say the words. "My husband recently passed away. Cancer."

Claire hesitated, still not looking at Eva, before finally saying, "I'm sorry."

"We were together eighteen years. Since high school." Eva blew her nose and stared into her drink. "His name was David." She took another sip, letting a piece of ice slip into her mouth and pressing it against the inside of her cheek, willing her heart rate to slow, for the story she was spinning to slow. Too fast and it would sound hollow and false. Lies needed to be doled out carefully. Planted and tended before the next one could be given. "He was wasting away to almost nothing, in excruciating pain. I couldn't watch it anymore." She let the image of a dying man shimmer in Claire's imagination before continuing. "And so, I told the nurse to go home, that I'd take the night shift. I wasn't very smart about it, but it's impossible to think clearly when the man you spent your whole life loving is suffering." Eva looked blankly across the terminal. "Now it seems they have questions. There might be consequences."

What Eva needed was a compelling reason why she, too, might want to disappear and never go home. Something other than the truth.

She felt the shift in Claire's body language, a slight turning toward her, no more than an inch, but it was enough. "Who is 'they'?" Claire asked.

Eva shrugged. "The coroner. The police." She gestured toward her phone. "That was my husband's oncologist. He told me they're asking everyone to go downtown in a week to answer questions." She looked out the windows toward the tarmac. "Nothing good ever happens downtown."

"Are you from New York?"

Eva looked back at her and shook her head. "California." *Pause. Breathe.* "He's only been gone twenty-one days, and every day I wake up and relive it. I thought a trip to New York would help. A change of scenery, the opposite of home."

"Did it?"

"Yes. No." She looked at Claire with a wry smile. "Can both be true?"

"I suppose."

"I've already lost everything that mattered to me. My husband is gone. I quit my job to take care of him. It was just the two of us—neither of us had any family." Eva took a deep breath and said the truest thing she'd said so far. "I'm alone in the world, and I don't want to go back. My flight leaves in an hour, and I don't want to be on it."

Eva dug around in her purse and pulled out her boarding pass to Oakland, laying it on the bar in front of them. A prop. A temptation. A silent suggestion. "Maybe I'll go somewhere else. I have savings. I'll buy a new ticket to some place I've never been and start over." Eva sat up straighter on her stool, as if the decision she'd just made had released something heavy inside of her. "Where do you think I should go?"

Claire's voice was quiet next to her. "It won't take them long to find you. You'd be traceable no matter where you went."

Eva took a few moments to think about that before saying, "Do you think it's possible for someone to disappear? Vanish without a trace?"

Claire didn't answer. The two of them sat in silence, watching people make their way toward their gates or toward baggage claim. Hurried travelers, giving each other wide berth as they avoided eye contact with everyone around them, too absorbed in where they were headed to notice two women sitting side by side at the bar.

In the distance, a child's wail grew louder as a frustrated mother passed them, pulling her sobbing daughter behind her, saying, "I'm not letting you watch *Parent Trap* for the hundredth time when you haven't done your reading for Mrs. Hutchins."

Eva watched Claire's eyes track them up the concourse until they were gone. Then she said, "Nice to know a new generation is still appreciating the work of Lindsay Lohan." She took a sip of her drink. "What was that other one she made? Where the mother and daughter trade bodies and live a day as each other. Do you know it?"

"*Freaky Friday*. My sister loved that movie," Claire said, staring down into her drink.

Eva counted to ten inside her head. She'd reached the very edge of where she needed this conversation to go. Then she said, "Who would you trade with? Who would you want to be?"

Claire's head turned slowly toward Eva and their eyes locked, but Claire didn't answer.

"*Freaky Friday* would sure help me right now," Eva continued, her voice growing distant. "Slipping into someone else's skin, being able to inhabit a totally different life. I'd still be me, but no one would know it."

Next to her, Claire lifted her glass to drink, and Eva noticed the slight tremor. "I'm supposed to go to Puerto Rico," she said.

Eva felt the alcohol finally hit her bloodstream, warm and low in her belly, easing the knot that had been steadily growing for the past forty-eight hours. "Nice time of year for it."

Claire shook her head. "I'd do anything to not be on that plane," she said.

Eva let the words hang in the air, waiting to see if Claire would offer more details. Because what Eva had in mind was risky, and she needed to be sure Claire was desperate enough. She swirled the ice in her glass, vodka and tonic melting into a clear liquid, the lime crushed and wilted around the edges. "Sounds like we both need a *Freaky Friday*."

Eva knew two things. First, Claire needed to believe this was her idea. And second, Eva didn't want to be a person who lied and deceived anymore. This was the last time.

Claire lifted Eva's boarding pass off the bar top and studied it. "What's Oakland like?" she asked.

Eva shrugged. "Nothing special," she said. "I live in Berkeley, though. People there are kind of nuts. If you rode down Telegraph Avenue on a unicycle blowing a trumpet, no one would look twice at you. It's just that kind of place. Easy to blend in because everybody's a little weirder than you are."

Just then, the bartender approached and said, "Can I get you ladies anything else?"

For the first time, Claire smiled. "I think we're good, thanks." To Eva she said, "Follow me."

———

They left the bar and walked shoulder to shoulder, forcing people to move around them, falling into a line of weary travelers in the women's room without saying more. Several stalls opened up, and Claire let people behind them go ahead, until the handicapped stall was available. She pulled Eva in after her and locked the door behind them.

Claire kept her voice low. "What you said back there, about whether I thought it was possible to disappear. I think there's a way to do it."

Toilets flushed, water ran, flights were announced over the loud-speaker, as Claire dug around in her purse and fished out her phone, pulling up her e-ticket and handing it to Eva. "If we trade tickets, flight records will show each of us boarding our respective airplanes," Claire said. "But in Puerto Rico, there will be no trace of me. And in Oakland, there will be no trace of you."

Eva tried to look skeptical. It wouldn't work if she agreed too quickly. "Are you crazy? Why would you want to do something like that for me?"

"You'd be doing it for me," Claire said. "I can't go home. And I'm a fool if I think I have the skills to disappear in Puerto Rico."

Eva's eyes shot up to Claire's face. "What do you mean?"

Claire said, "You don't need to worry."

Eva shook her head. "If I'm going to do this, the least you can do is tell me what I'm stepping into."

Claire looked toward the stall door and said, "I had a plan to leave my husband. It fell apart, and he found out about it. I have to disappear before..."

"Before what? Is he dangerous?"

"Only to me."

Eva studied the e-ticket on Claire's phone, as if she were thinking. "How can we trade tickets if we don't even look alike?"

"It won't matter. We're already through security. You'll have my phone, with my boarding pass. No one will question you." She stared at Eva, her eyes bright and desperate. "Please," she whispered. "This is my only chance."

Eva knew what it was like to almost have something within her grasp, only to have it yanked away again. It made you desperate, a hunger so fierce it blinded you to all the ways it might go wrong.

---

The plan turned out to be simple. They quickly transferred the contents of their bags, Claire pulling an NYU cap from hers and tucking her hair underneath. Then she took off her sweater and handed it to Eva. "My husband is going to leave no lead unfollowed. Every minute of this day will be unpacked and studied. Including airport security footage. We'll need to trade more than just tickets."

Eva slipped off her coat and handed it to Claire, hesitating for a moment. It was her favorite, an army-green hooded one with all the zippers and inner pockets that had served her well for many years.

Claire put it on, still talking. "When you land, use my credit card to pull out cash, or buy a ticket somewhere else. Whatever you want. Just leave a trail my husband can follow." Claire tucked a computer case into Eva's duffel, now resting at Claire's feet. Then she opened her toiletry bag and pulled out a plastic travel toothbrush, slipping it into one of the pockets of Eva's old coat, which Eva found odd. Oral hygiene seemed a strange thing to be prioritizing right now. From her wallet, Claire took a wad of cash and shoved it into another pocket, then dropped the wallet back into her own purse and held it out to Eva. "Do it fast, though, before he cuts everything off," she said. "My PIN is 3710."

Eva took it, though she didn't need Claire's money. Then she handed Claire her own purse, not even bothering to look through it, happy to be rid of all of it. The only cash she needed right now was tucked in a pouch against her skin, the rest of it far away, waiting for her.

Eva slid her arms into the pink cashmere sweater, feeling her escape drawing nearer, hoping Claire wouldn't lose her nerve. In ninety minutes she'd be in the air, on her way to Puerto Rico. Once on the ground, Eva knew a hundred ways she could disappear. Alter her appearance, then get off the island as fast as possible. Charter a boat. Charter a plane. She had enough money to do whatever she needed. She didn't care what Claire ended up doing.

A conversation she'd had with Dex a week ago floated back to her, spoken offhand at a basketball game. *The only way to get a fake ID is to find someone who's willing to give you theirs.* Eva nearly laughed aloud, Dex's words manifesting before her eyes in the handicapped stall at JFK's Terminal 4.

Claire fiddled with one of the zippers on the coat she now wore, and Eva thought about who might be waiting for her on the ground in Oakland. They might pause for a moment when they saw Claire exit the airport wearing Eva's familiar coat. But that's where the similarities ended.

"I hope you don't mind," Eva said, pressing her prepaid phone to her chest, "but this has all my pictures. A few saved voicemails from my husband…" She couldn't risk Claire discovering that it had no contacts, no photos, and only one number in her call history. She held up Claire's. "But I'll need you to disable your password so I can scan the e-ticket. Unless you want to print a ticket and keep your phone?"

"And let him track me that way? No thanks," Claire said, swiping through her settings and disabling her password. "But I do need to grab a number first."

Eva watched as Claire took a pen from her purse and scribbled something on the back of an old receipt.

Just then, the flight to Oakland was announced. Boarding had begun. They looked at each other, fear and excitement mingling on their faces.

"I guess this is it," Claire said.

Eva imagined Claire boarding the flight to California and getting off at the other end. Walking out into the bright sunshine without a clue of what she might find there, and she tried not to feel guilty. But Claire seemed scrappy. Smart. She'd figure something out. "Thank you for helping me start over," Eva said.

Claire pulled her into a hug and whispered, "You saved me. And I won't forget it."

And then she was gone. Out of the stall, disappeared back into the busy airport, security cameras recording a woman in a green coat and NYU baseball cap pulled low over her eyes, walking toward a different life.

Eva locked the door again, leaning against the cool tile wall, and let all of the adrenaline from the morning leak out of her, leaving her limbs weak and her head fuzzy. She wasn't free yet, but she was closer than she'd ever been.

———————————

Eva waited inside the locked stall as long as she could, imagining Claire flying west, racing the sun toward freedom.

"Boarding for Flight 477 with service to Puerto Rico has begun," a voice announced overhead, and she stepped out and strode past the long line of women waiting. Out of the corner of her eye, she watched her reflection in the mirror and marveled at how calm she appeared, when inside she felt like dancing. She pushed up the sleeves of Claire's pink cashmere sweater, washed her hands quickly, and hitched her new purse over her shoulder before exiting back onto the concourse.

At the gate, she waited on the periphery, her eyes scanning the crowd out of habit, and wondered if she'd ever learn how to be in a space without having to assess it for risks and danger. But everyone around her seemed to be absorbed in their own thoughts, anxious to escape the frigid New York temperatures for a warmer climate.

A harried gate attendant pulled a speaker close to her mouth and said, "Our flight this morning isn't full, so any travelers wishing to fly standby should check in at the counter."

People in vacation clothes jockeyed for spots in line, wanting to be first in their boarding group, but with only one gate attendant on duty, things were chaotic and slow to begin. Eva made sure to position herself on the edge of a loud family of six. Inside her purse, Claire's phone buzzed. Curious, she pulled it out.

**What the fuck have you done?**

It wasn't the words that stopped her, but the vitriol behind them, poisonous and familiar. Then the phone rang, jolting her nerves and making her nearly drop it. She let it go to voicemail. It rang again. And then again after that. She peered toward the Jetway, counting the people ahead of her, urging the line to move faster. To board and get into the air, to be on her way.

"What's the holdup?" a woman behind her asked.

"I heard the hatch wasn't opening right."

"Great," the woman said.

When it was Eva's turn, she handed the phone to the flight attendant, who scanned her e-ticket without even glancing at the name. She handed it back to Eva, who promptly turned it off and dropped it back into Claire's purse. The line crept forward, Eva on the threshold of the Jetway, buried in a long line of impatient travelers. Someone's bag bumped her from behind, knocking her purse to the ground and sending Claire's things skittering in different directions.

As she bent down to gather everything, she glanced back toward the concourse. Above her, the line had closed around her, blocking her from the gate agent's view, and she realized how easy it would be to slip away. The flight wasn't full. They might not notice her empty seat. She was scanned onto the flight, and Claire was already on her way to Oakland.

Eva had only a split second to make the decision. She could see how she'd do it. Step to the side and lean against the wall and fake another phone call. She'd be just another traveler, consumed with her own life, on her way somewhere new. She could leave the airport, head into Brooklyn and find a hair salon willing to take a walk-in wanting to dye her hair brown. Then pay cash for a later flight using Claire's ID. There could easily be two Claire Cooks, traveling to two completely different destinations. And once she landed and disappeared, the data would become irrelevant.

And so would she.

# CLAIRE

Tuesday, February 22

It isn't until an hour into the flight that my heart stops pounding, that I take the first deep breath I've had in years. I glance at my watch. The plane I'm expected to be on is somewhere over the Atlantic right now, thousands of miles away. I picture it landing in Puerto Rico, taxiing into the terminal and discharging vacationers, Eva slipping by everyone, invisible. Rory will have discovered what was in the FedEx package by now, and when he starts to look for me, he'll be searching for Claire Cook or Amanda Burns. He doesn't have a clue who Eva James is. It was almost too easy.

A memory arrives, of a night when I was thirteen, sitting on the porch with my mother. I'd been the target of a group of popular girls for several weeks. They followed me, whispering cruel things, waiting until I was alone in the hallway or the bathroom to deliver their cutting remarks. My mother had wanted to intervene, but I wouldn't let her, believing that would only make it worse. "I wish I could just disappear,"

I'd whispered. Together we watched a three-year-old Violet run around the small yard, the roses swaying in the slight evening breeze.

"If you pay attention, Claire, solutions always appear. But you have to be brave enough to see them," she'd said, plucking my hand out of my lap and squeezing it in hers.

Her words had confused me then. But I realize now she'd been giving me advice to hang on to, for later. I'd been trapped between two terrifying choices—Rory's anger or the kind of people Nico might have sent to help me—and then Eva came along and pulled me out.

I think about Eva, of what she's lost, and I hope that wherever she ends up, she can find a way to be at peace with herself. I picture her escaping to a remote village somewhere, finding a small house by the ocean, her blond hair contrasting with skin darkened by a sun that cascades like forgiveness across her shoulders. Far away from everything. A fresh start, like the one I'm hoping to create for myself.

How extraordinary that we found each other.

A bubble of joy tumbles around inside of me, and I laugh out loud, startling the man sitting next to me. "Sorry," I say, and turn toward the window, watching the land below us transform from city into large stretches of farmland, the miles between me and Rory growing with every second.

———

Six hours later, the plane bumps down in Oakland. We circled over San Francisco, and though the pilot pointed out landmarks such as the Bay Bridge and the Transamerica building, they'd barely registered amidst my excitement. I wait my turn to deplane, the crowd of people pressing in on me, and close my eyes, thinking of a game Violet and I used to play called Would You Rather. We'd spend hours creating impossible, hilarious choices: *Would you rather eat ten cockroaches or have liver for dinner every night for a year?* I smile to myself, wondering what Violet and I might come up with now. *Would you rather be married to an abusive but rich man or start over somewhere new, with no money and no identity?* The decision seems easy to me.

Finally, the door opens and people start to file off the plane. I take my place among them, pulling my cap low over my eyes, at least until I'm out of the airport and away from security cameras. The first thing I need to do is call Petra and tell her I'm in Oakland. And then find a cheap motel that won't ask a lot of questions. With only four hundred dollars in my wallet, I have to be smart.

When we deplane, I slip around everyone and go in search of a pay phone. But when I get beyond the gates, I realize something's different. Several clumps of people are gathered around television monitors in the various bars and restaurants, hushed.

Something must have happened.

I sidle up to a group outside Chili's and peer over people's shoulders. The television is set to a cable news station, but the volume is turned down. A somber-looking woman is talking, and the screen flashes her name—Hillary Stanton, NTSB Senior Communications Officer. I read the closed-captioning at the bottom of the screen.

**We don't know yet what caused the crash, and it's too early to say.**

The screen cuts to a news anchor, and I get a glimpse of the headline banner that was previously covered by the black closed-captioning text.

**The Crash of Flight 477.**

I read it again, trying to rearrange the words to mean something different.
Flight 477 was my flight to Puerto Rico.
I push closer. More text flashes up, this time from the anchor.

**Authorities won't speculate on the cause of the crash just yet, though they have indicated the unlikelihood of any survivors. Flight 477 was heading to Puerto Rico, with 96 passengers on board.**

The picture flashes to a live shot of the ocean, pieces of wreckage floating on the surface.

The ground seems to move beneath me, and I wobble into the man standing next to me. He steadies my elbow and hangs on long enough to make sure I don't fall. "You okay?" he asks.

I shake him off and push through the crowd, unable to reconcile what I'm seeing on the television screen with the memory of Eva still sharp in my mind—whose voice I can still hear, whose smile I can still see as the bathroom stall door closed behind me.

With my head down, I make my way through the concourse, suddenly aware of how many television screens there are, all of them broadcasting what's happened. I swallow the bile creeping up the back of my throat and locate a pay phone next to the restrooms.

With trembling fingers, I pull out the receipt where I'd jotted down Petra's number and dial. A voice directs me to insert one dollar and twenty-five cents. I dig around in Eva's wallet until I've counted out five quarters and slip them into the slot, one at a time, my heart racing.

But instead of ringing, I hear three tones and an automated voice saying, *We're sorry, this number is no longer in service.*

In my haste to reach her, I must have misdialed, double-entered a digit by accident, so I take a deep breath, willing my hands to stop shaking. I collect the quarters from the change receptacle and dial again, slower this time.

Again I'm told the number is no longer in service.

I replace the receiver, feeling as if I've separated from reality, lifting straight out of my body. Wandering over to a deserted bank of chairs, I collapse, staring across the concourse. People move in and out of my field of vision, pulling suitcases, corralling children, speaking into cell phones.

I must have copied the number wrong. I think back to the bathroom stall, scribbling Petra's number, adrenaline causing my attention to spread thin like scattershot.

And now, I'm completely cut off.

Across the way the television screens change again, pulling my attention back.

> **The names of the passengers have not been released yet, but NTSB officials say they will be holding a press conference later this evening.**

I realize how vulnerable I'm about to become, how things like this take hold, grabbing the heartstrings of the nation. First, the grisly details, the speculation about what went wrong. Then the human interest. The victims. Their lives, their hopes. Their faces, smiling, laughing, unaware of how it will end. Because of who Rory is, my story will be amplified, my minutes of anonymity slipping away at an alarming rate. My image will soon be splashed across the media, recognizable to anyone looking. I'm about to become as infamous as Maggie Moretti. Yet another tragedy Rory will have to bravely endure. And I'll be stuck, with very little money, no identification, and nowhere to hide.

My eyes land on Eva's purse, and I reach into it and pull out a ring of keys and her wallet. I pocket the keys and open the wallet, memorizing the address on her license. *543 Le Roy.* I don't hesitate. I walk out of the airport, into the bright California sun, and hail a cab.

---

We speed along a freeway, the San Francisco skyline peeking between industrial buildings on the east side of the bay, but it barely registers. Instead, I'm remembering Eva's final moments in the bathroom stall with me, determined to carve out a second chance for herself, not imagining that she never would. I rest my head against the window and try to focus on the cold glass pressing against my skin. *Just a little bit longer.* I can't let myself fall apart until I'm behind closed doors.

Soon, we've exited onto streets crowded with college kids, colorful and upbeat. I try to imagine what Rory might be doing right now. Most likely, he's on his way back to New York, having canceled the event in Detroit. Quietly depositing the forty thousand dollars back into the bank and hiding everything else in his secret drawer.

I stare out the window as we pass the university, students crossing the street in a haphazard way, oblivious the way only college students can be. We skirt around the eastern edge of campus and into a residential neighborhood on the north side with hills and winding streets. Houses, duplexes, and apartments sit side by side among tall redwood trees, and I think about what I'll find when I unlock Eva's front door. An intruder stepping into the home she shared with her husband, forever frozen exactly as she left it. Looking at their photographs. Using their bathroom. Sleeping in their bed. I shudder and try not to think that far ahead.

The driver leaves me in front of a white, two-story duplex with a long front porch and two identical doors anchoring each end. The right side is curtained, closed off from prying eyes. A large pine tree casts part of the porch in shadow, the soil beneath it looking dark and fresh. The left side is vacant, the windows bare, revealing empty rooms with crown molding, a red accent wall, and hardwood floors. I'm relieved I won't have to answer any questions from a neighbor, asking who I am or where Eva went.

I fumble with the keys, finally finding the right one, and push the door open. Too late, I realize there might be an alarm, and I freeze. But all is silent. The air smells of closed rooms and a faint trace of something hovering between floral and chemical—there and then gone.

I close and lock the door, stepping carefully past a pair of shoes that look as if someone kicked them off a few minutes ago, straining my ears for any kind of noise, any sound of another person. Yet despite the clutter, the house feels utterly still.

I set my bag down by the front door in case I need to leave quickly, and creep over to peek into the kitchen. Empty, though there's an open can of Diet Coke on the counter and some dishes in the sink. A door leads to the backyard, but it's locked with a chain across it.

I take the stairs slowly, listening hard. Only three rooms—a bathroom, an office, and a bedroom, clothes dropped on the bed and floor as if someone had left in a hurry. But I'm alone in the house, and I let out the breath I'd been holding.

Back downstairs, I collapse onto the couch and tip my head forward, resting it in my hands, and finally allow the day's events to catch up to me. The panic I felt, followed by the thrill of having slipped past everyone.

And then I think of Eva somewhere on the bottom of the Atlantic Ocean. Whether it hurt when the plane hit the water, if the moments leading up to impact were long, filled with terror-filled screams and crying, or if they were cut short by lack of oxygen. I take several deep breaths, trying to calm down. *I'm safe. I am okay.* Outside, a car passes through the silent neighborhood. In the distance, some bells chime.

I lift my head and take in the framed abstract prints on the wall and the soft armchairs flanking the couch. The room is small but cozy, the furniture high quality but not extravagant. Exactly the opposite of the home I just left behind.

There is a well-worn groove in the armchair angled toward the television, but the rest of the furniture looks pristine, as if no one has ever sat there. Something about the room nags at me, and I try to put my finger on it. Perhaps it's the way it was left, as if someone had just stepped away for a few minutes. I scan the space, trying to figure out where her husband's hospital bed might have been. Where the hospice workers might have counted pills, measured medication, washed their hands. But all evidence is gone. Not even a divot in the carpet.

Against the far wall, a bookshelf is crammed with books, and I wander over and see titles about biology and chemistry, with a few textbooks on the very bottom shelf. *I quit my job to take care of him.* Perhaps she was a professor at Berkeley. Or maybe he was.

From the kitchen comes a buzzing sound, loud and jarring in the silent house. When I get to the doorway, I notice the black cell phone on the counter, tucked between two canisters. I pick it up, confused, remembering the one Eva used at the airport in New York. The push notification is from one of those text apps that disappear after a set amount of time, from a contact named D.

**Why didn't you show up? Did something happen?**

The phone buzzes in my hand with another message, nearly making me jump.

**Call me immediately.**

I toss it back on the counter and stare at it, waiting for another text, but it remains silent, and I hope whoever D is, they're done asking questions for the night.

I step toward the sink and look through the small window overlooking a tiny backyard. It's surrounded by shrubs and bisected by a brick walkway leading to a gate in the back fence. I imagine Eva standing here, watching twilight fall as it is now, coloring the shadows in deep purples and blues as the sky darkens, while her husband lay dying.

The phone buzzes again, the sound reverberating around the empty kitchen, and a sense of foreboding descends. The empty house offers itself up to me, yet reveals nothing.

# EVA

Eva waited for him outside his dorm. It wasn't the same one she'd lived in, so many years ago, but a newer one, with softer edges and dark wood trim, as if they wanted students to feel like they were living in an Italian villa instead of student housing. Her gaze traveled upward, over windows that were open to catch the cool morning air, posters of bands she'd never heard of, taped picture-side out. From the center of campus, the Campanile chimed the hour, and students with early-morning classes passed by her as she stood on the sidewalk, leaning against a car that didn't belong to her. No one looked at Eva. They never did.

Finally, he exited, his backpack slung across one shoulder, his nose buried in his phone. He didn't notice Eva until she fell into step beside him.

"Hi, Brett," she said.

He looked up, startled, and a flash of worry crossed his face when he saw who it was. But then he plastered on a smile and said, "Eva. Hey."

Across the street, two men eased out of a parked car and started walking in their same direction, slow and silent. Trailing them.

Eva began. "I'm sure you know why I'm here."

They crossed the street, past coffee shops and bookstores, and skirted the southern edge of campus. She stepped in front of Brett to stop him when they'd reached the opening of a narrow brick walkway that led to the entrance of a small art gallery that wouldn't open until eleven o'clock. The men behind them stopped too, waiting.

"Look, Eva," Brett said. "I'm really sorry, but I don't have your money yet." As he spoke, he searched the faces of the few people on the street this early, looking for a friend. Someone to step in and help him. But Eva wasn't worried. To anyone who might be watching, Brett was just a student, chatting with a woman on the sidewalk.

"That's what you said the last time," Eva said. "And the time before that."

"It's my parents," Brett explained. "They're getting a divorce. They cut my allowance by half. I can barely afford beer."

Eva tilted her head sympathetically, as if she could relate to a problem like that. As if she hadn't been forced to live on a minuscule per diem in her three short years at Berkeley, pocketing extra food from the dining hall to tide her over long weekends. No one gave her an allowance. Paying for beer had never been on Eva's long list of worries.

She pressed on. "That's a sad story. Unfortunately, it's not my problem. You owe me six hundred dollars, and I'm tired of waiting."

Brett hitched his backpack higher on his shoulder and watched a bus rumble down the street, his gaze trailing after it. "I'll get it. I swear. Just…it's going to take some time."

Eva reached into her pocket and pulled out a piece of gum,

unwrapping it carefully, and stuck it in her mouth, chewing slowly, as if she were considering what he'd said. The men who were trailing saw Eva's signal and began making their way toward them.

It took Brett almost no time to notice them. To see the purpose in their stride, to see that he and Eva were their final destination. He took a step backward, as if to run, but the men closed the distance quickly, boxing him in.

"Oh my god," he whispered, his eyes wild with fear and panic. "Eva. Please. I swear I'll pay you. *I swear.*" He began to back away, but Saul, the bigger of the two men, placed a hand on Brett's shoulder to stop him. Eva could see his large fingers squeezing, and Brett began to cry.

She eased back toward the street, her part finished. But Brett's eyes stopped her, silently pleading with her to change her mind, and Eva hesitated. Perhaps it was the way the morning light slanted down on them, autumn just a hint in the air, reminding her of a new semester with new classes and new things to learn. Reminding her of a life she'd once loved, not yet snatched away from her.

Or maybe it was how young Brett looked. The way he whimpered, a pimple bright red on his forehead, the hair on his face still soft and thin. He was just a kid. And she remembered she'd been one once too. Making mistakes. Begging for another chance.

No one had given it to her.

She stepped back, allowing them to lead Brett down the walkway, away from the sidewalk.

A voice startled her from behind. "Had to be done."

Dex.

He emerged from the shadowed doorway of a closed shop and lit a cigarette, gesturing for her to walk with him. From behind them came the sound of fists hitting flesh, Brett's cries, pleading for help. Then a particularly loud blow—perhaps a kick to the stomach, or his head slammed into the wall—and no more sounds from Brett.

Eva kept her gaze steady, knowing Dex was studying her. "What are you doing here?"

He shrugged and took a drag on his cigarette. "I know you don't like this part. Thought I'd swing by and check on you."

A lie? The truth? With Dex it was hard to tell, but Eva had learned over the years that Dex didn't get out of bed this early unless their boss, Fish, told him to.

"I'm fine," she said.

Together they ambled up the hill toward the stadium, passing another coffee shop, its white awning covering a patio of empty tables and chairs still stacked in a corner. The interior was crowded with professors and university employees getting their morning coffee before heading to work. Outside, a panhandler sat in a wheelchair playing a harmonica. Eva tossed him a five-dollar bill.

"Bless you," the man said.

Dex rolled his eyes. "Bleeding heart."

"Karma," Eva corrected.

They stopped at the top of the hill, outside the International House, and Dex looked past her toward the bay, as if admiring the view, and she followed his gaze. The two men had emerged from the walkway and were moving west toward Telegraph Avenue. There was no sign of Brett, whom they'd probably left in a bloody heap. The gallery owner would come across him in a couple hours and call the police. Or perhaps Brett would somehow manage to get up and stumble back to his dorm. No classes for him today.

When the men disappeared from view, Dex turned back to her, handing her a small piece of paper. "New client," he said.

*Brittany. 4:30 p.m. Tilden.*

Eva rolled her eyes. "Nothing says 'child of the nineties' like the name Brittany. How did you find her?"

"Referral from a guy I know in LA. Her husband just got transferred up here."

Eva pulled up short. "She's not a student?"

"No. But you don't need to worry," he assured her. "She's legit." He dropped his cigarette on the ground and crushed it beneath his shoe. "See you this afternoon at three."

He headed back down the hill, not waiting for confirmation from her. None was needed. In the twelve years she'd worked with Dex, she'd never once missed a meeting. She watched him until he was past the walkway, still no sign of Brett, and then she turned north toward home.

As she crossed through the center of campus, memories flitted along the edges of her periphery. The end of summer in Berkeley. Eva's own rhythms, so deeply tied to the ebb and flow of the university, now felt off kilter, pulled to the side by Dex, as she wondered what his true purpose was in joining her that morning.

From behind her, Eva heard someone say, "Excuse me."

She ignored it and crossed over a small bridge covering a stream that wound its way through the center of campus.

"Excuse me," the voice said again, louder.

A young girl, a freshman by the look of her—skinny jeans, boots, and what appeared to be a new backpack—stepped in front of Eva, panting. "Can you tell me where Campbell Hall is? I'm late and it's the first day and I overslept..." She trailed off as Eva stared at the girl, so bright-eyed, with everything still ahead for her.

Another Brett, not yet happened. How many months would it take before the pressure of Berkeley began to crack this girl in half? How long until her first failed test, or her first C on a paper? Eva pictured someone sliding a scrap of paper with Dex's name and number across a wooden study carrel in the library. How long until Eva was meeting her outside of Campbell Hall?

"Do you know where it is?" the girl asked again.

Eva was so fucking tired of it all. "*No hablo inglés*," Eva said, pretending she didn't speak English, wanting only to be rid of this girl and her questions.

The girl stepped back, surprised, and Eva slipped past her and up the path. Let someone else help her. Eva wasn't ready to take her turn yet.

---

The unexpected appearance of Dex that morning was still bothering her several hours later, as she stood at the kitchen sink, washing dishes. As she rotated a glass under the hot water, it slipped from her fingers and shattered, sending shards flying into the porcelain basin.

"Shit," she said, turning off the faucet and drying her hands on a dishtowel before carefully picking up the larger pieces and dropping them in the trash. She could feel things rearranging and shifting, the way animals could sense an earthquake, tiny tremors deep beneath the earth's crust, warning her to pay attention. Seek safety.

She grabbed some paper towels and swept up the rest before checking the timer she'd brought up from the basement. Five minutes left.

She tossed her empty Diet Coke can into the recycling and stared out the kitchen window overlooking the backyard. The green shrubbery and roses were overgrown and in need of pruning. In the far corner, she spotted a cat, crouched and motionless, beneath a low-hanging bush, eyes locked on a small bird splashing in a shady puddle left from the morning sprinklers. Eva held her breath and watched, silently urging the bird to look around, to leave the danger of the yard behind.

Suddenly, the cat lunged. In a silent flurry of wings and feathers, it grabbed the bird, pummeling it to the ground and stunning it with a few swift blows. Eva watched as the cat slunk off carrying the bird in its mouth and felt as if the universe was sending her some kind of message. The only problem was, she didn't know whether she was the cat or the bird.

The timer rang, jolting Eva from her reverie. She looked at the clock on the stove, then glanced one more time through the window at the backyard, empty except for a scattering of feathers on the brick walkway.

She pushed herself off the counter, past the rolling shelving unit filled with things she never used, a prop to obscure the door hidden behind it, and slipped down to the basement to finish up.

# CLAIRE

Eva's house is so still, I feel as if it's watching me, waiting to see if I'll reveal who I am and why I'm here. When I open the fridge, the top shelf is crowded with cans of Diet Coke and not much else, just a misshapen take-out container shoved to the back. "Diet Coke anyone?" I mutter before closing it again, my gaze sliding over the shelves that line one wall, filled with cookbooks and mixing bowls, to the cupboards on the left of the sink. I begin opening them, revealing glasses, plates, and bowls, finally finding where Eva kept her dry goods. Ritz Crackers and a Diet Coke will have to be good enough for tonight.

When I've eaten enough to quiet my growling stomach, I move back to the living room. The clock on the wall reads six. I pick up the remote, trying not to think about Eva and her husband, snuggled under a blanket watching a movie or sitting in companionable silence scrolling through their phones, and I scan the room, looking for the evidence of a happy marriage. Photographs. Mementos from vacations. But none of it is visible.

I find the Power button and flip past the networks, finally landing on CNN.

The screen shows a close-up of the airport in New York, with an inset of the search and recovery team, a bobbing Coast Guard boat surrounded by dark water illuminated with floodlights. I turn up the volume. Kate Lane, political commentator, host of the show *Politics Today*, is speaking, her voice low and somber as the screen fills with an image of me and Rory at a gala function last year. My hair is swept up in an elaborate french twist, and I'm laughing into the camera, my face heavy with makeup. Kate Lane's voice says, "Authorities have confirmed the wife of philanthropist Rory Cook, son of Senator Marjorie Cook and the executive director of the Cook Family Foundation, was traveling to Puerto Rico on a humanitarian trip and was a confirmed passenger on Flight 477."

And then my picture is replaced with a live shot of the exterior of the airport, the camera panning in on what looks like a restricted area behind large, plate glass windows. "Representatives from Vista Airlines are meeting with family members this evening, while off the coast of Florida, search and recovery teams work late into the night. NTSB officials have been quick to dismiss terrorism as a cause of the crash, citing unstable weather and the fact that this particular plane had been grounded just four months ago."

The camera zooms in to show people hugging and crying, consoling each other. I move closer to the television, straining my eyes to see if Rory's there. But I needn't have bothered. As if on cue, the scene cuts to a bank of microphones, and Rory emerges from the room, stepping behind them. "I've been told we'll be getting a brief statement from Mr. Cook on behalf of the families."

I pause the TV and study him. He's wearing an expensive pair of jeans and one of his button-down shirts in a shade of blue that looks good on camera. But his face is etched with grief, his eyes hollow and red. I sit back on my heels, wondering if he's truly devastated or if this is all an elaborate act, that far beneath the surface he's livid, having surely discovered the truth by now.

Leaving the TV paused, I grab my computer from my bag and take the stairs two at a time up to Eva's office. The internet router blinks its green lights from a corner of the desk, and I turn it over, finding the password on the back, praying she never bothered to change it. It takes me three tries to match the password with a network name, but I'm in.

I click on the window I opened last night and take a quick look through Rory's inbox while he's on live TV. There are several messages from Danielle, cc'd copies of emails she sent this morning, letting the Detroit hotel know Rory will be using my reservation, informing the school that Rory would be the one doing the event.

And one message exchange between Bruce and Rory, shortly after the news of the crash broke.

I think we need to delay the announcement.

Rory's reply was brief.

Absolutely not.

But Bruce would not be deterred.

Think about the optics. Your wife just died. There's no way you can announce next week. It's insane. Let the NTSB recover the body. Have a funeral. Then announce after that. Tell them it's what Claire would have wanted.

Even though it doesn't surprise me, the fact that they're worrying about the Senate announcement right now still hurts. Despite our problems, despite his temper, I know Rory loved me, in his own broken way. But underneath is a tiny thread of satisfaction that I'd been right to break away now. That if given the choice, Rory would never pick me over his ambition.

I open a new tab and Google *Petra Federotov*. A long list of what appear to be art catalogues pop up, with brightly colored graphics and names I can't pronounce. Page after page of them. I revise my search to *Petra Federotov phone number*, and the list grows slightly longer—a pizza parlor in Boston, links to sites offering people-finding software for a thirty-dollar fee. But I'm certain Nico has made sure their information is scrubbed from those databases, and most likely scrubbed from the web as well.

I leave my computer open and go back downstairs, where Rory is still frozen on the screen, his arm about to swipe a chunk of hair that has flopped over his forehead. In another lifetime, I would have reached out to smooth it back, my touch gentle and loving. I stare at his face, remembering what it felt like to love him. The early days, when he'd pick me up from the auction house and surprise me with a dinner at Le Bernardin or a summer picnic in the park. His mischievous smile as he'd sneak us in the back door of a club, the tender way he'd brush the edge of my lip with his thumb, right before he'd kiss me.

Those memories aren't lost. Just buried. Maybe someday I'll be able to pick them up again. Hold them in my hand and examine them objectively, keeping the good ones and discarding the rest.

I press Play. Rory clears his throat and says, "This morning, like many of the families behind me, I kissed my wife, Claire, goodbye for the last time." He pauses, taking a deep, shuddering breath before continuing, his voice cracking and wobbling over the words. "What was supposed to be a humanitarian trip to Puerto Rico has thrust me, and the families of ninety-five other passengers of Flight 477, into a living nightmare. Be assured we will not rest until we get answers, until we fully understand what went wrong." He swallows hard and clenches his jaw. When he looks into the camera again, his eyes shine brighter, filling with tears that tip over the edges of his eyes and slide down his cheeks. "I don't know what to say, other than I'm devastated. On behalf of the families, we thank you for your thoughts and prayers."

Reporters shout questions at Rory, but he turns away from the cameras, ignoring them. I think about how effortlessly he lies. He didn't kiss me goodbye. He didn't say goodbye at all. And I realize, now that I'm dead, Rory can tell whatever story he wants about me, about our marriage. There is no one left to refute it.

The scene shrinks to an inset, and we see Kate Lane again, her familiar short gray hair and black-framed glasses filling the screen. I'd met her several years ago when she was interviewing Rory for the segment she was doing on Marjorie Cook's legacy, and I remember being struck by how cool she'd been toward Rory. She'd smiled and laughed in all the right places, but I sensed a part of her watching him, as if from a distance. Examining all his shiny surfaces and flourishes, and deciding they weren't real.

Her expression now is both somber and steadying. "Mr. Cook has been a frequent guest on this show, and I, along with everyone else at *Politics Today*, extend our deepest sympathies to the Cook family and all of the families affected by today's tragedy. I've had the good fortune of meeting Mrs. Cook on several occasions, and I knew her to be a smart and generous woman, a tireless advocate for the Cook Family Foundation. She will be deeply missed." In the inset picture over her shoulder, a man appears at the bank of microphones Rory just left and Kate says, "It looks like the director of the NTSB is going to answer some questions. Let's listen in."

The crowd of reporters begin shouting questions, but I silence the noise by turning the television off and, staring at the faint outline of my reflection in the dark screen, wonder what happens next.

———————

I carry my bag back up the stairs and into the master bedroom, pushing aside a discarded pile of clothes on the bed—a pair of sweatpants and a T-shirt—and sit. A dark wood dresser, drawers tightly shut, and a closet door that isn't closed all the way, revealing a jumble of clothes inside. And that's when it fully hits me: Eva will never laugh, or cry, or be surprised again. She won't grow old, with sore hips or a back that aches. Never lose her keys or hear the sound of birds in the morning.

Yesterday she was here, a beating and broken heart, a mind with secrets and desires she kept to herself. But today, every memory she'd accumulated across a lifetime has vanished. They simply don't exist anymore.

And what about me? Claire Cook is also gone, lifted up in the memories of those who knew me, no longer walking among the living. And yet, I still get to carry everything that belonged to me. My joys, my heartaches, memories of people I loved. And I feel a sense of privilege I don't deserve. That I get to keep it all and Eva does not.

I press my fists into my eyes, trying to stop my leaping thoughts, ping-ponging from moment to moment—the maid unpacking my suitcase. The phone call to the hotel in Detroit. Petra's voice on the phone at JFK. And Eva in the bathroom stall, handing me her bag, believing I was the solution to her problems, as I believed she was the solution to mine.

I need to sleep, but I don't think I can bring myself to pull back the covers and climb into the bed. Not tonight at least. Instead, I take the blanket and grab a pillow, carrying them back downstairs to the couch. I kick off my shoes and settle myself, turning the TV back on for company. I flip away from the news channels until I find a station showing *I Love Lucy* reruns and let the canned laughter carry me to sleep.

———————

I'm yanked awake by the sound of Rory's voice, speaking quietly in my ear. I leap off the couch, the dark room flickering in the blue light of the television screen, confused and disoriented, forgetting for a moment where I am and what happened.

And then I see him on the screen of the TV, smaller than in real life, but no less terrifying. A replay of the press conference. I collapse onto the couch again, fumbling for the remote to turn it off, letting the sounds of Eva's house—the low hum of the refrigerator, a quiet dripping from the kitchen faucet—slow my heart rate. Reminding myself that there's no way Rory could know where I am.

I stare at the ceiling, watching shadows from the streetlight dance across it, and realize how hard disappearing will be. It won't matter where I hide or what name I use. Every time I turn on a television, open a newspaper, or flip through a magazine, Rory will still be hiding there, waiting to leap out at me. He will never go away.

# EVA

**Six Months before the Crash**

Eva's hands moved automatically under the bright lights, while high above, the fan whirred, a white noise that dulled her senses, venting the air from her basement lab into the backyard. She couldn't seem to erase the image of that cat, how quietly it waited, how quickly things had ended for the bird.

She shook her head and forced herself to concentrate. She had to finish this batch before noon. She was meeting Dex at three to give him Fish's portion and was meeting her new client shortly after that.

She measured ingredients, carefully weighing and adjusting, and felt herself relax. Even after all these years, after everything that had happened, it was still magic, that you could combine substances, add heat, and create something entirely new.

She brought the mixture to a thick, pasty consistency on the camping stove, immune now to the bitter chemical stench that burned the inside of her nose and clung to her hair and clothes, long after she'd finished. Because of this, she invested in expensive lotions and shampoo, the only things that could cover the smell of what she made.

When it was ready, she poured the liquid into the pill molds and set the timer again. Using various cough and cold medicines mixed with some common household items, what she made was similar to Adderall. However, it was much safer to make, avoiding the explosive nature of most methamphetamines. The result was a tiny pill, simple to produce, with a powerful punch that kept subpar students like Brett awake and sharp-minded for hours on end.

When she was done, she washed the equipment at the sink in the corner, loading the portable dishwasher she'd bought several years ago. Her chemistry professor's voice floated through the years: *A clean lab is the mark of a true professional.* She was a professional by definition, but no one was going to come down here and make sure she was following standard lab protocol. She wiped the counters, making sure no traces of her work—or the ingredients she drove all over the Bay Area to purchase—were left out for prying eyes.

Not that anyone would come down here. Long ago she'd figured out the best way to hide the door to this old laundry room was to roll a shelf in front of it. From the outside, you'd never know it was there. At least six feet tall with a solid back, the shelves were filled with the tools of an amateur chef—cookbooks, mixing bowls, canisters that held flour and sugar, and several large utensil holders stuffed thick with spatulas and oversized spoons that Eva never used. She moved through the world similarly—appearing to be a bland, thirtysomething server who worked hard to make ends meet, who lived in a North Berkeley duplex and drove a fifteen-year-old Honda. When in reality she was the opposite, single-handedly responsible for keeping the students at Berkeley awake and on track to graduate in four years. And dealing quickly with the ones who caused problems.

Grabbing the timer off the counter, she headed up the basement stairs, flipping the light and fan off behind her. The silence folded over her, and she paused in the kitchen, waiting for the sounds of the neighborhood to settle into the space between her ears.

Next door, she heard her new neighbor, an older woman with close-cropped white hair, unlocking her front door. When she'd moved in a few weeks ago, Eva could tell she wanted to be friendly. Her eyes would linger on Eva, and though Eva was polite, with one- and two-word greetings, she could feel the woman's gaze, heavy and waiting for a deeper interaction.

Mr. Cosatino, the old man who'd lived there since the beginning of time, had been so much easier. They'd only spoken once, last year when she'd paid him cash to purchase her half of the duplex. She wondered what happened to him, whether he got sick or if he died. One day he was there, the next day, he was gone. And now this woman, with her friendly smiles and eye contact.

Eva left the bookshelf pushed aside and took the stairs two at a time, up to her home office. A tiny room overlooking the front yard, it wasn't used by Eva for much except paying bills and storing her cold-weather coats. But she'd decorated it like the rest of the house—warm tones of yellow and red that were a far cry from the institutional gray walls of the group home she'd grown up in. She'd picked each piece—the pine desk, the deep red rug, the small table and lamp that sat under the window—as an antidote to the coldness that had embedded itself inside of her as a child.

She settled in front of her laptop, pulling up the Singaporean bank log-in page, and entered her account information by memory. She was diligent about checking her balances, watching the number steadily increase over the past twelve years, going from five figures to six figures to a comfortable seven. The financial district in San Francisco was filled with handsome men who knew how to bend the law to suit their purposes, and it had been easy to find a tax attorney who was willing to set up a fake LLC, who knew which banks abroad would look the other way and not ask too many questions, and who could help her funnel her illegal income somewhere safe.

At some point, she was going to have to stop. No one could do this forever. And when that time came, she'd buy a plane ticket to somewhere far away and simply disappear. She'd leave everything behind. The house. Her things. Her clothes. Dex and Fish. She'd shed this life like an old skin, emerging newer. Better. She'd done it before, and she would do it again.

———————

When the pills were ready, she popped them from their molds and into separate bags. She wrapped the ones for Dex in blue paper, tied a ribbon around them, and drove to the park in North Berkeley where they were supposed to meet. She'd learned over the years how to be invisible. How to slip between the layers of the outside world, just a woman on a walk or meeting a friend in the park with a beautifully wrapped present. This wasn't a hard job, if you were smart. And Eva had always been smarter than most.

She found him sitting at a picnic table overlooking a small, dingy play area. Young kids were scattered across the equipment, each minded by a parent or nanny. Eva paused, still outside of Dex's line of sight, and watched the kids. That might have been her, if her mother had been a different person. Maybe she would have brought Eva to a park like this to blow off steam after school or to kill a few hours on a weekend. Over the years, Eva had searched her memory for an image, any memory at all from the short time she lived with her birth family, but her first two years were blank.

As a child, Eva had imagined them so many times and in so many ways, the images almost seemed like real memories. Her mother, with long blond hair, looking over her shoulder at Eva, laughing. Her grandparents, old and frail, worried about their wild daughter, scraping their pennies together to pay for another trip to rehab. A quiet family with a big problem. She tried to feel something for them, but she felt removed, like an unplugged lamp. There was no power behind it. No connection. No light.

But mothers and daughters always caught Eva's eye, snagging her attention like a sharp fingernail, scraping her in places that should have healed over long ago.

She knew only two things about her mother: her name was Rachel Ann James, and she had been an addict. The information had arrived unexpectedly in a letter from Sister Bernadette in Eva's sophomore year of college. The page had been filled with her precise cursive, so familiar it had lifted her up and carried her back in time to the girl she'd once been.

It had felt like an intrusion, the answers to questions she'd long since given up asking, suddenly landing in her mailbox. Just when she was beginning to feel like she might be able to rise above who she'd always been.

Eva had no idea where that letter was now. Tossed into a box or buried in a drawer. It was easier to pretend that part of her life had never existed, just a few short miles away in San Francisco, that she had instead emerged, fully formed, the day she started at Berkeley.

---

She tore her eyes away from the kids and walked the final few yards to where Dex sat.

"Happy birthday," she said, handing him the package of pills.

He smiled and tucked it inside his coat. "You shouldn't have."

She sat next to him on the bench, and together they watched the kids play—jumping from the slide, chasing each other around the swings—always lingering for a little while, just two friends enjoying the sunshine. Dex's mantra so many years ago now their routine—*You only look like a drug dealer if you behave like one.*

"I did my first solo deal at this park," Eva said, pointing toward the parking lot. "When I got here, there were two police cars parked at the curb, the officers standing next to them, as if they were waiting for me."

Dex turned to face her. "What did you do?"

Eva thought back to that day, how scared she'd been, how her pulse had raced and her breath shortened when she'd seen them, in full uniform, all guns and billy clubs and shiny badges. "I remembered what you told me, about how I had to walk with confidence, how I had to keep my eyes straight ahead and not hesitate."

Eva remembered passing the officers, meeting their eyes for a fleeting second and smiling through the fear, before walking toward the playground, where a third-year law student was supposed to meet her. "I imagined I was someone who worked in a windowless office, coming here to get a little sunshine and fresh air on my lunch break."

"The advantages of being a woman."

Eva didn't feel like it was much of an advantage, but she knew what he meant. People who looked like her didn't make or sell drugs. They were teachers or bank tellers. They were someone's nanny or mother. She remembered the moment when she handed over the drugs and pocketed her first two hundred dollars, how awkward it was. She had no finesse, the entire transaction silent and stilted. She remembered walking away and thinking, *It's done. I'm a drug dealer.* And feeling like the person she was only just starting to become had died.

But she'd gotten over it. Embraced what her life had become. A part of her was set free—all those years of conforming to the expectations of others. She'd been told that life was a single track, carrying you forward. If you worked hard, good things happened. But she'd always known it was more like a pinball, careening and racing. The thrill was in the unexpected. In the freedom to create her own destiny. Her life had turned to shit, and yet she'd made something out of it. That was fucking something.

Dex interrupted her thoughts. "I sometimes regret getting you into this. I thought I was helping, but…" He trailed off.

Eva picked a splinter from the table and held it between her fingers, studying the wood before dropping it to the ground. "I'm happy," she said. "I have no complaints."

And it was mostly true. She looked at Dex, the one who had stepped into the wreckage of her life and pulled her out. It had been Wade Roberts's idea to make drugs in the chemistry lab her junior year of college. But Eva had been the one with the skills. The one who said *yes* when she should have said *no*.

She tried hard not to think of that day in the dean's office, of the way Wade had slipped past everything and landed back in his charmed life, throwing touchdowns and luring girls too stupid to know better into doing things they shouldn't.

After they'd escorted her from the building, after she'd packed her bags and turned in her dorm key, panic had swept through her, deep and immobilizing. She had no one to turn to, nowhere to go. And then Dex appeared, sliding up next to her as she stood on the sidewalk outside her dorm, the same way she'd slipped alongside Brett that morning.

At the time, she only knew Dex as someone who hung around Wade and his friends, dark hair and startling gray eyes. He wasn't a student, and Eva could never figure out how he fit in. Like her, he rarely spoke, but he watched everything.

"I heard about what happened," he'd said. "I'm sorry."

She looked away, ashamed at how naive she'd been. How easily Wade had manipulated her. And how he'd gotten off and she'd gotten expelled.

Dex looked over her shoulder at some unseen object and spoke. "Look, it's a shitty situation. But I think I can help you."

She shoved her hands into her pockets against the cool fall night. "I doubt that."

"You have a skill that I think can benefit both of us."

She shook her head. "What are you talking about?"

"The drugs you made were great. I know a guy who can set you up with the equipment and the supplies to keep making them. His chemist is leaving the business, and he needs someone immediately. It's a great opportunity, if you want it. Totally safe. You make the drugs, he'll let you keep half to sell yourself. You can make more than five thousand dollars a week." Dex laughed, a bitter sound puffing into the air around them. "A school like this always has a need for uppers. Little pills that will get these kids through the next test, the next class, whatever." He gestured toward a group of students passing them on their way to the next bar or party, already drunk, laughing and in love with themselves. "They're not like you or me. They take Daddy's money, or the donor's money, and think nothing can touch them."

He looked into Eva's eyes, and she felt a flicker of hope. Dex was throwing her a lifeline, and she'd be stupid not to take it. "How?" she asked.

"I have a place near here," he said, "with a spare room you can crash in for a while. I help you, you help me."

"How would I be helping you?"

"You're exactly the kind of person my boss is looking for. Smart, and off everyone's radar."

Eva wanted to say no, but she was broke. She had no place to live. No skills with which to get a job. She imagined herself slinging her duffel bag over her shoulder and heading down to Telegraph Avenue, positioning herself among the other panhandlers, begging for money. Or returning to St. Joseph's, the weight of Sister Bernadette's disappointment, Sister

Catherine's curt nod, as if she'd always known Eva would turn out like her mother.

Eva had always been a survivor. But it was easy to be fearless when you'd already lost everything. "Tell me what I have to do."

––––––––––––––

Dex's voice pulled her back to the present. "A bunch of us are going into the city tonight to hear this new band, Arena, play. Come with us."

Eva shot him a sideways glance. "Pass."

"Come on, it'll be fun. I'll buy you Diet Cokes all night long. You need to get out more."

She studied the way his stubble was beginning to turn gray near his jawline. The way the ends of his hair curled up near his collar. She sometimes had to remind herself that Dex was her handler, not her friend. This was his attempt to keep an eye on her, not give her a fun night out. "I get out plenty," she said.

"Really?" he pressed. "When? With who?"

"Whom," she corrected.

Dex gave a soft chuckle. "Don't distract me with a grammar lesson, Professor." He nudged her arm. "You need a social life. You've been doing this long enough to know that you don't have to hide from the world. You're allowed to have friends."

Eva watched a mother sitting under a tree with her son, reading a book. "I'd spend all my time trying to hide things from them. Trust me. This is easier."

But it was also what she preferred. She never had to explain anything, or answer the get-to-know-you questions that people always asked. *Where did you grow up? Where did you go to college? What do you do now?*

"Is it easier, though?" Dex didn't look convinced. "What's that saying about work?"

"I never met a dollar I didn't like?"

Dex grinned. "No, the one about all work and no play."

"All work and no play makes Eva a rich girl," she finished. When he didn't laugh, she said, "Thanks for worrying about me. But really, I'm fine." She pulled her coat tighter. "Now, if you'll excuse me, I'm meeting that new client in a half hour, and then I'm working a shift at the restaurant."

For years, Eva had worked two shifts a week at DuPree's, an upscale steak and seafood restaurant in downtown Berkeley. The tips were great, and it allowed Eva to pay taxes, which kept her off the IRS's radar.

"I don't know why you bother with the charade," Dex said. "You don't need the money."

"The devil is in the details." Eva rose from the bench. "Have fun tonight. Don't do any drugs."

As she walked away, Eva glanced again at the playground. A small girl was standing at the top of the slide, frozen, fear plastered across her face. As tears began to fall, her cry grew into a loud wail that sent her mother running to help her. Eva watched the woman lift the little girl from the slide and carry her back to the bench where she'd been sitting, kissing the top of her daughter's head as she walked.

The girl's cries echoed in Eva's mind long after she closed her car door and drove away.

# CLAIRE

## Wednesday, February 23

I wake early and let my body and mind adjust to my new surroundings. My first full day of freedom. My head feels foggy, desperate for caffeine. But when I rummage around in Eva's kitchen, I can't find a coffee maker or coffee of any kind, and Diet Coke is not going to cut it. My stomach gurgles, reminding me I also need more than just crackers to eat, so I go upstairs to use the bathroom and grab Eva's purse, again tucking my hair under the NYU baseball cap.

Back downstairs, I stand in front of the mirror that hangs on the living room wall, my reflection staring back at me, blotched from a restless night of sleep. I'm still too much myself, recognizable to anyone who might be looking for me. *But no one is looking.* The thought slices through me, a brilliant flash of opportunity, impossible to ignore.

The street is dark and silent, the sound of my steps bouncing against the dark houses and echoing back to me, until I hit the edge of campus.

On the corner is a coffee shop, lights on, a young woman moving behind the counter, making coffee and setting pastries into the display case. I watch her from the safety of the shadowed sidewalk, weighing my need for caffeine and food against the risk of someone recognizing my face from the news.

But my stomach growls again, pushing me through the doors. Eclectic music swirls around the space, something Eastern and meditative. The smell of roasted coffee travels straight through me, and I inhale, savoring it.

"Morning," the barista says. Her long dreadlocks are held back with a colorful scarf, and her smile is bright. "What can I get you?"

"Large drip coffee, room for cream, and a ham and cheese croissant if you have one. To go please."

"You got it."

As she begins making my drink, I look around. Outlets dot the walls, and I imagine the place later in the morning, crowded with students studying and professors grading. As the barista finishes up my order, my eyes are drawn toward a stack of newspapers. *San Francisco Chronicle* and *Oakland Tribune*. The headlines are hard to avoid.

"The Fate of Flight 477" reads the *Tribune*.

"Crash of Flight 477 Leaves No Survivors and a Lot of Heartache" reads the *Chronicle*. Luckily, the editors have decided to go with action shots of the wreckage and not human-interest stories that would surely put my face on the front page. I hesitate for a split second, before sliding them both on the counter along with a twenty-dollar bill.

The barista sets my drink and a bag with my croissant next to them and hands me my change. "Sad, isn't it?"

I nod, unable to meet her eyes from under the brim of my cap, and shove the change in my pocket. Tucking the papers beneath my arm, I push out onto the dark street again.

I cross the empty road and follow a sidewalk that leads me into the center of campus. Beautiful redwoods tower over me, the sidewalk dotted with lamps still illuminated, casting pools of light beneath them. I follow a path through a thick stand of trees and emerge onto a wide expanse of grass leading down toward an enormous stone building. I settle on a bench and sip my coffee, letting it heat me from inside out. The place is deserted, though in a few hours it will probably be crowded with students, making their way across campus to morning classes or study halls. I open the bag and take a bite of my croissant, my mouth aching from the rich flavors. It's been nearly twenty-four hours since I've had anything substantive to eat, and it's been years since I've had anything as heavy as a ham and cheese croissant. I finish it quickly, then crumple the bag in my fist.

The birds in the trees around me begin to wake up, soft at first, but growing louder as light creeps over the hills to the east. Behind me, a street cleaner makes its way up the empty road, while overhead, a plane flies, its lights blinking. I think about the people on board, no different than the ones on Flight 477, who got on a plane thinking they'd get off at their destination, a little tired, a little wrinkled, but no different than taking the subway from point A to point B, trusting they'll arrive where they're supposed to.

The plane passes behind the trees, and I study the buildings that surround me and think about my own years at Vassar. My mother had been so proud of me, the first of our family to go to college. Violet had sobbed when I left, holding on to me so tight my mother had to pry her arms from around my waist.

I'd been ten when Violet was born, the product of a short and volatile relationship with a man who left town shortly after my mother told him she was pregnant. I was relieved, and I think my mother was too. She had a talent for finding unsuitable men whose only skill was their unreliability, like my own father, who disappeared when I was four. *I got the better end of the deal*, she'd always say. My mother never seemed to think we needed anyone but the three of us. But I always wished she had found someone to share the burden, to make us feel more like the families I read about in books and saw on TV. I knew she was lonely and often worried about money, exhausted from working two jobs and doing everything on her own.

And so I tried to make things easier for her. I was a hands-on sister from day one, feeding Violet, changing her diapers, carrying her for hours when she fussed. I watched her while our mother worked, taught her how to play Monopoly and how to tie her shoes. Leaving home was the hardest thing I ever did, but I needed to see who I might be, apart from a dutiful daughter and devoted sister. My high school years had been rough, and I was eager to reinvent myself as someone new, to build the life for myself I'd always dreamed of. I feel the weight now, the cost of wandering too far away from home. Of wanting too much.

I could have gone to college locally. Worked part-time. Spent the evenings with my mother and sister around our wobbly kitchen table, where we could have sat in the warm, yellow light, my mother doing a crossword while Violet and I played endless games of gin rummy.

Instead, I'd left, and I never went home again. Not in any real sense.

---

The sky is streaked with pink clouds, and the lamps on the walkway flicker off for the day. It would be easy to sit here and wallow—to rail against all that has happened to me—but I don't have that luxury. I need to stay focused and make some decisions. What do I need?

*Money, and a place to hide.* One out of two isn't bad.

I won't be able to stay at Eva's for very long. As soon as Eva doesn't show up downtown next week, people are going to come looking for her, and I want to be gone by the time that happens. But for now, it's my best option. It's free, and it's safe.

I stand and toss my empty coffee cup and crumpled bag into a nearby trash can, making my way back toward the edge of campus, the newspapers tucked into Eva's purse. Behind me, bells toll the hour, and I pause, listening. The chimes seem to vibrate through me, and I think of what it would be like to live here. To walk these streets on my way to a job I don't yet have, living the quiet life I always imagined for myself when I dreamed about leaving Rory. Of all the scenarios I imagined, the glitches I prepared for, the mistakes I knew were inevitable, I never imagined a break as clean as this. Not a single person knows what happened to me, and I have to guard this opportunity—for that's what this is, an incredible and heartbreaking opportunity—with every ounce of cunning I've got.

---

I find a twenty-four hour pharmacy a few blocks west of campus. The bright lights assault my eyes when I enter. I angle my head down, keeping my cap pulled low, and find the hair-care aisle. So many different shades, from bright reds to jet blacks, and everything in between. I think of Eva's blond pixie cut and choose something called Ultimate Platinum. On a lower shelf is a complete hair-cutting kit—*Easy to use clippers! Color-coded combs! A step-by-step guide to the most popular hairstyles!*—on sale for twenty dollars, and I grab that too.

At the front of the store, there's only one person working the registers, a pimply undergrad who looks half-asleep at the end of his shift, with glazed eyes and earbuds shoved into his ears. I set everything down on the counter and mentally calculate how much of my meager savings this will eat up.

I hesitate before sliding Eva's debit card out of her wallet, tracing the edges of it, wondering if I can use it as a credit card. I cast a quick glance around the empty store before I slide it into the machine. It's not like Eva's going to come back and accuse me of stealing from her.

I bypass the request for a PIN and select credit, my heart beating out a frantic rhythm I'm certain this kid can hear through whatever music pounds in his ears.

But then the register does something I can't see, drawing the kid's attention back. "Credit? I gotta see your ID," he says.

I freeze as if I've been caught in a bright headlight, every vulnerable inch of me exposed. Thirty seconds. One minute. An eternity.

"You okay, lady?" he asks.

Then I snap back. "Sure," I say, and pretend to search through my wallet, finally saying, "I must have left it at home. Sorry." I tuck the card back into my wallet and quickly pull out cash to cover the cost. When he hands me my receipt, I scramble out of the store as fast as I can, my entire body vibrating with tension and fear.

———————

The brisk walk back to Eva's steadies me, and when I get there, I take everything upstairs to the bathroom and strip off my clothes, propping the directions to the hair clippers against the mirror, noticing for the first time the expensive hand lotions that line the counter. I open the cap on one and sniff—roses, with a hint of lavender. Then I peek in the medicine cabinet, expecting to see numerous prescriptions leftover from her husband's illness. Painkillers. Sleeping pills. But it's empty. Just a box of tampons and an old razor. I close it with a soft click, uneasiness poking at me, like a minuscule burr in my sock, a flash of warning and then gone, impossible to locate.

I take a last look at myself in the mirror, the way my hair tumbles and curls around my face, and take a deep breath before attaching the medium-sized comb to the clippers and turning them on. I remind myself that even if I mess up, it won't matter. Eva's words about Berkeley come back to me. *It's easy to blend in because everybody's a little weirder than you are.* No one will look twice at a bad haircut.

I'm surprised by how easy it comes off, leaving an inch and a half of hair resting against my scalp. My eyes look bigger. My cheekbones more pronounced. My neck longer. I turn one way, and then another, admiring my profile, before turning to the box of hair color. Not done yet.

---

The dye has to stay on for forty-five minutes, so while I wait, I spread the newspapers open on the coffee table and read, my scalp tingling and burning, the sharp smell of chemicals making me dizzy. The articles are filled with details of the crash, though they're incomplete, gleaned only from radio communication with the air traffic controllers. But it's enough to chill me, to force me to reckon with what I've done. Approximately two hours into the flight, after they'd crossed Florida and were over the Atlantic, one of the plane's engines went out. The pilots tried to turn around and radioed Miami, requesting an emergency landing. But the plane didn't make it, instead crashing into the water thirty-five miles off the coast. The article is filled with statements from NTSB officials, and of course, Rory's representative on behalf of the families. No details are given yet about recovery, other than to say it's ongoing.

I try to imagine my bag, my phone, my pink sweater, torn from Eva's body and floating in the water, waiting for someone to scoop them out and identify them. Or nestling onto the sandy bottom of the ocean, where they'll soon be lost forever. I wonder whether they will try to recover remains, or if that's even possible. And what might happen if they come across someone whose dental records don't match anyone on the flight manifest.

I take several deep breaths, focusing on the biology of it. Oxygen entering my bloodstream, feeding my cells, then releasing carbon dioxide into the quiet space that surrounds me. In and out, again and again, each breath a reminder: *I made it out. I survived.*

———————

Forty-five minutes later I stare at myself in the mirror of Eva's bathroom, astonished. Taken on their own—my eyes, my nose, my smile—I can still see my old self, looking back at me. But as a whole? I'm someone completely new. If I seem familiar to anyone, they're going to search different corners of their mind, different parts of their life—someone from work or college. Perhaps the daughter of a former neighbor. They won't see Rory Cook's wife, who died in a plane crash.

The look suits me, and I love the freedom it offers. Rory always insisted I keep my hair long, so that I could wear it up for formal events and down for casual ones, arguing it was more feminine. I grin, and am surprised to see flashes of my mother, of Violet, smiling back at me.

———————

On the nightstand next to Eva's bed, the clock flips to seven o'clock, and I can't help but think about what I'd be doing right now if I were still living my old life in New York. I'd be sitting across from Danielle in my office, outlining our schedule for the day. Morning Meeting, she called it. We'd discuss the calendar—meetings, lunches, evening events—and I'd give her the tasks I needed her to work on for the day. But if my plan had worked, I'd be somewhere in Canada. Maybe on a train, heading west. I'd be scouring the news for any hint of my disappearance, the plane crash just a sad story that might have caught my attention for a moment. Instead, it's the turning point for my entire life.

I return to my computer and pull up the CNN home page, clicking on a short human-interest piece titled "Rory Cook's Second Heartbreak," with my photo alongside Maggie Moretti's. They rehash her death over twenty-five years ago and the subsequent investigation into Rory's involvement, and for the first time I realize how similar Maggie and I are. Some of the information I'd already known about her—she'd been a track star at Yale, where she'd met Rory, and she, too, had come from a small town. But I hadn't known that her parents had also died, when she was even younger than I was. Looking at us side by side, it makes me wonder if Rory had a type, zeroing in on women alone in the world who might be eager to join an established family like the Cooks. I know I was at first.

---

We'd met at an off Broadway play two years after I'd graduated from college. He sat in the seat next to mine and struck up a conversation before the curtain rose. I'd recognized him immediately, but nothing prepared me for how charismatic and funny he was in person. Thirteen years my senior and well over six feet, Rory had light brown hair streaked with gold, and blue eyes that seemed to pierce straight through me. And when I was under his gaze, the whole world faded away.

At intermission, he bought me a drink and told me about an art program the Cook Family Foundation was bringing to inner-city schools. These are the things that made him three-dimensional and more than just a face I recognized from the pages of magazines. His passion for education. The fire he had to make the world a better place. At the end of the show, he asked for my number.

I'd kept my distance at first. Older men like Rory—with their money, privilege, and connections—were not my speed. I didn't have the cultural knowledge or the wardrobe. But he'd been subtly persistent, calling to ask my advice when the foundation hit a wall with an organization they wanted for their arts education initiative, or inviting me to a show at one of their project schools. I was lured in by his vision of philanthropy, of how he wanted to use his family's money to better the lives of others.

All of that impressed me, but I fell in love with Rory's vulnerability, the way he'd strived and failed to hold his mother's attention. "As a young boy, it was hard not to resent her long absences, the months she spent in DC," he'd told me once. "The constant campaigning—for herself, or for others—and the causes that would consume her. But now I can see why it was so important. The impact she had on people's lives. I still get stopped in the street by people wanting to tell me how much they loved her. How something she did years ago still affects them now."

But that kind of legacy always has a price. Whether he liked it or not, Rory was defined by his mother. When you Googled Rory Cook, she always popped up too. Images of her with a young Rory, on vacation or the campaign trail. Rory at age thirteen, scowling in the background at one of his mother's political rallies, all elbows and pimples and one eye squinted shut.

And hundreds of images of Rory doing the bidding of the Cook Family Foundation, his mother's dying gift to the world. People loved Rory because of who he almost was. And he'd spent his entire adult life trying to step out from behind her long shadow.

———————————

I click off the CNN home page and toggle over to take a look at Rory's inbox, careful not to open anything that isn't already read. He has at least fifty folders on the left-hand side, one for each of the organizations the foundation contributes to. Buried in that long list is one labeled *Claire*. I click on it and scan the condolence emails. Hundreds of them, page after page, from family friends, Senate colleagues of his mother's. People who have worked with the foundation, quick to offer their sympathy. *Let us know if there's anything you need.*

I open an email Bruce sent to Danielle several hours after the initial reports emerged about the crash, but before I'd been publicly named as one of the victims. He'd cc'd Rory. The subject line reads *Details*.

> I'm already drafting the statement and should have it
> ready well before any scheduled press conferences.
> Danielle, please handle the staff in New York. They are
> not to speak to anyone. Remind them that they all
> have active non-disclosure agreements.

Another folder, *Google Alerts*, is filled with mostly unread notifications. Every time Rory's name appears online, he gets an email about it. Danielle also gets them in her inbox, because it's her job to sort through them and brief Rory on anything important he might have missed. My mind leaps back to last week, Danielle and I on our way home from a Friends of the Library event, me staring out the window at the slushy streets of Manhattan while Danielle flipped through that day's alerts. "A fluff piece in *HuffPo*," she said, almost to herself. "Trash." I turned to see her deleting the alerts, one after the other, only opening the ones from major media outlets. She caught my eye and said, "We're going to need to hire an intern for this once the campaign starts. Hundreds a day are going to turn into thousands."

Now I scan the long list of unread notifications in the wake of the crash and smirk. Too bad, Danielle.

I click over to the Doc. Blank. At the top it now reads *Last edit made by Bruce Corcoran 36 hours ago.*

I take a sip of Diet Coke, the carbonation tickling my nose. No one would ever imagine I wasn't on that plane.

The sun is fully up now, and I study the room. The hardwood floor is covered with a deep red area rug, which contrasts beautifully with walls painted a warm shade of yellow that reminds me of the color of my mother's living room, and in this moment, I feel protected, like a hibernating bear. While the world races on without me, I'm tucked up here, invisible, waiting until it's safe to emerge again.

I ease open the top drawer of Eva's desk, curious. I'm living in her house. Wearing her clothes. I'm going to have to use her name—at least for a little while. It would help to know who she was.

I start tentatively at first, as if I'm afraid if I move things around too much, someone will know I was here. Most of what I find is generic—faded receipts I can't read. A few dried-out pens, a couple pads of paper from local real estate agents. As I begin to grow more comfortable, I reach my hand to the back, sliding the jumble of pushpins, paper clips, and a tiny blue flashlight to the front, trying to peer beneath the mess to the person who threw these items into the drawer, believing she'd have time to sort them out.

---

Two hours later, I sit on the floor of the office, papers strewn around me. I've emptied the desk and gone through everything in it. Bank statements. Paid utility and cable bills. All of them in Eva's name. I'd found a box in the closet containing files with more important documents. Her car registration. Her social security card. But I'm struck by what's missing. No marriage license. No insurance paperwork you'd expect after a long illness and a death. What had been nagging me about Eva's house yesterday returns, this time in sharp focus. There aren't any personal touches. No photographs or sentimental pieces anywhere. There is absolutely no evidence that anyone other than Eva lived here. For someone who couldn't bear to face all the belongings of a deceased and beloved husband, there are zero reminders of him to have left behind.

I work hard to find explanations for what's missing. Maybe her husband had bad credit and all the bills had to be in her name. Maybe everything related to him is boxed up in the garage, too painful to even have inside the house. But these feel flimsy, half-color fabrications that are simply not true.

I pull out the last file in the box and open it. It's escrow paperwork for an all-cash purchase of this side of the duplex, dated two years ago. At the top, her name only. *Eva Marie James.* And underneath it, the box next to *Single* is checked.

I can still hear her voice in my mind, the way she spoke of her husband. High school sweethearts. Together for eighteen years. The emotion in her voice when she described her decision to help him die, the way it broke, the tears in her eyes.

She lied. She fucking *lied.* About all of it.

# EVA

Ten minutes before her scheduled meeting with Brittany, Eva parked her car in a lot at the outer edge of Tilden Park, rather than driving into the interior. She preferred to walk in and out, arrive and leave silently. Tucking the package into her coat pocket, she turned toward a path that would take her to a tiny clearing where she used to come and study, a lifetime ago.

The full trees cast a dappled shade on the path, yet a cool wind kicked up from the bay, despite it being the last month of summer. Even though the sky above was clear, Eva caught glimpses of San Francisco Bay in the distance, of the marine layer gathering over the Pacific, and knew in a few hours that would change. She shoved her hands deep into the pockets of her favorite coat—army green with several zippered pockets—and felt the outline of the pills through their wrapping paper.

The trees that surrounded Eva were old friends. She recognized them individually, the shape of their trunks and the reach of their branches. She tried to place herself back in time, coming here after classes were over, spreading her books across the picnic table or on the grass if the weather was warm. Sometimes Eva caught flashes of that girl, like images from a passing train. Glimpses into a different life, with a regular job and friends, and she'd feel unsettled for days.

When she arrived at the clearing, she was relieved to see she was alone. The scarred wooden picnic table still stood beneath a giant oak tree, a concrete trash can chained to it. She wandered over to the table and sat on it, checking the time again, the familiar location drawing her mind back in time.

———

Fish ran the drug underworld in Berkeley and Oakland, and Dex worked for him. "Most drug dealers get picked up quickly," Dex had warned her at the very beginning. He'd taken her to lunch at a waterfront restaurant in Sausalito, so he could explain what she'd be doing. Across the bay, San Francisco had been swathed in a deep fog, only the tops of the tallest buildings visible. She'd thought of St. Joseph's and the nuns who'd raised her, buried under the fog and the assumption that Eva was still enrolled in school, still on track to graduate with full honors in chemistry, instead of where she was—three days post expulsion, sleeping in Dex's spare bedroom and getting a crash course on drug selling and distribution. Eva tore her eyes away and focused back on Dex.

"What you make has a very specific market," Dex continued. "You will only sell to people referred to you by me. This is how you'll stay safe."

"I'm confused," Eva had said. "Am I making or selling?"

Dex folded his hands on top of the table. They'd finished eating, and the server had tucked the check next to Dex's water glass and then disap-peared. "Historically, Fish has struggled to keep good chemists for long. They always think they can do better on their own and then things get complicated. So we're going to try something different with you," he'd said. "You will produce three hundred pills a week. As compensation for this work, you will keep half and Fish will let you sell them yourself, keeping one hundred percent of those profits."

"Who will I sell them to?" she'd asked, suddenly uncomfortable, imagining herself face-to-face with strung-out addicts. People who might grow violent. People like her mother.

Dex smiled. "You will provide an important service to a very specific clientele—students, professors, and athletes. Five pills should sell for about two hundred dollars," Dex had told her. "You can clear $300,000 per year, easy." He smiled at her stunned expression. "This only works if you follow the rules," he'd warned. "If we hear you're branching out, or selling to addicts, you put everything and everyone at risk. Understand?"

She'd nodded and cast an anxious glance toward the entrance. "What about Fish? I thought he'd be here today."

Dex laughed and shook his head. "God, you're green. I forget you don't know how any of this works. If you do your job well, you'll never meet Fish." She must have looked confused, because he clarified. "Fish keeps things compartmentalized. It's how he protects himself. If any one person knew too much, they'd become a target—of either a competitor or the police. I'll be your handler, and I'll make sure you stay safe." Dex dropped several twenty-dollar bills onto the table and stood. Their meal was over. "If you do as I tell you, you'll have a nice life. It's safe as long as you follow the rules."

"Don't you worry about getting caught?"

"Despite what you might see on TV, the police only know the ones they catch, and they only catch the dumb ones. But Fish isn't dumb. He's not in this for power. He's a businessman who thinks about long-term gains. And that means growing slowly, being selective about his clients as well as the people who work for him."

She'd been eager to get started. It had sounded so simple. And the system worked. The only hard part was being on campus among her peers, having to live alongside the life she'd just lost. Walking past her dorm where the same people still lived. The chemistry building where her classes went on without her. The stadium where Wade continued to shine, and one year later, the graduation ceremony that should have been hers. It was as if she'd stepped through some kind of barrier, where she could watch her old life still unfold, unseen. But as the years passed, the students grew younger and soon campus was populated by all new people. The loss had faded, as all losses did, replaced by something harder. Stronger. She could see now what she couldn't see then. All choices had consequences. It was what you did with those consequences that mattered.

———————

Eva's gaze tracked down the small service road that wound its way through the hundreds of acres that comprised Tilden Park. Something about this meeting felt off, and her instincts, finely tuned after so many years, were pinging. She'd give Brittany ten more minutes and then leave. Return to her car and drive home, closing the door and forgetting about this woman. Eva worked hard to stay sharp. To not grow complacent and careless. Despite how mundane the work could sometimes feel—the endless hours in the lab, the quick handoffs with Dex or a client—this job was dangerous.

Early on—it must have been some time in her first year—Dex had woken her, just before dawn, a quiet knocking on her door. "Come with me," he'd said, and she'd pulled her coat from the hook, following him across the deserted campus, the pathways still lit by lamps.

They'd walked west without talking, past the track stadium, restaurants and bars closed and shuttered at that predawn hour. She'd seen the flashing emergency lights from a block away. Police, ambulance, yellow crime-scene tape cordoning off the sidewalk outside a cheap motor court motel, forcing them to cross the street.

Dex had put his arm around her and pulled her close, as if they were a couple making their way home after a late night out. They'd slowed as they drew near, and Eva could make out a body, a puddle of blood seeping out from under it, a shoeless foot, the white sock practically glowing.

"Why are we here? Do you know that guy?"

"Yeah," he'd said, his voice rough. "Danny. He supplied Fish with harder stuff. Coke. Heroin."

Dex pulled her along, and they rounded the corner, the flashing red and blue lights still staining the backs of her eyelids. "What happened to him?"

"I don't know," Dex had told her. "Like you, I only see what I'm allowed to see. But if I had to guess, he was either double-dealing—working for one of Fish's competitors—or he fucked up somehow, got snagged by police." He paused. "That's the thing about Fish. He's not going to spend a lot of time asking questions. He's just going to fix the problem."

Eva couldn't erase the image from her mind, the twisted form of the body, the sheer volume of blood, more than she'd ever imagined, a black-red shade that only appeared in nightmares.

Dex had dropped his arm from around her, and cold morning air chilled the place where it had rested. "Fish is a strong ally, but a ruthless enemy. He will not hesitate to eliminate anyone who betrays him. Maybe it was a mistake to have brought you here, but I needed you to see for yourself what will happen if you cross him."

Eva had swallowed hard. Up until that point, she'd fooled herself into believing this job had been no different from any other—mostly

98

routine, maybe a little dangerous in some abstract way. But Dex had insulated her from the worst of it. Until that morning.

"Full transparency," Dex had warned, as they walked back up her street, the night sky finally shifting to a pale gray. He deposited her on the porch and disappeared, making her wonder if she'd dreamt it all.

———————

Eva was just about to hop off the picnic table and head back to her car when a Mercedes SUV pulled up at the curb, a polished woman behind the wheel. In the back, Eva could make out a child's car seat, thankfully empty. The license plate read *FUNMOM1*. Her lingering unease intensified, and she took a deep breath, reminding herself she was in control of the situation and could walk away at any time.

She watched as the woman got out of the car. "Thanks for meeting me!" she called. Her clothes were expensive casual. Chanel sunglasses tipped up on her head. Knee-high UGG boots, worn over designer jeans. This was not Eva's typical ramen-fed student.

Up close, Eva could see the woman's red-rimmed eyes, how her skin looked tired and stretched, though her makeup was flawless, and another tingle of apprehension zipped through her.

"Sorry I'm late. I had to wait for the sitter to show up." She held out her hand for Eva to shake. "I'm Brittany."

Eva let it hang there, keeping her own hands in her pockets, and Brittany finally let it fall to her side as she began digging through her purse as if she'd just remembered why she'd come. "I was hoping I could buy more than what we'd talked about. I know I asked for five pills, but I really need ten." She pulled a wad of cash out of her purse and held it out to Eva. "That's four hundred instead of two."

"I only brought five with me," Eva said, not taking the money.

Brittany shook her head, as if that were a minor detail. "I'd be happy to meet you again tomorrow. Same place, if that suits you."

The marine layer from over the bay finally rolled in, skirting over the sun, casting gray shadows and dimming the light. Wind kicked up, causing Eva to pull her coat tighter. Brittany looked over her shoulder and then lowered her voice, although they were the only ones around. "We're leaving on Saturday for a trip," she continued. "We won't be back until next month. I just want to make sure I'm not caught short."

Eva's body tensed. This woman drove a fancy car, wore expensive clothes, and had a big diamond on her finger. It was one thing to need the pills to push through a difficult task. This woman seemed to need pharmaceutical help to navigate her daily life. But Eva's resistance felt more personal, bubbling up from her darkest corners, surprising her with its heat. This was a woman like her mother.

"I don't think I can help you," Eva said.

"At least let me buy what you brought," Brittany said, her words loud, tearing through the empty clearing. "Please."

Eva's gaze snagged on several scabs dotting the backs of Brittany's hands, picked red and raw by nervous fingers. Brittany thrummed with manic energy, and Eva only wanted to leave.

"We're done here," Eva said.

"Wait," Brittany said, reaching out for Eva's arm. "Tell me what I can do to change your mind."

Eva yanked her arm back and turned to walk away.

"Come on," Brittany cajoled from behind her. "It's why we're here. You make the sale and get your money. I get what I need, and we both win."

"I don't know what you're talking about," Eva called over her shoulder. "You must have me confused with someone else." Then she strode toward the hiking trail that wound through the trees and down the hill to the lot where she parked her car.

As she passed the SUV, she looked in the window. The back seat was littered with Cheerios, an empty sippy cup, and a pink hair ribbon. Eva slowed for a moment, wondering what that child's life was like, living with a mother who begged for enough pills to be strung out for weeks. She wondered if her own mother had been like Brittany, buying drugs in a deserted park while Eva was stuck at home with a sitter. Beneath it all, she hated herself for the fleeting whisper of jealousy that this little girl still got to know her mother while Eva had not.

As she moved into the woods, Eva heard Brittany yelling obscenities after her. Then she heard the slam of a car door and the engine rev, before tires squealed away from the curb. She looked over her shoulder and saw the car swerve, skidding against the curb as it careened around a bend in the road. Eva held her breath, bracing for the sound of impact that didn't come, then hurried back to her own car.

———————

Eva saw her again, at the gas station directly across from the park exit, as she waited at a red light. That same SUV, and Brittany leaning out of her open window, talking to a man who stood next to a low sedan with tinted windows and government plates. Brittany handed the man a slip of paper, which he tucked into the pocket of his sport coat.

The light turned green, and still Eva stared, her unease from earlier crashing back into her, quickly morphing into a dark panic. Behind her, someone honked, jolting her attention back to the road, forcing her to drive forward. As she drew nearer, she tried to capture as many details as she could. The man's short brown hair and mirrored sunglasses. The outline of a holster beneath his sport coat. And as she drove away, she wondered what Brittany had just put into play.

———————

At home, Eva pulled her car into the small garage at the side of the house and closed the door, locking it with the padlock. She was desperate to get inside and call Dex, but her new neighbor was sitting on the front step, as if she was waiting for her. "Shit," she muttered under her breath.

Relief spread across the woman's face when she saw Eva. "I fell," she said. "Missed that last stair and took a tumble. I think my ankle is sprained. Could you help me inside?"

Eva glanced down the street, thinking again of the man at the gas station, of the piece of paper he slipped into his coat. She didn't have time for this. But she couldn't leave the woman on the porch. "Sure," she said.

Eva helped the woman stand and was surprised at how tiny she was. Barely five feet tall and easily into her sixties, she was wiry but strong. She gripped the railing and pulled herself up the steps as Eva supported her, hopping on one foot until she got to the top. Eva gave her a moment to catch her breath, and together they made it to the door and into her apartment.

Warm-colored rugs covered the floor, contrasting with a cream-colored couch. One wall in the dining room had been painted a deep red, and half-emptied shipping boxes cluttered the corners. Eva helped her to a chair, and the woman sat.

"Do you want some ice?" Eva asked, impatient to move things along. She needed to contact Dex, to figure out what was going on and what she should do, not play nursemaid to her neighbor.

"Let's start with names," she said. "I'm Liz."

Eva fought back a growing panic, feeling the minutes slipping away, caught in some kind of a small-talk time warp with her chatty neighbor. But she smiled anyways and said, "My name is Eva."

"Nice to finally meet you, Eva. Yes, I would love some ice. Straight through there, if you don't mind."

Dismissed, Eva entered the kitchen, which was bare except for a few plates and glasses on the counter by the sink. In the freezer, Liz had a tray of ice cubes that Eva broke apart and piled into a dishtowel, winding the top closed. She grabbed a glass from the dish rack next to the sink and filled it with water, noticing how her hands trembled as she carried them both back to the living room and handed them to Liz. She was about to make her excuses and leave when Liz said, "Have a seat. Keep me company."

With another quick glance toward the window and the empty street beyond, she lowered herself onto a chair that allowed her to keep an eye on things outside.

Liz's smile grew wider. "I don't know very many people here yet," she said. "I'm a visiting professor from Princeton, teaching two classes this semester."

Eva smiled politely, only half-listening as Liz talked about how much she was looking forward to a California winter, and ran through the encounter with Brittany again. What she'd said. The way her hands shook. How desperate she'd been to make the deal. Any deal. Gradually, Eva's mind began to slow, the panic subsiding. She'd been in tight spots before, and she reminded herself that she hadn't done anything illegal. She was safe for now in Liz's living room, with a clear view of the street, listening to Liz explain why she preferred to rent an apartment rather than subject herself to the politics of faculty housing. She could practically feel her blood pressure lowering.

"Now tell me," Liz said. "What do you do? Where are you from?"

Eva tore her gaze from the window and delivered her standard reply. "I grew up in San Francisco. I'm a server at DuPree's in downtown Berkeley." And then she swung the conversation back to Liz. "So you're a professor? What do you teach?"

Liz reached for her water and took a drink. "Political economics," she said. "Economic theory and the accompanying political economic systems." She laughed. "I promise you, it's a fascinating subject."

She pulled the ice off, and Eva watched as she studied her ankle, turning it cautiously. Liz looked up and grinned. "Not a sprain. Which is a relief, because launching a new semester on crutches would have been a challenge."

There was something about Liz's voice, deep and resonant despite her small size, that calmed Eva. It vibrated inside of her, causing her to breathe deeper. To listen harder. Eva imagined her at the front of a large lecture hall, her voice carrying into the very farthest corners. The scratch of pens on paper or the quick tapping on laptops, students eagerly recording everything she said.

From her position on Liz's couch, Eva saw the government sedan glide down the street and slow to a stop at the curb. The same man who'd been talking to Brittany at the gas station got out and walked up their front path.

Her mind began connecting dots she hadn't even known were there, passing over the question of how he'd found her house to its inevitable answer—there must have been someone else following her. Someone she hadn't seen.

Eva stood suddenly and moved toward Liz. Away from the window. "Are you sure you don't need to see a doctor?"

Liz put the ice back on her ankle and said, "I'll tell you what I need. I need you to dump out this crappy tap water and fill my glass with vodka. Get one for yourself too. It's in the freezer." The faint sound of knocking from next door caught Liz's attention. "I think someone's knocking on your door," she said.

Eva peeked through the blinds and saw the man slide something into her mail slot. Every nerve in her body tingled with fear, urging her to run. She glanced through the doorway and into Liz's kitchen, imagining herself tearing out the back door, through the back gate and down the alley, sprinting all the way to Dex's, demanding answers.

But she took a deep breath, reminding herself that all she'd done was talk to a woman in the park. She hadn't sold her anything, or even showed her anything. *Play through.* Advice Dex used to give her in the early days when she'd get scared. *Only guilty people run. That's exactly what they're waiting for you to do. So don't do it.*

"I've seen this guy before," Eva lied. "He's selling subscriptions to an alarm company. You have to pretend like you're not home, otherwise he'll talk your ear off."

"I hate door-to-door salesmen," Liz said. If she thought it odd he didn't come to her door next, she didn't mention it.

Eva stood and said, "I think I'll go get those drinks for us." A drink was the very least she deserved.

# CLAIRE

I leave Eva's office strewn with paper and move across the hall, determined to know for certain what I'm beginning to suspect—that nothing Eva told me about herself, or what she was running from, was true. I throw open the door to her closet, pawing through the hangers, looking for evidence of the husband she adored. At the very least, there should be big, empty spaces where his clothes used to be. But all I find are a few nice tops, a couple dresses, boots, and flats. All of it Eva's. I yank open dresser drawers, finding shirts, jeans, underwear, and socks, flashes of my unfamiliar new profile startling me in the mirror, so similar to Eva's I can almost believe for a moment she's returned. That she's here and I'm the one who died. *Freaky fucking Friday.*

I sink down on Eva's bed. Everything I believed—about Eva, about her life, about why she didn't want to be here, lay in pieces at my feet. If there was no husband, there will be no investigation of his death. And if there's no investigation, there has to be another reason why Eva was so willing to trade places and disappear.

I begin to laugh—the hysterical spiral of an exhausted woman teetering on the edge of sanity—and think of all the lies she told, straight-faced and sincere. And then I hear her voice in my head, and imagine her telling me to calm down and get the fuck out of her house, and I smirk at how sharp it is, how perfectly I can still recall it.

Neither of us could have guessed this was what would happen. We were only trading tickets. I wasn't supposed to drive to her house, unlock her door, and step into her life. Whatever I've walked into, I'm here because I chose to be.

———————

Back in Eva's office, with the Doc open on the screen in front of me, I take a closer look at one of Eva's bank statements, scanning her monthly expenses. Food, gas, coffee shops. Automatic payments every month for everything, including cable and trash service, with a balance of two thousand dollars. There are two direct deposits from a place called DuPree's Steakhouse, each for nine hundred dollars. Not nearly enough income to warrant an all-cash purchase of her home.

And as I expected, no medical bills, no copays. No pharmacies. I feel a sliver of admiration at the outrageous fabrication rendered with the finesse of a con artist. The smooth way she set her boarding pass on the bar between us, a quiet temptation I was too preoccupied to notice at the time, the way she described how easy it was to blend in to Berkeley. The subtle way she reflected my own desires and fears back at me, allowing me to fall into step alongside her.

According to her car registration, she drives an old Honda, which is most likely hidden in the attached garage. A woman smart enough to orchestrate something like this isn't going to leave her car parked at an airport or train station, identifying that as her starting point. I don't want anything to do with it, though. If someone's looking for her, they'll surely begin with her car. But it's nice to know it's there, if I need it.

I make quick work of the rest of Eva's desk. More dried-out pens and paper clips in a tangle, empty envelopes, a few charging bricks with no cords. But none of the other things you'd expect to find. No saved birthday cards or appointment reminders. No photographs, notes, or sentimental keepsakes. Not only was her husband a fabrication, I'm beginning to wonder if Eva was too.

I look to the left of the desk, where an empty trash can sits, and my gaze catches on a small piece of paper, partially concealed behind the desk, as if someone meant to throw it away and missed. I pick it up and smooth it. It's a small card, the handwriting a neat cursive, the slanted, loopy kind you don't see beyond elementary school. *Everything you ever wanted is on the other side of fear.*

I try to imagine the circumstances upon which Eva wrote this and then later discarded it. If perhaps she didn't need it anymore, or whether it stopped being something she believed to be true.

I carry it across the hall to Eva's bedroom, tuck the card into the edge of the mirror over her dresser, and begin to tidy the mess I'd made. As I refold her shirts, the smell of her—flowers with that chemical undernote—stirs in the air around me. I come across a Red Hot Chili Peppers T-shirt, and I hold it against my chest. Oversized and well worn, it's from their *Californication* tour. The Chili Peppers were one of Violet's favorite bands, and I had promised her that when she turned sixteen, I'd take her to a concert. One of the many things she never got to do. I drape the shirt over my shoulder and close the drawer. This, I want.

I finish tidying the dresser, confirming no hidden money or jewelry. No diary or love letters stashed away from prying eyes. Fictional husband aside, no one—except perhaps me, living in Rory's house—lives a life this empty.

Across the room, I sit on the edge of her bed and open the top drawer of her nightstand. Another tube of expensive hand lotion that smells like roses when I rub it into my arm. A bottle of Tylenol. But tucked along the inside edge of the drawer is a photo, the only one I've seen in the house so far. It's a novelty shot of Eva posing with an older woman outside a stadium in San Francisco. Enormous Giants Baseball banners hang behind life-sized cutouts of players, and the women pose, their heads tilted together, Eva laughing, her arm draped over the woman's shoulders. She looks light and happy, as if whatever shadows were chasing her hadn't shown up yet. I wonder if this was a friend, or someone else Eva had tricked. Whether everything Eva did had been calculated for her own benefit.

I imagine Eva, spinning her lies. Making this woman believe Eva was someone who needed help. I study the woman's face, wondering where she is now, whether she might come looking for Eva, and what she'd say to find me, with the exact same haircut and color as Eva's, living in Eva's house, wearing her clothes. Who's the con artist now?

At the back of the drawer, underneath a pair of scissors and some tape, I find an envelope. Inside it is a handwritten note dated thirteen years ago, clipped to some pages behind it. I remove the clip and flip through them, paperwork from a place in San Francisco called St. Joseph's. A convent? A church? The handwriting is spidery and faded, and I tilt it toward the window so I can read it better.

*Dear Eva,*

*I hope this letter finds you well, studying hard and learning a lot! I'm writing to let you know that after over eighty years, the St. Joseph's group home is finally being absorbed into the county foster system. It's probably for the best, as we are all getting older here—even Sister Catherine.*

*I remember you used to frequently ask about your birth family, and while we were prohibited from answering your questions at the time, now that you're over eighteen, I want to give you all the information we have. I'm enclosing copies of our notes on your intake and the general records from your years here. If there are any specifics you want to know, you'll have to petition the county for your official records. I think the social worker who worked on your case was Craig Henderson.*

*You should know that I tracked down your mother's family after your last foster placement failed, hoping they might have had a change of heart. But they hadn't. Your mother struggled with addiction, and her family was overwhelmed with the burden of monitoring and caring for her. That was a large part of why they surrendered you in the first place.*

*But despite that beginning, you've grown into an incredible person. Please know that we talk of you still—and are so proud of your many accomplishments. Sister Catherine scours the newspapers for your name in association with a magnificent scientific discovery, although I have to remind her you're still in school and that's probably a few years off yet. We would welcome a visit or a call to learn what kind of wonderful life you've built for yourself at Berkeley. You are destined to do great things.*

*Much love in Christ,*
*Sister Bernadette*

I set it aside, looking at the rest of the papers that were attached with the clip. They're photocopies of handwritten notes, dating back over thirty years ago. They describe the arrival and adjustment of a two-year-old girl at a Catholic group home.

*Child, Eva, arrived at 7:00 p.m.; mother, Rachel Ann James, declined interview, signed documents for termination of parental rights. St. Joseph's submitted paperwork to county, awaiting response.*

Another page, dated twenty-four years ago, was less clinical.

*Eva returned to us last night. This was her third placement, and I fear her last. We will keep her as long as the Lord guides us to, and give her a spot here at St. Joe's. CH is the social worker assigned to her case this time, which means we won't be seeing much of him.*

A student at Berkeley explains the science textbooks downstairs. Perhaps she never finished—either because she couldn't afford to, or her grades weren't good enough to graduate, leading her to become a server at a steakhouse. And a con artist, spinning lies in a New York airport.

It also explains why the house is so bare, empty of anything Eva might have accumulated from a family—photo albums, birthday cards, notes. I know what it's like to wake up alone every day, with no family to worry about your well-being. Your heart. Whether you're happy. At least I had that for the first twenty-one years of my life. It's possible Eva never did.

This is what it's like to die, having left so much unfinished. It still tethers you—like an unbreakable thread, always leading your thoughts back to *if only*. But *if only* is a useless question, a spotlight shining on an empty stage, illuminating what never was, and never will be.

I tuck the letter back into the envelope and return it to her drawer, trying to imagine this new version of Eva into existence. But she dances, like quicksilver—a flash and then gone. Never settling long enough to see her clearly, an ever-shifting shape just outside my peripheral vision.

---

I need a shower, stray pieces of hair making the back of my neck itch. The only clothes I own are the few items I grabbed from my suitcase in the bathroom stall at JFK. My jeans. One pair of underwear. No bra or socks other than the ones I'm wearing. I look between the bag and Eva's dresser, filled with clothes that don't belong to me. Not just jeans and shirts, but intimate things. And it hits me again. I have almost nothing. I hesitate before sliding open her underwear drawer again, my stomach clenching, steeling myself against the idea of wearing her clothes. I close my eyes, thinking of other people who have had to resort to much more horrific things to survive than wearing someone else's underwear. *It's just cotton and elastic*, I tell myself. *And it's clean.*

I pull my own clothes from the bag, wondering if a person can live indefinitely with only two pairs of underwear, and hurry into the hall where I pull a towel from the linen cupboard. In the bathroom, I run the water hot, letting the room steam up and obscure my reflection in the mirror until I'm just a faint outline. A blurry facsimile of an anonymous woman. I could be anybody.

---

When I'm done, I dress and stand in front of the mirror in Eva's room, the unfamiliar rose scent of Eva's soap and lotion hanging in the air around me. A stranger looks back at me with her cropped blond hair and sharp cheekbones. I step over to the dresser, where Eva's wallet sits, and pull out her license, comparing my face to hers, a flutter of optimism growing inside of me.

I recognize this feeling, the excitement of being on the cusp of a new life. I felt it when I met Rory, when everything seemed to glitter with possibility, standing on the edge between who I was and who I wanted to become.

A cover story starts to form, an explanation I can give to anyone who asks. *Eva and I grew up together in the group home.* I can speak with authority about Sister Bernadette and Sister Catherine. And if they ask where Eva went and why I'm here, I'll tell them I'm getting a divorce, and Eva is letting me stay here while she travels.

*Where did she go?*

I stare at my reflection in the mirror—not quite Eva, not quite Claire—and try out my answer. "New York."

---

Back in Eva's office, I begin to tidy up, sorting Eva's papers into stacks, unsure of what to do next, when text pops up on my computer screen. First, a single sentence, typed by Rory. *The Detroit trip.* Then, on the right-hand side of the computer, Rory adds a comment.

**Rory Cook:**
What did you do with the FedEx package?

---

A reply comes almost immediately.

**Bruce Corcoran:**
Money in the drawer. The ID, passport, and the rest of it have been shredded.

---

**Rory Cook:**
The letter?

---

**Bruce Corcoran:**
Scanned, then shredded.

---

**Rory Cook:**
How the fuck did she get her hands on a fake passport and ID?

---

Three dots show Bruce responding, and I hold my breath.

**Bruce Corcoran:**
No idea. Homeland security has cracked down on forgers, but what Claire had looked real. I checked her cell activity in the few days leading up to the trip. There was a number she called that morning that we can't match to anyone she knew. We're still looking into it.

---

I wait for them to continue, but nothing new appears. Then the comments disappear, one by one, and the text in the Doc itself also vanishes. In the upper right-hand corner, Bruce's icon disappears, leaving only Rory's behind. I need to be careful. There's no way to differentiate my presence in the Doc from Rory's, and if I start clicking things, that activity will show up on his computer with his name attached. So I'm stuck, a silent observer, unable to follow up or have my questions answered. All I can do is watch this play out on the screen in front of me.

Out of tasks, with still hours to fill until I can go to sleep, I open a new tab and navigate to CNN's home page and search for news coverage of the crash. There's a small item reporting that they've planned my funeral, scheduled for a Saturday three weeks from now. Plenty of time for Rory to plan something grand, probably in the city, a guest list thick with dignitaries.

Then I click on Kate Lane's picture. Her most recent television segments are there for me to rewatch. I scroll down and click on the news conference from last night so I can listen to the NTSB director answer reporters' questions.

After rehashing the details of what had already been released, he closes the press conference. *We are still in the search and recovery phase. More information will emerge in the coming days. I ask for your patience in this matter. Vista Airlines has been cooperative and is complying with all federal requests.*

It's as I expected—more questions than answers. But right before the camera cuts back to Kate in the studio, my eye catches on something in the crowd. I back it up and watch the end of the news conference again, hitting pause when I see it. In the lower left-hand corner is a familiar flash of color tucked in among the typical black and brown parkas and navy windbreakers. The blurred image of a platinum-blond woman wearing a bright-pink sweater decidedly out of place for a frigid February evening in New York.

# EVA

The man's name was Agent Castro, and over the next few days, Eva began to see him everywhere. She'd thrown away the business card he'd dropped through her mail slot, and tried to pretend he hadn't followed her to her house, walked up her walkway, and knocked on her door. But he kept cropping up. In the parking lot at the supermarket. Driving down Bancroft Avenue as she exited a coffee shop. He even showed up at DuPree's, taking a table in a different section and causing Eva to mess up several orders while he slowly ate a prime-rib dinner and drank a Guinness.

It worried her, how unconcerned he was about being seen. And it made her wonder how long he'd been watching her before deciding to make his presence known.

When Dex finally called her back, she demanded they meet immediately. "How did you get that Brittany referral?" she asked him. They were at a sports bar on Telegraph Avenue, sitting across from each other at a beer-sticky table in the basement dining room next to a pool table while semidrunk students around them watched a preseason football game on the big-screen TV.

"This guy I grew up with moved to Los Angeles. He knows her from down there. When she moved up here, he gave her my name. He told me she'd be a steady client. Why?"

Eva studied his face, looking for any signs of a lie, tension, or a flash of guilt. "I saw her talking to a federal agent after she tried to buy from me. Now he's following me. I see him everywhere."

Dex set his burger down, his expression serious. "Tell me exactly what happened."

Eva described how Brittany appeared to be strung out. The jittery way she spoke, and the scabs on her hands. "I guess my question is why you sent me someone you hadn't vetted yourself. That's not the way it's supposed to work."

Dex's gaze darkened. "What are you suggesting?"

"I'm pointing out that shortly after I met with a client you referred, I'm being tailed by a federal agent."

"Fuck." Dex tossed his napkin on the table. "I want you to stop everything. Don't make or sell anything until you hear from me."

"And how will you explain that to Fish?" she asked.

"I'll handle him," Dex told her. "My job is to keep you safe."

Eva stared at him, weighing his words, knowing how this game was played. At the end of the day, if the choice was jail or selling out a friend, people in their business did what they had to do. She didn't delude herself into thinking Dex would be any different, and she wasn't entirely certain she would be either.

And yet, Dex had been the one to teach her how to evaluate risks, to identify who might be an undercover agent or an addict who could expose her. She couldn't picture him leading her into an abyss that would surely pull him in after her.

———————

They'd been meeting someone, several months after her expulsion, while she was still living in Dex's spare bedroom and making the drugs on old equipment in his kitchen. They saw him, a shaggy-haired student, barely twenty years old, with headphones and sagging pants.

"Watch him," Dex had said. They were tucked behind a bus kiosk, as if they were checking the schedule. The man had a tic of some kind, shrugging his left shoulder, shaking his head, almost imperceptibly, as he waited. In a low voice, Dex said, "You always watch first. You look for anomalies, like whether they're wearing a sweatshirt in eighty-degree heat. Or if they're wearing a tank top when it's raining. These are clues, and you *have* to notice them. Check out his headphones. They're not plugged into anything. See the way the cord is tucked into his front pocket, but the outline of his phone is in his back pocket?" Eva had nodded, filing these things away, knowing her survival depended on remembering them. Dex continued. "When you see anything like that, you keep going, because something isn't right. Either he's an addict or a cop." He looked at her with a grave expression, his gray eyes locking onto hers. "Your number one priority— Fish's number one priority—is your safety. It's why he's lasted as long as he has in this business." Dex laughed quietly. "That and the ten people he has working for him inside the Berkeley and Oakland police departments."

They'd stepped out from under the cover of the kiosk and turned away from the man without making the sale, leaving him on the curb, waiting for drugs that would never show up.

"Did you sell her anything?" Dex asked Eva now.

"No. She was off. Crazy. I told her she had me confused with someone else and got the hell out of there."

Dex nodded. "Good. You're taking a vacation until we figure out what's going on."

"It's like this guy wants me to see him."

"He probably does," Dex said. "People make mistakes when they're nervous, and he obviously wants to make you nervous. The fact that he's so visible means he doesn't have anything on you and he's getting desperate."

"What am I supposed to do?"

"Let him follow you. He won't see anything, and eventually he'll look somewhere else."

Dex tossed a couple five-dollar bills onto the table for a tip. Around them, the room erupted in cheers, all eyes on the television, where someone had just scored a touchdown. Eva started to rise, but Dex said, "You should stay a little longer."

Eva sat back and watched him leave, fighting down a growing panic, like someone waiting her turn to get on a lifeboat and realizing she was going to be the only one left on the sinking ship. Dex was already trying to distance himself.

Around her, the college kids drank and laughed, their biggest worry whether Cal would go to a bowl game. She had never in her life felt that relaxed. Even when she was a student, she'd been guarded. Quiet. Growing up in a group home, she learned from a young age that it was safest to observe rather than jump in with loud laughter or a witty joke. The sisters at St. Joe's encouraged them to be studious. Respectful. Which Eva had become, all the while figuring out how to break the rules more quietly.

But it wasn't a home. The sisters were older. Strict and

uncompromising. They believed that children should be silent and compliant. Eva remembered the cold hallways of the dorm, tucked behind the sanctuary, smelling of candle wax and damp. She remembered the other girls. Not their names, but their voices. Harsh and bullying, or soft and scared. She remembered the crying at night. How, at the end of the day, each of them was alone.

Eva took a final sip of her beer and stood, weaving her way toward the stairs that led up to the main dining room. She eyed the emergency exit, imagining the sound of the alarm, which was already screaming inside her head. But she bypassed it, knowing now was not the time for anything so desperate. Not yet.

---

As she pulled into her driveway, she saw Liz locking her door and heading down the front walk toward her car. Eva glanced up and down the street, forcing herself to slow down and act normal.

"Hello!" Liz called.

Eva had grown curious about Liz since that first afternoon in Liz's apartment. She found herself listening for her. Watching her come and go. The sound of Liz's voice still reverberated in her mind, and Eva couldn't deny she felt drawn to the woman.

Eva locked her car and turned to her with a smile, pointing at Liz's New Jersey plates. "You drove all the way from New Jersey?" She tried to relax her shoulders and focus on Liz and not on the possibility that Agent Castro's car might turn the corner at any moment.

But today was not a day for talking, and she breathed easy when Liz said only, "I thought it would be a fun road trip, but already I'm dreading the drive back." She rounded her car and slid into the driver's seat with a wave, and Eva continued up the walkway, unlocking her door and slipping inside.

The silence was a relief. She made her way over to the couch and lay down, forcing herself to take several deep breaths, but she couldn't relax. She could feel Castro's presence like an audience, watching everything she did. Every coming and going, to the market, to DuPree's. Every interaction like the one she'd just had with Liz, recorded in someone's field notes. *4:56 p.m.: Eva chats with older neighbor on lawn.* She stared at the wall that separated her apartment from Liz's and wondered if Liz might be a useful person to have around. Become part of the story she wanted Castro to believe about her. That she was just a server who lived a small life filled with mundane details too boring to record. *Eva spends evening out with neighbor friend.* Or *Eva and neighbor friend do a guided tour of Berkeley Rose Garden.* What might bore them the most?

---

Later that evening, there was a knock on the door. A quick peek through the window revealed Liz on the porch, holding a casserole dish. "I don't know when I'm going to remember to cut a recipe in half," she said, though Eva suspected Liz preferred to have someone to cook for.

Liz handed her the dish and stepped inside, causing Eva to falter as she carried the casserole into the kitchen. She had just closed the refrigerator and turned around to see Liz bent over, reading the titles of the books on her shelf in the living room. It unsettled her, to have someone in her space, looking at her things. But she took a deep breath and smiled through her discomfort. *7:45 p.m.: Neighbor brings Eva food. They chat for twelve minutes.* She could do this.

"You're interested in chemistry?" Liz asked.

Eva shrugged. They were mostly old textbooks from her last year of college that Eva hadn't opened in years. Yet she couldn't bring herself to get rid of them, as if doing so would toss away a critical part of herself. "I studied it for a little while. In school."

"These are college texts," Liz said, pulling one out. She flipped it open, looking at the stamp of the Berkeley student store on the inside cover. "You went to Berkeley? You never mentioned that."

"For a bit," Eva said. "I didn't graduate."

"Why not?" Liz asked, as Eva knew she would.

"Stuff got in the way." Eva hoped that her half answers and deflections would end the conversation there.

On the counter, Eva's phone buzzed, lighting up with a text from Dex. Eva snatched the phone, pressing the Save for Later option on the screen before shoving it into her pocket.

Liz watched her, waiting for her to say something, and when she didn't, Liz pointed to the open can of Diet Coke on the counter. "That stuff is poison," she said.

Eva checked her watch, the charade suddenly draining her. How long would she need to entertain this woman? "I'd better get in the shower. I'm working a shift at the restaurant this evening."

Liz waited a beat, as if trying to read the truth beneath Eva's words, before saying, "You know, life is long. Lots of things can go wrong and still end up all right."

Eva thought about her lab, hidden beneath the room where they stood. And she thought it was a fitting metaphor. Liz saw only what was in front of her, while Eva worried about everything hidden beneath the surface that might float to the top, where Agent Castro waited to collect it.

"Thanks for the food," she said.

Liz replaced the textbook on the shelf, dismissed. "You're very welcome."

After she left, Eva pulled out the phone and read Dex's text.

Fish is dealing with it. Take a couple weeks off and this guy will be gone.

Relief flooded her. Like a missed collision, Castro would barrel past her, leaving her weak and shaky but in one piece.

"It's going to be fine," she said out loud to the empty room. Next door, Liz had turned on some music, and the faint sound of jazz wound its way around Eva, calling out to her, offering her a glimpse of a life she could have for a little while.

———————————

Later that night, she entered DuPree's from the alley and hurried to her locker, hoping Gabe, her manager, wouldn't notice she was late. When she emerged again, she found him directing a busser to clear some tables. "Finally," he said. "You're working section five."

Eva grabbed her notepad and ran through the specials with the sous chef in the kitchen before heading out into the large dining room.

She soon lost herself in work. Taking orders, chatting with patrons, delivering food. For a little while, she could be exactly who everyone thought she was. Just a server, working hard and saving her tips for a long weekend in Cabo or a new leather jacket. A lightness zipped through her, making her feel buzzy with anticipation, like a child released from school for the summer.

Gabe found her in the kitchen, giving directions to the cook for a vegetarian order. He was in his midforties, balding, with a shirt that always seemed to be straining at the edges. He was a fair boss who seemed gruff and impatient with his employees, but always gave them time off when they needed it. "Eva," he said. "When are you going to let me schedule you for more shifts? I need you more than twice a week."

"No thanks," she said. "It's too hard to pursue my hobbies otherwise."

"Hobbies?" Gabe said, perplexed. "What hobbies?"

Eva leaned against the kitchen wall, grateful for the short break, and ticked them off on her fingers. "Knitting. Ceramics. Roller derby."

One of the dishwashers snorted, and she winked at him.

Gabe shook his head, muttering under his breath about how no one appreciated him.

Someone called from across the kitchen. "Eva, table four looks ready to order."

She headed back into the dining room, emptier now that it was nearing nine o'clock. When she arrived at table four, she pulled up short. There sat one of her best clients, Jeremy, flanked on either side by what had to be his parents.

Jeremy was a third-year communications major whose father demanded straight A's in order to continue funding Jeremy's tuition and lavish lifestyle, which included a BMW, a loft apartment in downtown Berkeley, and the drugs Eva made. And unlike Brett, Jeremy always paid in full. Cash on delivery. It was a pleasure working with him.

Every now and then, she ran into her clients in the real world, and it always caused them to stumble in some way. Jeremy was no different. When he saw her, his face paled, his eyes darting for the nearest exit. His mother studied her menu while his father scrolled through his phone. Eva smiled, hoping to put him at ease. "Hi there. Let me tell you about the specials." She launched into her recitation, all the while Jeremy refusing to look at her. She understood his panic. It had taken her years to figure out that people couldn't see through her act, that they wouldn't know what she was doing when she met someone in the park or on the corner by the grocery store. The world was filled with people who carried secrets. No one was who they seemed to be.

Jeremy cornered her by the bathrooms before dessert. "What are you doing here?" he hissed.

"I work here."

He looked over her shoulder toward the dining room.

She followed his glance and said, "Look, Jeremy. You can relax. Take some advice: people will believe whatever you want them to, as long

124

as you don't hesitate. You don't know me, and I don't know you." She walked away, leaving him standing between the men's room and the emergency exit.

When her shift was over, she walked by Agent Castro's car in the lot, letting her gaze meet his for a split second before sliding away. Whatever game he was playing, she could play it too.

# CLAIRE

I stare at the frozen image on the computer screen until my eyes begin to water, until I see nothing more than an accumulation of pixels—shades of pink, dark shadows, platinum-blond hair where a face should be.

It was Rory's Aunt Mary who had given me that pink cashmere sweater for Christmas one year. "Something to keep you warm while living in the stone-cold center of the Cook family." She'd laughed, loud and wet, jiggling the ice in her nearly empty glass, as if to loosen whatever gin might remain on the bottom.

I'd held the sweater, soft and luxurious, on my lap, waiting for someone to jump in, to explain away Aunt Mary's words. But they'd just rolled past it, Rory giving me a tiny wink, as if I was now in on the family secret.

Later that same Christmas, Aunt Mary sidled up to me, drunk, and said, "The whole world loves Rory Cook." The oldest sister of Rory's father, Mary was unmarried and considered a family liability. Her voice lowered, the smell of gin heavy on her breath. "But you be careful not to cross him, or you'll go the way of poor Maggie Moretti."

"That was an accident," I said, my eyes glued on Rory, across the room from us, joking around with some younger cousins. I was still trying to believe I'd gotten the life I always wanted, with three generations of the Cook family gathered to celebrate the holidays. I wanted to embrace their traditions. The caroling at the children's hospital, the candlelight church service followed by a midnight supper, the family life I'd always craved as a girl, such a vibrant contrast to the quiet holidays of my childhood.

But my instincts pinged, forcing me to stay and listen to what she had to say, because my idea of Rory had begun to shift, the shine of his attention had begun to chafe. I was beginning to see the price I'd paid, missing the simple things I used to take for granted. The freedom to pick my own friends. To grab my car keys and go somewhere on a whim without having to clear it with at least two assistants and a driver first.

Aunt Mary cackled. "Oh, so you're in the *poor Rory* camp, alongside the rest of the world." She took a sip of her drink and said, "Let me tell you something. It's a poorly kept family secret that my brother paid off everyone involved. Why would he do that if there was nothing to hide?" She gave me a sly smile, and I could see her pink lipstick oozing into the crevices around her mouth. "The Cook men are dolls, as long as you do what they want. But step out of line and watch your back."

Across the room, Rory threw his head back and laughed at something one of the cousins said. Aunt Mary followed my gaze and shook her head. "You remind me a little bit of Maggie—a nice girl from a simple background. Like you, Maggie seemed to have integrity, which is something this family is sorely lacking. But she and Rory fought like dogs, about every little thing." She looked at me, her smirk somewhat blurred by alcohol. "She couldn't control him. I'm guessing you can't either."

"Why are you telling me this?" I asked.

Aunt Mary's watery eyes held mine, the years etched into the deep lines around them. "This family is like a Venus flytrap—shiny on the surface, but dangerous underneath. And once you know their secrets, they will never let you leave."

She was drunk. Bitter. A resentful old woman spreading poison. And yet, what she said haunted me through the years as Rory grew silent. Then angry. And eventually violent. I wanted to believe the version Rory meticulously fed to the world, but he beat that desire out of me, one bruise and broken bone at a time.

Aunt Mary died a few years later, the last of that generation of Cooks to pass. But her words trailed after me every time I wore that sweater, a whisper—or a warning—that Maggie Moretti's fate might also be mine.

---

Somewhere outside, a dog barks, pulling my attention back to the room and to my computer. I drag the cursor backward to replay the video from the beginning, staring so hard at that blurred figure in pink, my eyes begin to burn. No matter how I try, I can't see anything else. Just some blond hair—long or short, I can't tell. Just a flash of pink—there and then gone—and I try to remind myself that plenty of people wear pink sweaters, in all kinds of weather, and that Eva was scanned onto the flight. You can't fake that.

---

"One drip coffee, room for cream please," I tell the barista early Thursday morning. I keep my eyes averted, and I still wear my NYU cap, too nervous to show my entire face. Will it always be like this, terrified to look anyone in the eye and smile?

I tossed and turned all night, my mind replaying the flash of pink at the news conference, but no matter how many ways I imagined an alternative for Eva, I kept coming up against the fact that my ticket was scanned onto the flight. It's unlikely she had enough time to talk someone else into switching with her, and the flight crew would have noticed when they did the headcount if she'd gotten off the plane before takeoff. I woke this morning convinced it was just a coincidence, that it was only guilt, wishing it had turned out different for Eva.

I pay for my coffee and settle into a soft leather armchair with a clear view of the door and the street outside.

Last night, wanting to try calling Petra again, I'd Googled how to reset the password on a prepaid phone and was able to unlock Eva's. As I expected, it didn't reveal much. No photographs, no emails. She used an app called Whispr, and the texts that arrived my first night were gone, vanished into the ether. If any others had been received since then, they were gone as well.

Once I was in, I dialed Petra's number again, imagining the relief I'd feel to hear her voice. To see her standing on Eva's front porch, hired car idling at the curb, ready to lift me out of this nightmare and deposit me somewhere safe. A fancy hotel in San Francisco where we'd order room service and wait for Nico's guy to make a new set of documents for me.

But the call ended again with the three tones. No longer in service. I tried a few variations, transposing numbers, swapping different ones in. I reached a deli, an older woman who spoke only Spanish, and a preschool before I gave up. Nico's words floated back to me: *You can never go back. Not once. Not in any way, ever.*

I look out the coffee shop window and watch Berkeley come to life. A small trickle of people enter, order, and leave again, the morning rush aligned with a college town's later start. By six thirty, it's empty again, my coffee nearly gone.

The barista comes out from behind the counter and begins wiping down the table next to me. "You from out of town?" she asks.

I freeze, unsure how to answer, afraid that I've somehow been recognized. But she keeps talking a steady stream, giving me time to catch up. "I know just about everyone who comes in here—if not by name, then by face. But you're new."

"I'm just passing through," I say, gathering my things and preparing to leave.

She gives the table one last swipe and looks at me. "No need to go," she says. "Take your time." Then she moves behind the counter and starts a fresh batch of coffee. I lean back in my chair and watch the light at the intersection blink from red to green and back again.

Around seven thirty, the shop grows crowded and I leave. The girl behind the counter gives me a wave and a smile as I exit, and I return it, feeling a tiny tendril of pleasure wrap around me.

———————

I decide to push myself out into the world and go for a walk, knowing I can't hide forever. So instead of heading back to Eva's, I turn west on Hearst Avenue and trace the northernmost perimeter of campus, marveling at the giant redwood trees that stand, thick among the buildings and grassy expanses. When I hit the western edge of campus, I turn south, and circle back east again, this time on the south side. This is the Berkeley you see on television and read about in books. A drum circle has positioned themselves outside the student union, and people swarm past them, on their way to class or their offices, heads down in the brisk morning air. As I make my way up the hill toward the old stone stadium, I turn and look west, a sharp wind cutting through my thin sleeves. I shiver, staring at the white expanse of San Francisco, the gray water contrasting with the deep greens and golds of the hills to the north, the Golden Gate Bridge a dusty-orange silhouette. Somewhere out there is the convent where

Eva grew up. An entire childhood lived and lost among the buildings that seem to shimmer in the distance.

As I cut across campus, I imagine what it would be like to be a student here, one of the many people hurrying to class, and try to picture Eva among them. I slow down as I approach a bridge that traverses a small stream and lean against the railing, looking down into the swirling water making its way downhill toward the ocean. Above me, the breeze whispers through the tall trees, a quiet rush that makes my thoughts slow. I can't imagine ever wanting to leave a place like this.

I push off the railing and continue my walk back to Eva's, past the coffee shop, where the barista is still working the morning shift, and past several other closed businesses—a used bookstore, a hair salon— until I'm back in Eva's neighborhood again. My breath comes faster as I make my way up the winding hill, past apartment buildings and small houses and duplexes similar to Eva's. I peer into them as I pass—a woman sitting at her dining room table, feeding a baby in a high chair. A messy-haired college student, eyes puffy and barely awake, staring out his kitchen window.

As I round the corner onto Eva's street, I collide with a man walking toward me. He grabs my arm to keep me from falling. "Sorry," he says. "Are you okay?"

He has dark hair, with a few flecks of early gray, but he doesn't look much older than me. Sunglasses cover his eyes, and he wears a long coat, with a flash of color under it. Dark pants, dark shoes.

"I'm fine," I say, and I look beyond him, up Eva's street, wondering where he came from, whether he's a neighbor of Eva's.

"Beautiful morning for a coffee and a walk," he says.

I give him a tight smile and step around him, feeling his gaze press against my back until the street curves and I'm out from under it.

It isn't until I've closed and locked the door behind me that it registers.

How would he know I'd just been for a coffee and a walk? I feel a heavy thump of apprehension pass through me, a low tremor that leaves me even more unsettled and on edge.

---

Back in front of my computer, I check Rory's email and see a new one from the NTSB that he forwarded to Danielle. A request for a DNA sample and my dental records. His directions are short and to the point: *Handle this.*

I look toward the window, bright morning light flooding through it. If they're recovering bodies, it's only a matter of time before they figure out I'm not there. And that someone who isn't supposed to be is.

I toggle over to the Doc in time to catch the tail end of a conversation between Rory and Bruce, and I have to scroll up to find the beginning. But it's not about the body recovery like I expected. It's about an email that arrived late last night from someone named Charlie.

I can practically hear Rory's sharp tone, the clipped words of his directions.

**Rory Cook:**
This was dealt with years ago, with cash. You need to remind Charlie what coming forward will cost.

---

*Charlie?* The only Charlie I can think of is Charlie Flanagan, a senior accountant with the foundation who retired two years ago. I read the rest of their conversation, noticing Rory's words agitating upward, Bruce's becoming placating and conciliatory. But it's Rory's final comment that puzzles me the most, because buried inside his usual bullying tone is a flash of vulnerability.

**Rory Cook:**

I cannot afford for this to come out now. I don't care how you deal with it. Or how much it'll cost me. Just fix it.

---

I do a search of Rory's inbox for any emails from Charlie. There are many, but not the one Rory and Bruce are discussing, and nothing recent. And as far as I can tell, every one of Charlie's emails have at least two other foundation personnel cc'd on them.

I plug in the thumb drive and search there, but all that comes up is the standard nondisclosure agreement all employees sign. So I organize the folder containing the thousands of documents I copied from his computer alphabetically, focusing on the C's and F's. The only thing that would have Rory scrambling like this is if Charlie knows about some kind of financial misstep or fabrication that might derail Rory's run for office. Information showing that the golden child of Marjorie Cook isn't so golden after all. It's why I copied the hard drive in the first place. Like a bear in the woods, you don't have to see one to know it's there.

But most of what I'm reading is unrelated. Memos about new tax laws. Quarterly reports. Occasionally, my name crops up in strategy notes. *Claire might be better here*, one says, in reference to an opening of a downtown art gallery. I click through documents, one by one, but it's all junk, useless noise, like looking through someone's garbage.

After an hour, I give up. Whatever Charlie knows that has Rory spooked, I'm not going to find the answers so easily. For now, I have to be satisfied with watching. Waiting for them to say more.

# EVA

"Put on your shoes," Liz said one sunny Saturday in late September. "I'm taking you to a baseball game."

*Eva and her neighbor attend a baseball game.* "Baseball?" Eva asked.

Liz said, "Not just baseball. The Giants. At home."

"We live in the east bay. Shouldn't we be going to an A's game?"

Liz shrugged. "My department chair has season tickets. She invited a few of us, and I asked if I could bring a friend."

In the three weeks since Eva had been on hiatus, she had been enjoying her very first vacation. Working extra shifts at DuPree's and spending a lot of time with Liz, she felt the way she imagined a bookkeeper or an accountant might feel on a long-overdue holiday, how they might forget the spreadsheets and financial records after a few weeks on the beach somewhere, the heat of the sun leaching the stress from their body.

But the threat of Castro was never very far from her mind. She found herself playing to an audience of one, walking slower, laughing louder, lingering longer. She made it a game. Every time Liz invited her to do something, she had to say yes. A tour of the UC Botanical Gardens. A movie and shopping on Solano Avenue, pizza at Zachary's afterward. Every invitation, an opportunity to show whoever was watching that she was no one special.

They talked about philosophy, politics, history. Even chemistry. Eva had shared the bare bones of her own past, what it was like growing up at St. Joe's, sticking to the truth whenever she could, to better keep track of her lies. She'd made up a story about why she'd never finished college— the money had dried up because of a problem with her financial aid. But this allowed Eva to talk freely about her time as a student at Berkeley, and the two of them bonded over what campus life was like. The various quirks of the community, the ferocious rivalry with Stanford, traditions that wouldn't make sense to anyone who hadn't lived inside of it.

"Do you have a family back home?" Eva had asked one evening.

"My daughter, Ellie," Liz said, staring into the flickering flame of a candle. "I raised her on my own—her father left when she was seven." Liz had sighed and looked down into her wineglass. "It was hard on both of us, but now, looking back, I think we're better for it." Liz described her ex-husband's exacting nature, the precise way he'd demand his steak to be cooked, or the unrealistic expectations he placed on his young daughter. "I'm glad she didn't have to grow up with that kind of relentless pressure."

"Where is she now?" Eva had asked, curious about the woman who was lucky enough to be Liz's daughter.

"She works for a nonprofit. Long hours, rarely a day off. She sublet her apartment in the city to housesit for me while I'm in California, but I'm worried she'll isolate herself out there in New Jersey, away from her friends," she'd said, giving Eva a sheepish smile. "A mother's heart is always worried."

Eva had stared at her, wishing it were true.

Other times, Eva would ask Liz questions about the classes she was teaching and then sit back and let her talk. Liz was a gifted teacher, able to make complex concepts seem simple, and it was like being back in college. Maybe better. Dex, who had been a daily presence in her life, had all but disappeared, replaced by this talkative, diminutive, brilliant woman from Princeton.

So when Liz stood before her on this bright September Saturday, two baseball tickets in her hand, Eva was ready to say yes again. Maybe even happy to.

"Sure," she said. "I just need a minute."

She left Liz in the living room while she raced upstairs to change. As she slid her feet into tennis shoes, she glanced at her phone and saw a text from Dex.

> It's fixed. F wants you back to work immediately. Plan
> to meet at Tilden Monday with full supply.

She stared at the message until the Whispr app made it fade and disappear.

Eva sat down hard on her bed, surprised that the first feeling she had wasn't relief but sadness. This was what she'd been waiting for. All her time with Liz had been to get this exact outcome—Castro gone, and Eva back to work. But it felt like an empty victory, one she no longer wanted, now that she had it. Her gaze flicked toward the doorway, where Liz waited downstairs, unaware that she was no longer necessary.

But Eva would go to the game and play the part a little longer. She tossed her phone onto the dresser, harder than necessary, surprised by the sharp sound it made as it slid across the polished wood and hit the wall.

They took the BART across the bay, walking with crowds of people toward the stadium. As they waited in line, Liz nudged her toward a photo station, where people could pose next to cutouts of players Eva didn't recognize. "Come on," she said. "It'll be fun. My treat."

Eva hesitated. She wasn't the kind of person who had her picture taken, aside from school photos that no one ever bought. She couldn't remember a time anyone had pointed a camera at her and said *Smile*. But Eva went along with it, a small part of her glad to have a souvenir.

Inside, they found their seats, Liz's colleagues from the political science department greeting her warmly. There was Liz's closest friend, Emily, and her partner, Bess, plus their department head, Vera. Eva took the seat on the end and let their conversation flow around her—gossip about who was getting grants and who wasn't, who was getting published and who wasn't. Complaining about who always burned popcorn in the office microwave.

To Eva, it was like getting a glimpse into the life she'd once dreamed she'd have herself. There had been a time, before everything went wrong, that she'd imagined herself a professor at Berkeley. Delivering lectures in Gilman Hall. Supervising graduate students. Striding across campus, smiling a greeting as students said *Hey, Dr. James*.

Eva felt a sharp stab of regret, surprising her after so many years of believing she'd made her peace with how things turned out. That was the funny thing about regret. It lived inside of you, shrinking down until you could almost believe it had vanished, only to have it spring up, fully formed, called forward by people who meant you no harm.

Eventually they turned their attention toward the game. Vera kept score, talking about player statistics and upcoming trades, while the rest of them debated whether spitting sunflower shells was any better than tobacco juice. Eva cheered when the Giants scored, drinking a beer and eating a hot dog. It was a slice of life Eva thought only existed in movies, this idea that everything could be so perfect—the grass, the sun, the players in their crisp white uniforms, hitting home runs over the fence and into San Francisco Bay, where a cluster of people with baseball gloves in kayaks waited to catch one of them.

Right before the sixth inning, Emily leaned over and said, "I'm so glad you could come today, Eva. Liz has been talking about you nonstop for weeks."

A ripple of pleasure passed through Eva, but she offered her shyest smile, the one she reserved for bank tellers and police officers. "Thanks for inviting me," she said.

Liz was quick to jump in. "I've seen a lot of brilliant minds in my time, but Eva's is one of the sharpest I've ever encountered," she said. "The other night, she nearly had me convinced Keynesian economics might be better than free market."

Emily looked impressed. "That's no small feat. Where did you go to college?"

Eva hesitated, imagining the questions they'd have if she said Berkeley. *What was your major? Who were your professors? What year did you graduate? Do you know Dr. Fitzgerald?* And how quickly one of them would discover the truth—an innocent comment at the faculty club, someone quietly recounting her story. The chemistry department was small, and people didn't move on from Berkeley to better jobs elsewhere. There were probably several people still there who would remember her.

Luckily, Liz must have sensed her discomfort. "She studied chemistry at Stanford," she said, giving Eva a tiny smile. "Try not to hold it against her."

---

"You didn't have to lie for me," Eva said later, after they'd said goodbye and were strolling along the Embarcadero, making their way back to the

BART station. The evening air was gentle on her skin, faint traces of the afternoon sun still present.

Liz waved her words away. "They're all a bunch of aunties. They would have given you a ton of unwanted advice about going back to school and finishing your degree. It wouldn't have mattered to them that you're smart enough to have figured out how to do that if you wanted to."

Eva thought about what was waiting for her on the other side of the bay. Certainly not the possibility of going back to college. That would never be an option for her. Until Liz came along, Eva had been happy. But now there was a hunger rumbling deep inside of her, a desire for more time with Liz and her friends. But not as a visitor passing through. She wanted to be a part of it, to live inside of it. Eva wanted to complain about why women didn't have the kind of grant opportunities that men did. She wanted to feel the thrill of announcing another article placed in a peer-reviewed journal. She wanted to be the one who burned popcorn in the office microwave.

The idea of resuming work—the hiding, the lying, the vigilance that accompanied her every time she left the house—descended, pressing her into a tight knot, and a grief she hadn't felt since her expulsion from Berkeley swirled around inside of her, as a part of her brain began to map out what needed to be done. Buy more ingredients. Clean the equipment. Start setting the stage for her withdrawal from Liz. She'd have to start talking about picking up more shifts at the restaurant, or perhaps invent a boyfriend who would soon consume her free time.

But there, in the darkening twilight, the water of the bay lapping against the pier pilings, the lights of the Bay Bridge sparkling in a graceful arc above them, shooting like an arrow into the dark, Eva felt the urge to reveal something more of herself. To tell Liz something completely true. "My last foster home was just on the other side of that hill," Eva told Liz, pointing west, toward Nob Hill.

Liz looked at her. "What happened?"

Carmen and Mark had been the closest Eva had ever come to having a family. When she was eight, the couple had come to St. Joe's, interested in adopting a young girl. They were accompanied by her social worker, Mr. Henderson, a pasty man with wispy hair and a briefcase full of files. The woman, Carmen, was bright and vibrant. When Eva met her, she seemed to glow with energy. Carmen's husband, Mark, was more reserved and deferred to his wife, keeping his eyes down. Eva wondered if he, too, knew that it was best to always hold a piece of himself separate from others.

"Carmen and Mark," she told Liz now. "At first, it was great. They pushed to get me into the gifted program at school. Bought me tons of books, clothes, took me to museums and the science center."

"They sound wonderful. What happened?"

"I started stealing. First money, then a charm bracelet."

Liz gave her a sharp look. "What made you do that?"

This was the tricky part. Eva wanted to explain it to Liz, to help her see an essential part of who she was. That she had depended, from a very early age, on being able to hide behind a curtain of lies, never trusting anyone enough to let them see who she really was.

"Being unwanted is a heavy burden," she said quietly. "You never fully learn how to engage with the world. To allow others to see you."

A large group of people walked toward them, laughing and talking over each other, and Eva waited for them to pass. How could she explain the way it made her feel, to listen to the way Carmen and Mark bragged about how smart she was, how lucky they were to have her? It had felt like they were covering her in plastic wrap. People could still see her, but the essence of who she was got trapped beneath their expectations, and she worried about what would happen when the truth seeped out. "It was easier to push them away," Eva finally said. "When they looked at me, they saw the child of an addict. Everything I did—good or bad— was viewed through that lens, and as long as I was with them, that would

140

always be my whispered story. *It's amazing how much Eva has overcome in such a short time,* or *You can hardly blame her, considering what she's gone through.* I needed to show them they couldn't fix me. That I didn't want to be fixed."

"You wanted to be the one to define who you were," Liz said. She linked her arm through Eva's, and Eva leaned into her, loving the solid feel of Liz's shoulder against her own, wanting to drag that moment out until infinity, to never descend into the BART station, to never return across the bay to her old life, stale and rotten at the center. "And so you stayed at the convent until you graduated?" she asked.

Eva nodded. "Until I turned eighteen and started at Cal."

Wind whipped up from the bay, growing stronger as it funneled between the tall buildings, and Eva hugged her other arm tight around her, thinking about the family she'd almost had, if she'd been a different person. A better person. But that possibility had fractured long before Carmen and Mark showed up. Cracked down its center, the pieces rough and jagged. She'd insulated herself from the sharpest parts, but Liz had reached in and gently unwrapped them, showing her she didn't need to be afraid to think about her past. That she could hold the pieces in her hands without hurting herself. That she could do something with them if she wanted to.

They were quiet as they descended the stairs and passed through the turnstile and onto the platform. The faint sound of a far-off train carried through the dark tunnel, and Eva pictured the people on the street above them, driving, walking, working in the high-rise buildings of the financial district. It was a miracle the whole thing didn't come crashing down on top of them.

"Have you ever thought about looking for your birth family?"

Eva shook her head. "After things went down with Carmen and Mark, the nuns made another attempt to reunite me with them." She looked down the tunnel, looking for their train, but all was quiet. "They said no."

"It's possible they did the best thing they could for you."

Eva knew that was probably true, that she wouldn't have had any kind of life growing up with an addict, but that knowledge sat alongside the rejection—it didn't cancel it out. "I don't know that I'll ever truly forgive them," she said.

Liz shook her head. "You don't know what they were dealing with at the time. Your mother's problems probably took up every inch of space inside of them. I can only imagine what kind of hell that must have been." She glanced down at the platform and then back at Eva. "You can't blame them for knowing their limits. Even if those limits included you."

The sign above them flashed with their train number, and beneath her feet Eva could feel the rumbling of its arrival. Liz placed a hand on her arm and said, "Look. Obviously, you know what's best for you. But I sense an unhappiness, a hole that makes you hold yourself apart from the rest of the world. And I hate to see you hurting. Seeking them out doesn't mean expecting a happy ending. I don't think that's why you should do it. But information is power. And once you hold it, you get to decide what to do with it. That's all I want for you."

They waited in silence as Eva considered her words, turning them over in her mind. She wondered what it would be like to know people who were related to her. Who looked like her. Who carried family memories and knew where they got their sharp noses or their blond hair. She'd never had that kind of connection with anyone.

Liz continued, her voice low. "You aren't the only adopted child to want answers from her biological family."

"I was never adopted."

Liz closed her eyes briefly, then opened them, turning to face Eva. "I'm sorry. You're right, and this is none of my business."

"Look, I appreciate what you're saying. I really do. But that kind of rejection does something to a person. It breaks you, all the way down to your core. And makes it impossible to be vulnerable. To open yourself up to anyone."

Liz looked at Eva, her gaze steady and knowing, forcing Eva to look away. Just then, the train pulled into the station and people pressed in on them from behind, pushing them forward and through the opening doors.

———————

On their way back to Berkeley, she studied Liz next to her, the short white hair and regal set of her shoulders, and thought about what Liz was suggesting. Eva imagined her birth family out there, trying to forget what they'd left behind—the pain of an addict daughter, the granddaughter they'd sacrificed in order to save her. And what would they get if she showed up? More heartache. More pain. A reminder that they'd been right to give her up when they did.

What Eva did was worse than anything her mother had ever done. Her mother had a disease. Eva was just a drug dealer who barely blinked at the idea of having a nineteen-year-old beaten to a bloody pulp over a few hundred dollars. Eva pictured her phone at home, waiting to yank her back down. Pulling her away from Liz, who had no idea what kind of a person Eva really was.

The train rumbled and swayed, her ears popping as they dropped below the bay, the lights flickering and creating dim shadows around them, thinking about the next day when she'd have to roll the shelf in her kitchen aside and get back to work, and she felt the beginning tendrils of tension take root and start to spread outward. She wished she could turn back time, go back to that morning when Liz stood in her doorway infused with an excitement that nearly filled her up. Or maybe earlier. To that afternoon at Tilden waiting for Brittany. To have listened to her instincts and gone home. Gotten ready to work her shift at DuPree's, far removed from Agent Castro and Brittany's collaboration. Or maybe even further still, to the sidewalk outside her dorm, saying *no thanks* to Dex. Saying *no thanks* to Wade. That was the problem with wishes. They always led to others. Bigger ones. Trailing back in time, knot after knot needing to be untangled, never noticing how they wrapped around you until they pulled you down.

But as she stared at her dim reflection in the dark train window, Eva was struck with a thought so clear, so pure, it sent a shiver through her. *I'm not going to do this anymore.*

An impossible wish. Fish and Dex would never let her walk away. Not just because of what she could do, but also what she knew. Even though she was compartmentalized, she still knew too much.

*Could I find out more?*

Castro's presence had felt like a threat. But she saw now how it could also be an opportunity. The chance to become the person Liz saw when she looked at Eva. She fingered the photo of the two of them at the entrance to the stadium, already looking like a relic from another time. As the train rose again on the east side of the bay and outside light filled their car again, Eva felt it slip into her, creating space where there had been darkness, hope where there had been despair.

Eva would do what was expected of her—she'd go back to work, she'd deliver the drugs—but underneath it all, she'd do what she did best: She'd watch. And wait. And exploit everyone's complacency. Because she knew without a doubt Castro would be back. And this time Eva would be ready for him.

# CLAIRE

At the coffee shop Friday morning, I wander over to the job board while I wait for my coffee. My tentative plan is to take Eva's social security card, her birth certificate, and any other relevant documents and move somewhere else. Which will require more money than the three hundred fifty dollars I have left.

There are plenty of minimum wage jobs I'm qualified to do—data entry, waiting tables, or even working in a coffee shop—but I feel paralyzed with fear, constantly weighing the risks against the benefits of applying. It would mean committing to being Eva in a very real and public way. There's a difference between using her name to order a coffee and writing her name and social security number on a W-2 form.

And whatever Eva was running from tumbles around in my mind, a riptide of questions that pull me in unforeseeable directions. I can never work a job requiring a background check. I will always have to be on the move, never settling, always wondering when Eva's past will finally crash into me.

Through the window, students are beginning to make their way to class. A crowd of them emerges from a bus, some carrying coffee cups and wearing earbuds, while others look tired and drawn, up too early on a Friday morning.

When they've dispersed, I see him again. The man from yesterday, standing on the corner, waiting to cross the street. He wears the same long wool coat, with a paper tucked under his arm, as if he's heading to work. I stare at him, trying to figure out what it is about him that bothers me. He's just a man on his way somewhere. The longer I stay at Eva's, the more familiar the people in the neighborhood will become.

But as the light changes, he looks over his shoulder, directly at me, as if he knew I would be here, watching him. Our eyes lock, and I feel the weight of his gaze, curious and searching. He lifts his hand in a silent salute, meant just for me, before he crosses the street, disappearing onto campus.

"Eva?" the barista says.

I turn, still surprised I had the nerve to give her the name. It felt low stakes, to use it on a coffee barista who seemed more in tune with the local bands than the national news.

"Looking for a job?" She passes me my drip coffee, the cheapest item on the menu.

"Sort of," I say, handing her two dollars.

She raises her eyebrows as she gives me my change. "You either are or you aren't."

"I am." I turn away from her, doctoring my coffee with enough cream and sugar to fill me up for a few hours. I don't know how to tell her that I'm desperate for work, that I'm terrified I will run out of money and be stuck here forever.

"I work part-time for a caterer," she says, wiping down the counter next to the coffee machine. "He's always looking for extra people to be servers. You interested?"

I hesitate, trying to decide whether I have the nerve to say yes or not.

She glances at me and continues her cleaning. "It pays twenty dollars an hour. And"—she gives me a sly grin—"he pays under the table."

I take a sip of coffee, feeling the hot liquid scald the back of my throat. "He would hire someone he never met?"

"He's actually desperate for bodies. He's got a huge party this week-end and two of his servers flaked because they have some kind of soror-ity meeting." She rolls her eyes and tosses the rag into the sink behind her. "If it goes well, it could be a regular thing."

I've organized hundreds of catered events—both big and small—and wonder what it would feel like to work behind the scenes. To be one of the anonymous people I barely noticed when I was hosting an event. "What would I have to do?"

"Set tables. Carry trays of food. Smile at bad jokes. And clean every-thing up. The event begins at seven, but we start at four. Meet me here on Saturday at three thirty. Wear black pants and a white top."

I quickly do the math. Twenty dollars an hour, under the table, will earn me close to two hundred dollars for one night's work.

"Okay," I say.

"My name's Kelly," she says, holding her hand out to shake. Her grip is firm and cool.

"Nice to meet you, Kelly. And thanks."

She smiles. "No thanks necessary. You seem like someone who could use a break. I know a little something about that."

Before I can say anything else, she passes through the swinging doors into the back and I'm left standing there, amazed at my good fortune.

---

It's only seven in the morning, and the idea of going straight back to Eva's and hiding out for the rest of the day makes me feel twitchy. So instead, I walk across campus and over to Telegraph Avenue. I stand outside the student union, watching people move through the intersection and toward wherever it is they're going, unaware of how lucky they are to have the privilege of easy conversation with others. To debate, or laugh together at a joke. To share a meal, and maybe later, a pillow. And I feel the tug to be one of them, just for a little while.

I cross the street, keeping my head angled down and my hands shoved deep into Eva's coat pockets. Around me, panhandlers ask for money, people try to hand me flyers advertising bands, but I shake my head and keep walking.

I catch flashes of my reflection in shop windows as I walk, and I stop in front of a clothing store and stare at myself. With my short blond hair poking out of the bottom of my cap and Eva's coat, it's like looking at a ghost. People swirl on the sidewalk behind me—laughing students, homeless people, aging hippies—but all I see are strangers I can never know. I will never have the freedom to sit down and open myself up to someone else, never be able to talk freely about my mother and Violet, about who I am and where I'm from. This is the life I have ahead of me. Always being alert. Aware. Holding the most important parts of myself back.

I wait for a large group of students heading back toward campus and join them, walking close enough to give myself the illusion that I'm a part of them. That I'm not stranded in this new life alone. I follow them across the busy street that borders campus, peeling off as they make their way into the student union. I can walk among them, but I will never be one of them again.

---

On my way back to the house, I stop off at a supermarket to pick up a few basics. I grab a hand basket and find the cheap staples my mother used to buy—off-brand bread and peanut butter, a large grape jelly. I skip her other favorites—rice, beans simmered in water with onion and garlic. I don't want to be here long enough for leftovers.

In the checkout line, my eyes drift toward the magazine rack, and there it is on the cover of *Stars Like Us* magazine—a glossy tabloid somewhere between *People* and *Us Weekly*. "The Crash of Flight 477: Heartbreak as Families Try to Pick Up the Pieces." And in the upper right corner, surrounded by others who were on the flight, is my picture. The caption reads *Wife of philanthropist Rory Cook among the victims.*

The photo had been taken at a gala at the Met a couple years ago. I was laughing at something someone had said off camera. But even though there's a smile on my face, my eyes look empty. I understand better than most how secrets can live on your skin and how hard they are to hide, because the truth is always visible somehow.

I lay the magazine facedown on the conveyor belt and read the covers of the more scandalous tabloids. Rory hasn't been covered like this since Maggie Moretti. "Rory Ravaged by Grief Seeks Solace in Mystery Woman" reads one, with a picture of Rory and a woman I've never seen before. With a jolt, I realize that someday, Rory will fall in love again, and a part of me feels guilty for walking away and leaving that trap open for someone else.

"How you doing today?" the checker asks as she begins scanning my groceries.

"Great, thanks," I say, my voice quiet and strained, hoping to pay quickly before she takes too much notice of me. I hold my breath as she finishes and begins to bag everything, tossing the magazine in without a second glance. I remind myself that I don't look like that woman anymore. Someone would have to study my features closely, the shape of my eyes, the freckle patterns across my cheeks, in order to see it. I

149

look like Eva. I wear her clothes. Carry her purse. Live in her house. The woman on the cover of that magazine doesn't exist anymore.

---

Back home again, I set the groceries down and dive into the magazine. A rolling unease passes through me as I look at the smiling faces of people who weren't as lucky as I was. I force myself to imagine a picture of Eva, staring back at me from the page, the way she appears in my memory, frozen in time, determined, hopeful. And duplicitous.

It's a four-page spread, with full-color photographs of the crash site. The article is almost all human interest, dissecting the victims' lives, interviewing bereft loved ones. A newlywed couple embarking on their honeymoon. A family of six—the youngest only four years old— taking a long-awaited trip home. Two teachers on their way somewhere warmer for their annual February break. All of them lovely, vibrant souls extinguished in what was probably a long and terrifying descent into the ocean.

I save the feature about me and Rory for last. He's sent them a picture from our wedding, staring into each other's eyes, a background of twinkle lights and shadow. *Among the victims was the wife of New York philanthropist Rory Cook, son of the late Senator Marjorie Cook. His wife, Claire, was traveling to Puerto Rico to assist with hurricane relief efforts. "Claire was a shining light in my life," Cook said. "She was generous, funny, and kind. She made me a better man, and I will be forever changed by having loved her."*

I sit, trying to reconcile the words with the man I knew. Identity is a strange thing. Are we who we say we are, or do we become the person others see? Do they define us by what we choose to show them, or what they see despite our best attempts to conceal it? Rory's words alongside a happy wedding photograph paint one picture, but the people reading this magazine can't see what he was like before or after it was taken. And there are clues, if you know where to look. They're there, in the way he grips my elbow, in the angle of his head, the way he leans forward and I lean back.

I remember that moment, not because it was wonderful, but because of what happened shortly beforehand. I'd wandered over to the side of the room to talk to Jim, one of my former colleagues from Christie's. I'd been laughing, my hand on Jim's arm, when Rory joined us, interrupting Jim's story with a hard stare.

"Smile," I'd chided Rory. "It's supposed to be a happy day."

Instead, Rory wrapped his hand around my wrist, squeezing it so hard I nearly cried out. "If you'll excuse us," he said to Jim, "we're needed across the room for some photographs." His voice was smooth, giving Jim no clue that anything was wrong, but I knew, in the way he gripped my wrist, in the steel set of his mouth, in the narrowing of his eyes, that my flippant comment was something I'd pay for later.

I caught my college roommate watching us from across the room, where she and a few other friends were seated near the DJ's table, and I gave her a wide smile, hoping to convince her that everything was wonderful. That I hadn't just married a man who was beginning to terrify me.

Rory demanded I remain by his side for the rest of the reception. He made the rounds of the room, charming guests, cracking jokes, but never speaking a word directly to me. It wasn't until we were in the elevator, on our way up to our lavish suite, that he turned to me with ice in his eyes and said, "Never humiliate me like that again."

I stare at the photo of myself, barely recognizing the woman in it, and my finger traces the contours of her face. I wish I could tell her that everything was going to be okay. That she'd get out in the most extraordinary way, and all she needed to do was hang on.

———

After a quick peanut butter and jelly sandwich, I settle in front of my computer again, clicking over to check the Doc. It's blank, but I notice that Rory has been working on my eulogy. I open it and start to read.

> **My wife, Claire, was an incredible woman who lived an extraordinary life of service and sacrifice.**

I cringe. The pull quote from the magazine carried more emotion. This makes me sound like an octogenarian who has died peacefully in her sleep after a long and productive life. Not the vibrant person I was—and still am. And I wonder, what would I like Rory to say instead?

*I was incredibly hard on Claire—much more so than she deserved. I know I scared her. I sometimes hurt her. I loved her in a broken and warped way that made it impossible for us to truly be happy. But Claire was a good person. A strong person.* I shake my head. Even in my imagination, I can't make Rory say what I need him to say.

*I'm so sorry, Claire. What I did to you was wrong.*

But the eulogy on the screen in front of me doesn't say any of that. It talks about my childhood in Pennsylvania and goes on to describe my charity work, the many lives I touched, the people I've left behind. Even here, I feel a lack of any real grief or regret. But perhaps that's all I was to him. The wife from humble beginnings. The wife who tragically lost her family. The wife who was successful in the art world until she gave it up to join her husband's charitable foundation. And now, the wife who died too young. It reads like the plot points of a secondary character in a novel, not my life.

I imagine my former colleagues from Christie's, sitting in a back corner of the church at my funeral. People I haven't spoken to in years, thanks to Rory's isolation. How many will actually show up? Four? Two? In many ways, I feel like I died a long time ago. Nothing of my former self remains. The person in this eulogy is a stranger.

Just then, Rory's email pings with a new message, and I toggle over to his inbox. It's from the director of the NTSB, and the preview sends a chill zipping down my spine.

> Dear Mr. Cook, I wanted to follow up on our earlier conversation regarding the section of the plane where your wife...

I'm tempted to open it, read it, and then mark it *Unread*. I need to know how that sentence ends. But I force myself to wait.

I stand and pace the room, never taking my eyes from the screen, silently urging Rory to check his email. Finally, after fifteen minutes, the message shifts to *read*, and I immediately race back to the desk to click on it.

> Dear Mr. Cook, I wanted to follow up on our earlier conversation regarding the section of the plane where your wife was seated. I've just been informed that despite the relatively intact condition of the fuselage, recovery workers report that your wife's seat was empty. We will continue to prioritize the recovery of her remains, and I will update you on any new developments.

All the air leaves my lungs in a white-hot rush, everything I'd believed shifting and turning into something completely different.

Rory's reply pops up below this email immediately.

> What does this mean? Where is she?

I sit back in my chair, Rory's questions about what might have happened to my body tumbling around in my mind, evolving into questions about how Eva could have pulled it off. Who else she manipulated, and where she might have gone. A part of me isn't surprised at all. A woman who lies about killing her husband, a man who doesn't even exist, is certainly capable of this.

After a few minutes, a reply arrives.

> Until we recover the black box and get more details about the crash, it's impossible for me to speculate. There could be any number of reasons why your wife wasn't where we expected her to be. I apologize, and ask for your patience. Reconstructing events of a crash takes time. It will be a while before we have any answers.

I see it all again, that flash of pink at the news conference. For the first time, I let myself seriously consider the possibility that somehow, despite being scanned, Eva didn't get on that plane.

# EVA

Let's switch it up and meet at Chávez Park.

Eva hoped her text to Dex would give the impression she was feeling jumpy. Scared.

César Chávez Park was a giant stretch of grass that sat directly on the San Francisco Bay with a path that traveled around the perimeter. On weekends it was crowded with families flying kites, joggers, and lots of dogs. But at two o'clock on a Tuesday in late September, it was deserted. Eva found Dex sitting on a bench, his back to the sweeping views of the bay, hands shoved in his pockets. When he saw her, he stood.

"Let's walk," she suggested when she reached him.

Eva gripped her purse close to her side and reminded herself that

Dex was just a regular person. He couldn't read minds or peer through the side of her purse and see the voice-activated recorder she'd dropped in there before she exited her car, the red Record button illuminated. All he saw was a scared woman in front of him. That would be her advantage. It always had been.

Eva was preparing, the way others might prepare for a natural disaster, storing food and water, mapping their exit routes, packing their emergency kits. Castro would return, and Eva would cast her own net, trading the information she already knew and the information she would soon find out for a new identity. A new life in a new town. Castro could give her a backstory that didn't include drug-addict mothers, foster homes, and expulsion. She could wipe the slate clean. But first, she'd have to walk a razor's edge and hope she didn't slip up.

Together, they began a lap around the park on the cement path. A tall, grassy hill rose in the center of it, blocking their view of the Berkeley Hills and marina. "So what do you have for me?" he asked.

Eva crossed her arms against the wind that whipped up off the bay and said, "Tell me the truth. Is it really over?"

"I told you, Fish took care of it."

Eva looked at him, incredulous. "How can you possibly think that would be enough for me? They targeted me. Followed me to my house." Her voice rose, trembling with emotion. "Don't fucking tell me Fish took care of it and expect me to roll over."

Long ago, when she was a girl in the group home, Eva discovered that big feelings made most people uncomfortable, and she learned how to use anger or sadness to turn up the pressure, to maneuver people into a position where their only desire was to make the emotion go away. To stop the tears. To fix the fear. To placate the anger. Dex was no different. And Eva didn't have to reach too deep to find the fear, to make a compelling case for why she might need details to reassure her.

In the distance, two women walked toward them on the path, deep in conversation, and Eva continued. "Everywhere I go, I wonder if I'm being followed. The man in line behind me, the woman on her phone…" Eva gestured toward the two women, closer now. "Even them. How do I know they don't work for Castro?"

Dex took her arm and pulled her closer, hissing, "Calm down, Eva. Fuck."

They stepped to the side and let the women pass, and when they were out of earshot again, Eva said, "So tell me. What does it mean, 'Fish took care of it'? How? Because there's a difference between a duty officer losing some paperwork and a sergeant or lieutenant calling off a federal investigation."

Information about how Fish's people operated inside the department wasn't Eva's end goal. It would be useful, but Eva was using it to warm Dex up. To get him to start talking. Like a crack in a wall, it would grow wider with time and pressure.

Dex looked away from her, his voice low, and Eva stepped closer to him. "The woman you met in the park was freelance," he said. "Your instincts weren't wrong. She was an addict, trying to curry favor in exchange for a lighter sentence. Fish's people inside the department have successfully neutralized her as a source. Because you didn't sell her anything, and no money exchanged hands, they have nothing to go on. They're gone."

They'd resumed their slow stroll, shoulder to shoulder, the wind now at their backs, the green hills of Berkeley rising in the distance. Eva picked out the Campanile, the stadium, and the white shape of the Claremont Hotel, and let Dex think she was absorbing what he told her. "So what happened to her?"

"No clue," Dex said. "Jail or rehab, probably."

Eva turned to face him, placing a hand on his forearm. "Look, you know me. I'm not prone to hysteria. But there's no way I'm handing over drugs out in the open like this. Not until things settle down."

Dex's eyes narrowed. "You have an obligation. You don't get to set the terms."

"I think I do," Eva said. "I'm the one with the skills."

Dex peered down at her, anger radiating off him. "This isn't a fucking game. Brittany might be dealt with, but it isn't over. Now the cleanup starts, the deconstruction of what happened. Who else was involved, what they knew, and when. You being difficult right now puts me at risk too."

They walked in silence for a few minutes, the wind whipping and grabbing the edges of her coat, before Eva asked her next question. "What happened to the chemist Fish had before me?" Dex looked at her, surprised. "You told me he was leaving the business. But that wasn't entirely true, was it?"

"He refused to do what he was told," Dex finally said. "I don't want the same to happen to you."

Again Eva let the panic she felt bubble to the surface, where Dex could see it, and pressed her lips together, as if she were battling to stay calm. "That body you showed me at the motel? Was that him?"

Dex shook his head. "No, that was someone else. The chemist was gone before you even came on board." He lowered his voice, and Eva stepped closer to catch what he'd say next. "You've got to pull it together. For me as well as yourself. This is how mistakes are made."

Eva nodded, as if she were making her peace with how things were going to be. She had enough for now. They'd reached the outer edge of the park, with nothing but black asphalt littered with trash between them and her car, and she reached into her pocket and pulled out an envelope. "Football tickets for this Saturday," she explained. "We're taking things in-house for now."

*In-house* was a term she and Dex used when they felt it was too risky for Eva to pass him his weekly supply in a park or restaurant. Many years ago, Eva had begun buying season tickets to football and basketball, though she rarely used them. But the purchase also included access to elite club-level venues that gave its members a sense of entitlement and security. Access to places an undercover cop couldn't easily follow them.

At this point, she couldn't stop making drugs for Fish. But if Castro was still watching, she wasn't going to do anything to incriminate herself until she had something to offer him.

Dex slipped the tickets into his coat and put his arm around her shoulders, pulling her close. "Whatever you need to get the job done."

# CLAIRE

Friday, February 25

> Recovery workers report that your wife's seat was
> empty.

I stare at that line from the NTSB, trying to make sense of it, my mind leaping between two competing questions—could Eva have somehow gotten off the plane, and what might Rory do when recovery workers tell him there isn't any trace of me.

I open a new tab in my browser and Google *Recovery of remains in a plane crash, ocean.* At least twenty articles pop up about the crash of Flight 477, all of them written in the last four days. "The Latest: Searchers Recover Remains and Debris." Another one is titled "Vista Airlines Crash: Flight 477 Goes Down off the Coast of Florida." I try something else. *How are human remains recovered after a plane crash?* Again, I get a long string of articles updating the search and recovery efforts, outlining Vista's poor safety rating, speculation as to the cause of the crash, but nothing that will tell me what I need to know—whether they will be able to definitively say I wasn't there, or whether it's possible that they can't recover everyone.

And the bigger question: How could Eva have gotten off that plane? I try to imagine her out there somewhere, using my name as I'm using hers, flashing my driver's license to check into hotels. Or perhaps she sold it the minute she landed somewhere else. I paid Nico ten thousand dollars for my Amanda Burns documents. I have no idea what a real driver's license would sell for. Maybe identity theft was Eva's side business, how she paid cash for a duplex in Berkeley.

I turn to Google again. *Can you scan onto a flight but not get on it?* I find a thread on a discussion board where someone is wondering if they can do this in order to get enough miles to bump them up to the next frequent flier level. But responses are not encouraging:

> No way to get around the final head count. If it doesn't match, everyone deplanes and they run everyone through security again. There's no way to achieve that without screwing yourself and every other passenger on the plane.

Another response reads

> It's impossible to have your boarding pass scanned and then not get on the flight. Think about it. You get scanned about six feet from the Jetway. You think a flight attendant is going to scan your pass, then watch you walk away? This entire thread is stupid and a waste of mental energy.

Right. The head count. Eva had to have gotten on that flight.

I'm startled by the buzzing of Eva's phone on the desk next to me. A call from *Private Number*. I stare at the bright screen as it rings two times. Three. Four. I picture myself answering it. Pretending to be Eva. Asking questions that might lead to answers about who she really was. What she did. Why she might approach a stranger in an airport bar with an outrageous story about a dying husband. The buzzing stops, and silence fills the room again. After a minute, the screen lights up with a new voicemail. I punch in the new code I set the other day and listen.

It's a woman's voice on the other end. *Hi, it's me. Checking in to see how it went. If you're okay. I thought I'd hear from you by now, so call me.*

That's it. No name. No callback number. I listen to the message again, trying to grab at any details—the age of the woman, any background noise that might tell me where she's calling from—but there's nothing.

My mother once took Violet and me on a trip to the beach in Montauk. She gave each of us an empty egg carton, telling us to fill the spaces with treasures. Violet and I walked for miles, searching for sea glass and intact shells that looked black on the outside, but when you turned them over revealed the pearly pink of cotton candy and ballet slippers, or the purply blue of music boxes and baby blankets. We sorted our treasures by type, by color, and when we'd filled our cartons, we returned to the rental house to show our mother.

Trying to figure out Eva's life is like trying to fill one of those cartons. Some spaces are filled with things that don't make sense—a prepaid cell phone left behind. A lack of any personal items. A house paid for in cash. A woman, waiting for a phone call from Eva, inquiring about *how things went*. And others are still empty, waiting to connect it all. To make sense of everything.

A heaviness descends. This isn't how I thought it would be. Maybe it was naive, but I never considered the stress of trying to live a lie. I only thought of how it would feel to be free of Rory.

And here I am. I'm free, but far from liberated.

Saturday morning, I'm up early, eating a vanilla yogurt and watching Rory and Bruce debate whether to release a printed version of the eulogy Rory wrote for me after the funeral is over. Bruce—yes. Rory—no.

And then:

**Rory Cook:**
What did Charlie say when you met?

I sit up and carefully set my yogurt aside while I wait for Bruce to respond.

**Bruce Corcoran:**
I did as you asked. I explained that you were too devastated by Claire's death to come yourself, that it was incredibly opportunistic to come forward now, violating the terms of an ironclad nondisclosure agreement. Doing so would force us to bring a lawsuit, which no one wanted to do. Especially now.

**Rory Cook:**
And?

**Bruce Corcoran:**
Didn't make a difference. Kept saying if you're going to run for office, the voters need to know what kind of a criminal they're voting for. That what happened to Maggie Moretti needs to be brought out into the open. The people who loved her deserved to know the truth.

And just like that, all of my assumptions rearrange into something new. I feel a rush of adrenaline pass through me at the mention of Maggie and I hold my breath, waiting.

**Bruce Corcoran:**
What do you want me to do now?

I can practically hear Rory yelling as words appear next to his name.

**Rory Cook:**
I want you to do your fucking job and make this go away.

**Bruce Corcoran:**
I'll put together a package, see whether that might silence this. Try to be patient.

**Rory Cook:**
I don't pay you to tell me to be fucking patient.

And then they're gone, leaving my mind spinning, trying to figure out how Charlie Flanagan, Rory, and Maggie Moretti intersect.

When I was young, I used to ride my bike across town and into a small wooded area. I loved the way the sidewalk would just end, picking up the beginning of a dirt trail, rutted and winding through patches of shade and dappled sunlight, riding beneath tall trees that kept my secrets.

But my favorite part was when I'd emerge again, my entire body vibrating after so long on the rough terrain, and what it felt like to glide back onto the asphalt—all the bumps smoothed flat again.

I feel that zip now, after so many days of rough riding. I've come out again and can see a path forward.

I return again to the thumb drive, finding a file buried in the M's, labeled simply *Mags*. But when I open it, there isn't much. Rory and Maggie dated pre-internet and pre-email. So there are only about twenty scanned images—photographs, notes on lined paper, cards, a hotel bar napkin. Each one labeled with a meaningless IMG number. Clicking through them, an eerie shiver passes through me, Maggie's handwriting as personal as a fingerprint, as quiet as a whisper in my ear.

It doesn't surprise me that Rory kept these images, long after he'd destroyed the hard copies. I know he loved her, in the only way he knew how. Like a road map, they trace the path of their relationship from the bright and shiny passion of new love into something more complicated, and reading them is like listening to an echo of my own marriage, musical notes that are both familiar and hollow at the same time.

Near the bottom of the folder, I open a scanned image showing the blue lines and ragged edges of a page torn from a spiral notebook. It's dated just a few days before she died.

*Rory,*

*I've thought a lot about your suggestion we spend the weekend upstate, to work things out. I don't think it's a good idea. I need space to figure out whether I want to keep seeing you. The last fight we had scared me. It was too much, and right now I don't know if it's possible to continue as we have been. Please respect my wishes, and I'll call you soon. No matter what, I will always love you.*

*Maggie*

I read the note again, feeling like a wheel yanked out of alignment, steering me in a new direction as I remember that dinner from so long ago. *Maggie wanted us to get away for a quiet weekend. To reconnect and really talk without the distractions of the city.*

But Maggie didn't want a weekend away to reconcile. She wanted to break up. And I know firsthand how Rory reacts when a woman tries to leave him.

It's a gruesome irony that both Maggie Moretti and I had to die to finally be free from him.

# EVA

It didn't take long for Liz to start asking questions. First, it was a comment about a smell in the backyard she couldn't place, which forced Eva to work at night, after she was certain Liz was asleep.

"Are you sick?" Liz asked her another day, after three consecutive all-nighters, dark circles under her eyes. Eva had tried to deflect the questions as best she could, blaming the neighbors across the alley for the smell and a sinus infection for her haggard face.

In the few weeks she'd been on hiatus, the landscape of Eva's life had shifted, and she was struggling to navigate back to normal. She began thinking about her life as two parallel tracks, the one she was living, with her late-night lab work and the demands of Dex and Fish taking up her time, and the life she'd had just a couple weeks ago. Dinners with Liz. An uncomplicated window of time that had felt lighter and brighter than she'd ever imagined.

And now, as she wove her way through the crowds dressed in blue and gold, up the hill that led to Memorial Stadium, her mind was fuzzy, her eyes gritty. She waited in line at the gate, her eyes trained on the security guards asking everyone to open their purses and bags for inspection. She pressed her arm against her side, feeling the outline of the package of pills, safely tucked into an inner pocket of her coat.

Eva hadn't contacted any of her clients to let them know she was back to work. She would make the drugs for Fish, but as far as her clients were concerned, she was still on hiatus and would remain so indefinitely. Her singular goal was to gather as much information about Fish and the way his organization was structured as she could, not make money she didn't really need.

When she reached the front of the line, she opened her purse and watched the guard's eyes scan the contents—a wallet, sunglasses, and small voice recorder—and held her breath as she always did, waiting for someone to finally see through her act, to finally see her for what she really was.

But that wasn't going to happen today.

As she passed through the entrance and into the stadium, the field spread out below her, each end zone painted with a yellow *California* set against a dark blue background, the trademark script *Cal* centered on the fifty-yard line. Eva ignored the people in the seats around her, instead staring across the field as the marching band played and students filled the section next to it, feeling more isolated and alone than she'd felt in years.

As an undergrad, Eva had only been to one game, and the memory of it haunted her every time she returned. *Meet me in the north tunnel afterward*, Wade had said. She'd been shocked to see the number of people lingering there, waiting for players. Hangers-on, followers, sorority girls flipping their hair and checking their lip gloss. She'd hung back, watching as she always did, from the perimeter. When he came out, his eyes scanned the crowd and landed on her. As if she glowed. He passed through the crowd of people and claimed her, putting his arm around her and leading her away, the smell of his soap mixing with the redwood trees that surrounded the stadium. She knew then that she was lost, that Wade Roberts had chosen her, and she was bound to follow whether she wanted to or not.

She'd first met him in the chemistry lab she was TA'ing. At the beginning, she'd assumed he was just another jock, trying to flirt his way to a better grade. But every time Wade had looked at her, she felt an electric zing pass through her.

Early in the semester, she'd been walking them through some basic chemical reactions when Wade had said, "Why are we doing this? When are we ever going to need to know what substances react with calcium chloride?"

She should have redirected him back to the task. But Eva knew she needed to be someone unexpected if she hoped to hold his attention. "Do you like candy?" she'd asked him. And then she'd shown them all how to make strawberry-flavored crystals, a simple procedure that anyone could find on the internet if they wanted to.

That was how it started. A pin in the map that marked the beginning of a journey she never wanted to take. Wade had begun pressuring her to try making drugs shortly after they started dating. At first, she didn't want to. But what he was asking was so simple, she figured she'd do it once and get him off her back. Science had always been where she felt the safest— among the laws of physics and chemistry. Unlike life, which could dump you at a group home at the age of two with no warning or second chances, chemistry was predictable, its actions absolute. Wade was the person everyone wanted to be close to, and he wanted to be close to her. And so, when he asked her to do it again, she did. And then again after that.

The stadium was filling up. Eva checked her watch and reached into her purse to activate the voice recorder. Across the field, the marching band drums pounded a rhythm, the same one from that day so many years ago. The people around her pressed closer, making her feel smothered, and she tried to shrink down inside herself, to just hang on. Wait. To do her job and be ready.

"Been here long?" Dex asked, sliding into the seat next to her.

"Maybe five minutes." Her eyes traveled up the hill where the cannon that fired after every touchdown poked through the trees on its platform, a white California banner fluttering in the wind. Tightwad Hill, open to anyone willing to hike up there and sit in the dirt. Fucking Berkeley. "God, I hate this place," she said.

"Then give me what you've got and let's get out of here." He twisted around, looking into the crowd behind them, and then faced forward again, his knee bouncing a jittery rhythm.

Eva shook her head. "Not a chance. We do this my way." She knew that just because Dex said Castro was gone, it didn't mean he wasn't still out there, watching her. Waiting for her to make a mistake.

"You really don't need to worry."

"Your lack of detail does not inspire confidence," Eva said. She pulled her purse from underneath her seat and inspected the bottom of it, wiping dead leaves and an old gum wrapper off of it before placing it next to her armrest. "You need to give me specifics. Who was following me. Why. And how it is they're gone now."

Dex slouched down in his seat, his gaze leaping from one thing to another, never landing, never still. "Fine," he said. "It was a joint task force, DEA and locals, looking to grab Fish. Which they've been trying to do for years. The whole thing got disbanded two weeks ago."

"How is it possible Fish can call off a joint task force?" she asked.

Dex squinted across the field where the band launched into a version of "Funky Cold Medina." Finally, he said, "It costs a lot of money to run surveillance, and you weren't giving them anything. They can't keep watching you forever. Higher-ups pulled the money, and with no evidence pointing anywhere, Fish's friends inside the department began rumbling about *better uses of resources* and bitching about the budget. They had no choice but to fold."

"Listen to yourself," she said. "Federal agents. Joint task forces. And you're telling me not to worry?"

"I'm telling you this topic is closed. You need to drop it."

She studied his profile, softer around the contours of his jaw, laugh lines framing his eyes and mouth. She'd known Dex for twelve years. And something was off about him today.

Just then, the cannon fired as the Cal team burst out of the north tunnel, and next to her, Dex nearly leaped out of his seat. He covered it by rising along with the rest of the crowd as the band launched into the fight song, but Eva wasn't fooled. "Are you okay?" she asked.

"Yeah," he said, shoving his hands in his pockets as they sat again and the first quarter started. "Just a little rattled."

"You just finished telling me all was well. What the hell, Dex?"

He shook his head. "It's fine. Just, Fish is looking into that guy I told you about. My friend who referred Brittany."

"Are you in danger?"

Dex gave a hollow laugh and looked at her, his eyes sad. "When am I not?"

At halftime, they headed back into the mezzanine. As people made their way toward the bathrooms or the concession stands, Eva led Dex toward the doors labeled *Stadium Club*. She handed her badge to the guard at the door, who scanned it and waved them through. The noise of the stadium faded as she led Dex up a set of stairs and into a large room that overlooked the campus, all the way to the San Francisco Bay and the Golden Gate Bridge in the far distance.

"I'll get drinks," Dex said, leaving Eva to stare out the window and think about another time, an office with an almost identical view, the ghost of Wade Roberts still following her.

---

It had been the nicest office Eva had ever seen in all her years at Berkeley. Set high on the hill at the top of campus, its window offered sweeping views all the way to the Golden Gate and beyond. In a corner, a clock ticked, measuring Eva's fate in seconds. The dean had flipped through her file, and she'd glanced at the door again, wondering when Wade would show up and deliver the pardon he promised.

"I see you're a scholarship student." The dean looked up, waiting for her to confirm. She stared at his nose, a sharp beak that propped up a pair of bifocals, and said nothing. He resumed his reading. "You came from St. Joe's in the city?"

The first glimmer of sympathy. She could almost time its arrival. When people found out she grew up in a group home, they either took a step back or a step forward. But it almost always changed how they viewed her. She'd shrugged and looked at the door again. "It's all in the file." Her tone was more abrupt than she'd intended, and she wished she could reel her words back in and start over. Tell him how attached she'd grown to her life as a student, that Berkeley was a place where potential seemed to shine down and touch her shoulders. But Eva had never been able to offer honesty like that. So she said nothing and waited for the rest to happen.

"It seems foolish to throw it all away by making drugs in the chemistry lab," he'd said.

Eva was saved from responding when the door swung open and the dean's assistant ushered Wade in. The breath Eva had been holding released. Wade had promised her he would tell the dean that making the drugs had been his idea, and would assume all of the blame. As the

172

quarterback of the football team, he'd get a slap on the wrist, maybe a one-game suspension, but nothing that would ruin his career.

But her relief quickly vanished as Wade was followed by Coach Garrison. Eva had only seen his picture in the paper, or once as a tiny, pacing ant on the sidelines of the only football game she'd ever been to, at Wade's behest. *I want my girlfriend to watch me play.* It had been the word *girlfriend* that had done it. Eva had never been anything to anyone—not daughter. Not friend. Certainly never girlfriend. She had felt foolish that the betrayal struck her so deeply, that she'd allowed herself to believe Wade might be different.

———————

"All they had was white," Dex said, handing her a small plastic cup of wine. Eva tore her eyes away from the view and refocused on the present. She'd believed she'd risen from the ashes, making a life for herself. But it had all been an illusion. A delusion. Nothing had changed at all. Dex had stepped into the space Wade had vacated, and things continued as they'd begun, only on a much larger scale.

Dex drank from his cup and grimaced. "How much do you pay every year for the privilege of drinking shitty wine?" he asked.

The last thing Eva needed was a recording filled with musings about bad wine. "Sometimes I wonder whether I've ever encountered Fish and not known it. Like, maybe he's one of those high-rolling donors over there." She pointed to a group of older men, clustered near a trophy case, clad in dark blue and gold. "It makes sense, really. For him to hide in plain sight like that." Dex stared at her over the top of his plastic cup and she continued. "You know him. What's he like?"

Dex shrugged. "A regular guy, I guess. Nothing special. Scary as fuck if you make him mad." A shiver passed through him, and he turned to look at Eva, his expression sad. "Don't start asking questions now."

Eva took a sip of her wine, the sharp tang biting the back of her throat. "Don't worry. I know you can't tell me anything. But I've been thinking about what happens after I give you the pills. I never considered until now whether any of it could somehow be traced back to me. They can do some crazy shit with forensics."

"It doesn't stay local, if that's what you're worried about."

"I guess my worry hinges on what you consider local. Sacramento? Los Angeles? Farther?"

Dex took another sip of wine before dumping the rest into a nearby trash can. "Let's finish this and get out of here."

They walked down a small side hallway toward a restroom with a gender-neutral icon on the door, where they fell in line behind a mother and small child. An older man exited and the mother and child entered, locking the door behind them. A server passed them in the hallway and said, "If you guys want, there are bigger bathrooms around the corner. No wait."

Dex and Eva smiled and assured her they were fine. After another five minutes and some muffled crying behind the closed door, it was finally her turn. She locked the door and checked the recorder in her purse, frustrated Dex hadn't told her more. She leaned against the wall, the cool tile seeping through her shirtsleeve, trying to figure out what she could ask, what she could do, to get Dex to tell her something more specific. Where they sent the drugs, and who bought them. Details about Fish she could trade. Finally, she flushed the toilet, only pulling out the brightly wrapped package of pills after she'd washed and dried her hands.

She placed it on top of the towel dispenser and exited, letting Dex slip in after her. When he came out, he patted his coat and said, "Hope you don't mind, but I'd rather not stick around for the second half."

"I get it," she said. They made their way out of the club and back down the stairs, exiting the stadium.

They paused outside. "Look," he said. "We're both a little wound up, and you're right to want to be cautious." He gestured toward the stadium behind them, where the game had resumed. "We'll do this your way until we're both comfortable again."

She looked at him, his expression softer now that he'd gotten what he wanted from her. He was both comrade and captor. Protector and prison guard. Regardless of how he behaved, Dex was not her friend. She had to remind herself he wasn't worried about her comfort; he was worried about himself.

She gave him a grateful smile and said, "Thanks, Dex." As long as he believed he was handling her, he wouldn't notice how she was handling him.

———————

Later that night, instead of working, Eva sat in front of her computer, staring at a blank search field. Being at the stadium today, remembering how it felt to sit there alone, with no one to fight for her, to say *Eva is a good person. She deserves a second chance* made her wonder if a second chance would have even been possible. Liz's words floated back to her. *Information is power.* Liz had poked through the boundaries she'd constructed for herself, and she wasn't sure if this would help resurrect them or destroy them completely.

Eva tried to prepare herself for the most painful outcome—her mother, recovered, living a happy life with a family and friends—and entered her mother's full name into the search field, the only light in the room the glowing of the screen, illuminating her face. Outside a car glided by, quiet tires humming on the pavement, then silence filled with the relentless chirp of crickets.

She pressed return.

A long list of hits popped up. Rachel Ann James on Facebook. Images.

Twitter. A Rachel Ann James at a college in Nebraska. She scrolled down and clicked on a free people-finder link, which brought up eighteen potential matches. But none of the ages matched. Her mother would be in her early fifties, and these people were either too young or too old.

Her body vibrated with anxiety, more than her most stressful drug deals, and she was tempted to stop. To close her computer, get back to work, and forget about all of it. But she navigated back to a new search and entered *Rachel Ann James obituary, California.*

This time, it was the first link in her results. It was a short paragraph from a local paper in Richmond just a few miles north of Berkeley. No details were given about how she'd died, just the year and her age, twenty-seven. *Rachel is survived by her parents, Nancy and Ervin James of Richmond, California, and brother, Maxwell (35).* No mention of her, the granddaughter they didn't want.

Eva stared at the screen, listening to the blood pump in her ears. Eva had been eight. She tried to match up the childhood she remembered with this new information. Her time with Carmen and Mark. The return to the convent, when the nuns had reached out to her family again. Somewhere in there, her mother had died. And yet, her grandparents, Nancy and Ervin, finally freed from the nightmare of having an addict daughter, had still said no.

She thought about printing the obituary, taking it downstairs and knocking on Liz's door. Asking her how any of this gave her power. As far as she was concerned, it felt like a thousand tiny cuts piercing her skin, a pain with no center, just a radiating fire that consumed her.

But instead, she cleared her search and closed her computer, settling herself into the darkness, and got to work fitting this new rejection, this new heartbreak alongside all the rest.

# CLAIRE

That Rory lied about his last weekend with Maggie is interesting, but not incriminating in a legal sense. Of course, he would make himself look sympathetic when recounting the story to me, his new girlfriend, and I can't begin to guess why Maggie might have changed her mind and gone anyways. But Maggie's reference to a scary argument chills me, because I know what Rory's temper looks like, how easily she could have ended up at the bottom of that staircase.

But the note doesn't prove anything other than they fought. Which was widely reported at the time. What nags at me is how Charlie Flanagan is connected to that weekend in 1992. That's the key to figuring out everything. Perhaps he was the one to organize the payoffs Aunt Mary mentioned, illegally skimming them from the foundation's account.

A quick check of the time tells me I have just a half hour until I'm supposed to meet Kelly, so I go into the kitchen and grab a Diet Coke from the fridge and take a sip, staring out the back window. As I wait for the caffeine to hit my bloodstream, I imagine Charlie releasing whatever he has to the media. Huge exposés in the *New Yorker*, *Vanity Fair*, the *New York Times*, stripping Rory of all his power. I know it's a leap, but the fantasy still energizes me.

I set the can on the counter and head upstairs in search of a pair of black pants and a white top.

---

When I arrive at the coffee shop, Kelly is already there, waiting in her car, and I open the door and slide in.

"Ready?" Kelly asks.

"Let's do it."

Kelly's phone rings as we hit the end of the block. "Jacinta," she says into the phone. "I'm on my way to work." She listens for a moment, and then curses. "Okay, I'll be there in five minutes."

She hangs up and turns the car around. "Sorry," she says. "My daughter, Jacinta, has been working on this project for her art history class and she left the poster supplies in my trunk."

"I don't mind," I tell her.

"Normally, I'd leave her to sweat it out, but she's working with a partner and I don't want to punish her for Jacinta's carelessness." She sighs. "This project has been a pain in the ass from day one."

"What is it?"

"Compare and contrast two twentieth-century artists. Deliver an oral presentation with visuals." She rolls her eyes. "Berkeley takes its arts education very seriously."

"How old is your daughter?" Kelly can't be much older than her late twenties.

"Twelve."

She glances at me, catching my surprised expression. "I had her when I was only seventeen."

"That must have been hard."

Kelly shrugs. "My mother nearly killed me when she found out I was pregnant. But then it was buckle down to business." We stop at a red light, and she glances at me. "My mom is my rock. I couldn't work or go to school without her. And she and Jacinta are tight. Where I get attitude and eye rolling, my mother gets giggles and secrets."

"You must be busy, working two jobs and going to school," I say.

Kelly smiles as the light turns green. "I suppose. But I've always worked, so I'm used to it. I have the early morning shift at the coffee shop, take classes during the day, and do catering events for Tom at nights and on the weekends. I'm saving money so Jacinta and I can get our own place. Right now, we live with my mother and it's crowded."

I bite my lip, wishing I could tell her not to be in such a hurry to leave.

———————

Kelly's house is in a neighborhood of small, one-story houses so similar to my mother's in Pennsylvania, I could squint my eyes and believe I was back home again. When we pull into the driveway, she turns to me and says, "Come in and meet my family."

I hesitate, knowing I should stay in the car. There's a difference between being one of many black-and-white-clad servers at an event and shimmying up to Kelly's family with a name and a handshake. But it would be strange if I refused.

And I'm overwhelmed by how much I want to go inside. After so many days of being alone, I want to sit in someone's kitchen and talk about art. "I know a bit about art history," I finally say. "Maybe I could help."

"We can use all the help we can get," Kelly says.

It's exactly as I imagined it would be. The living room is spare, just a couch, a reclining chair, and a television. Through an open doorway is a small kitchen and eating area where two girls sit, hunched over the table. Beyond the living room is a short hallway that probably leads to a couple small bedrooms and a bathroom. My mother's house had the same feel to it, frayed and scarred around the edges, but polished to a high shine. I can imagine the three of them here in the evenings, each of them in her favorite spot. Kelly's mother in the armchair, Kelly and Jacinta on either end of the couch, their legs in a tangle the way Violet and I used to watch TV.

An older woman stands at the counter, chopping vegetables, while on the stove, pots simmer, the air thick with the smell of rosemary and sage.

One of the girls looks up as we enter. "Sorry, Mom," she says.

Kelly leads me into the kitchen and says, "Let's practice some manners, Jacinta. This is Eva."

"Nice to meet you," I say.

Jacinta smiles, and I can see Kelly in the set of her brown eyes and the sharp structure of her cheekbones. "Nice to meet you too."

"And her friend, Mel."

The other girl raises her hand in a half wave, then turns to Kelly and says, "Thanks for coming back, Kelly."

Kelly squeezes her shoulder and says, "Only for you, Mel."

The older woman chimes in from the counter. "I'm sorry I didn't check in with her before you left." She shoots a look at Jacinta. "She told me she had everything she needed."

Kelly turns to me and says, "Eva, this is my mother, Marilyn."

I brace myself, waiting for a flash of something in her eyes, a flicker of a question, knowing this is how it will always be when I meet someone new. But she smiles and wipes her hands on a towel before shaking my hand. "Nice to meet you."

I'm struck by the power of belief. How easily it transfers from one person to another. Kelly believes I'm Eva, and now her mother does too, without question. I look between them, their bond as familiar as an old, favorite coat. It wraps around me, making me want to sit down at the table and never leave. "Tell me what you've chosen for your project," I say to the girls.

Jacinta slides her laptop so I can see two paintings side by side on the screen. Jasper Johns's *False Start* and Jean-Michel Basquiat's *Boy and Dog in a Johnnypump.*

"Great choices," I say. "Basquiat started on the streets of New York as a graffiti artist, commenting on the social injustices he saw and experienced. He's responsible for graffiti being the legitimate art form we know it to be today."

"I think we read something about that. But it's all kind of blending together," Jacinta says. "This is the project from hell."

"Jacinta," Marilyn warns.

"Sorry, Grandma. It's just…look how different they are. It's easy to contrast them. But how are they similar? They're not. At all."

I sit down in the chair next to them and lean my elbows on the table, which wobbles in the same way my mother's used to. "Here's a tip. Don't get tied up in the images. Art is all about emotion. Teachers want to know what you take away from the piece and how you apply that to your own life. It's totally subjective, so have fun with it." With the light streaming in from the windows, the rich smell of a cooking meal filling the room, and the reassuring sounds of Marilyn behind us, opening the refrigerator, moving between the sink and the stove, I feel as if I've traveled back in time. All my edges matching up with the space around me.

I spend five more minutes filling the holes in their research. Background about each artist, their childhoods and early influences, before Kelly tells me we have to leave.

"I like your family," I say as we pull out of the driveway.

Kelly smiles. "Thank you. It's not always easy, trying to raise a child under my mother's thumb. Because I had Jacinta so young, my mother sometimes forgets that I'm Jacinta's mother, not her. I appreciate her help, but that house is too small for the three of us."

I want to tell her that the tangle of their crowded life should be a comfort, not a burden. I'd been in such a hurry to redefine myself, not knowing that I'd be carving away a piece of my heart. I assumed my family would always be there, waiting for me. Sometimes I can trick myself into believing my mother and Violet are still in our house, moving around each other, waiting for me to finally come home.

---

"How'd you know all of that?" Kelly asks as we turn onto the on-ramp of the freeway.

I've been silent for most of the ride, my mind still back at Kelly's house, sitting at that table, feeling as if the farther we drive from it, the farther I'm traveling away from myself. Who I'm supposed to be.

"I was an art history major in college." I don't feel I'm risking too much to tell her that, and it feels good to say something true.

Kelly looks at me, impressed. "You should be looking for jobs at museums or auction houses."

"It's complicated," I say, suddenly afraid if I keep talking, I'll tell her everything.

Kelly laughs. "Show me someone whose life isn't complicated." When I don't respond, she says, "No pressure. I get it."

"I'm leaving a bad marriage," I finally admit, before tacking on a lie. "Hiding out at a childhood friend's house while she travels. It's temporary, until I can figure out what's next. But my husband will be looking for me, so I can't work in my field anymore."

The car feels like a protective layer, safe and warm as we speed down the freeway toward Oakland. I look out the window, at the people in the cars around us. So many secrets playing out in their minds. No one is going to look too closely at mine. And as far as Kelly is concerned, my story has been lived a hundred times already.

"It takes a lot of courage to start over," she says.

I don't respond. Nothing about what I've done feels brave or courageous. Kelly reaches across the center console and squeezes my hand. "I'm glad you're here."

---

Kelly wasn't kidding when she said tonight's party was a big one. There are twelve of us hired to set up and work the event, which is being held in a giant warehouse in downtown Oakland. Nearly forty tables fill the enormous room, each one seating eight. When she introduces me to her boss, Tom, I only hold his attention for a split second before someone calls for him from the kitchen. "Thanks for giving me the job," I say as he begins to hurry away.

"Thanks for helping out in a pinch," he calls, just before disappearing back into the kitchen. "Kelly will show you what to do."

Soon we're busy with linens, table settings, and flowers. "I've been waiting for this event for months," Kelly says.

"Why?"

Her eyes sparkle. "It's a banquet for the Oakland A's." She looks around the room. "In a few hours, this place is going to be crawling with professional athletes. I'm hoping to at least get an autograph." Then she winks at me. "Maybe a phone number."

She slides away again, leaving me to my napkin-folding, but I'm suddenly unable to make my fingers work. My gaze leaps to the exit and then back to my pile of linens. I've run events like this before, with big names in a big location. And one of my first calls was always to the media. The more photographers, the better.

I finish the napkins with trembling hands and begin the table settings, trying to remind myself that I look different now. And in my black pants and white shirt, I'll be just one of many faceless workers sliding between the crowd, paid to remain invisible.

———————

An hour into the party, I feel more relaxed. The photographers were clustered near the entrance, taking people's pictures as they arrived. There are only two inside, and they're easy enough to avoid. I feel my chest loosen again, and I navigate the large space, offering appetizers and napkins. Some people smile and thank me, while others take what I'm offering without even making eye contact or stopping their conversations at all.

I'm surprised by how physical the work is.

"You're a natural," Kelly says as she passes me, carrying a tray of dirty glasses toward the kitchen.

I massage a knot in my shoulder. "It seems pretty simple. Keep the food moving, stay in the background." I think of Marcy, the caterer I always used in New York. A tiny woman who had the grace of Jackie Kennedy but the countenance of a bulldog. She commanded the respect of all who worked for her and had a gift for making any event sparkle. Her staff was always impeccable, though until tonight, I had no idea how hard they worked. I wonder what Marcy thinks of my passing. Whether she will cater my funeral.

———————

As I circulate among the guests, offering bacon-wrapped scallops, I pass a beautiful woman in a tight blue dress, holding a whispered argument with a well-built man who must be one of the players.

"Just stop, Donny," the woman hisses.

"Don't fucking tell me what to do."

My nerves tighten reflexively, even though I know he's not speaking to me. But the way he spits the words at her, his voice laced with venom, makes me hurry past them, eyes cast downward, fear zapping all my nerve endings and making my skin buzz. I know what it's like to be on the receiving end of that kind of anger. And I wish I could turn back, help that woman in some way. I wonder how many people here know this is how he treats her. The other players. Their wives and girlfriends. Do they see it and look away, as so many people did with me? Do they whisper about it to each other, but do nothing to help? I feel impotent with rage, at the careless way people discard other people's problems, and how I'm no better. Watching it happen and doing nothing.

My eyes track them as they move away from me and become swallowed by the crowd, the way his hand remains on her lower back, and how easily that can shift from solicitous to a shove.

———

Midway through dinner, a man approaches the microphone set up at the front of the room, and the crowd claps. I take my tray and stand alongside the back wall to listen. He has the voice of a radio announcer and talks about his years of working inside the booth at the stadium. But my attention is soon drawn back to that same couple, now directly in front of me. At first he's trying to silence her with what looks like platitudes and promises, but she's having none of it. Her anger spirals upward, and I tense, waiting for him to react. *Don't make him mad*, I silently plead with her. *You still have time to turn this around.* My palms grow sweaty, and my breath comes in short gasps that I try to elongate, reminding myself that all couples argue. Just because my husband used to hit me doesn't mean this man will hit her. And yet my body is reacting. Tensing. Preparing.

The man at the microphone draws another laugh, which covers the sound of their argument for a moment, but when it dies down again, their words slip into the silence.

Heads turn toward them. The woman begins to step away, but Donny grabs her arm, yanking her toward him, the people nearest them gasping.

I'm close enough to see the fear flash through the woman's eyes. It's just a split second, but it's long enough to tell me that this has happened before. That she knows what will come next.

Without thinking, I drop my empty tray to the ground and push off the wall, taking two giant steps until I'm between them, doing what no one ever did for me. I press my palm against the man's shoulder and say, "You need to let go of her."

Surprised, his grip loosens, and the woman yanks her arm away. She rubs it, staring daggers at him over my shoulder and says, "You're a fucking liar, Donny."

More people turn away from the speech at the sound of her voice and stare at the three of us.

"Cressida," he says. "I'm sorry. I didn't mean it."

"Don't follow me. Don't call me. I'm done." She pushes past me toward the entrance, and I finally step back.

And that's when I see them. Three separate cell phones, pointing at us, recording.

# EVA

Eva rewound the tape and listened again to Dex's voice. *He refused to do what he was told. I don't want the same to happen to you.*

It still wasn't enough, so she began to keep a log, writing down the number of pills made and the dates she passed them over to Dex. She couldn't always risk recordings, and she didn't even know if Castro could use them. It was like trying to drive blind. She had to intuit her way toward what she'd need through instinct and guesswork.

And throughout it all, she tried hard not to think about what might happen if she was discovered. Despite her efforts to remain focused, images flashed like a movie behind her closed eyes, jerking her awake at night, sweaty and panicked, certain it would never work. Convinced they already knew. But she used that fear, allowing her to get even more work done, her sleepless nights growing more and more frequent as she waited to see if Castro would return. She could feel him out there, a heavy presence that lurked in the dark corners, biding his time, and she only hoped she'd be ready when he showed up again.

Downstairs, someone knocked on the door. She and Liz had plans to shop for a Christmas tree at a special tree farm Liz had found online. Eva had declined—not once, but twice—citing reasons that Liz stepped around. She'd badgered until Eva capitulated, rationalizing that it was easier to accommodate Liz than to keep avoiding her. Liz would only be there for another month, and then she'd be gone, back to Princeton for spring semester. Eva tried hard to ignore the sharp stab of sadness she felt every time she imagined Liz's apartment quiet and empty. But if all went well, Eva would be gone shortly after that and it would no longer matter.

She hurried down the stairs, reaching for her coat as she swung the door open. But it wasn't Liz. It was Dex.

"What are you doing here?" she asked.

He didn't waste time with a greeting. Instead, he stepped into her house, kicking the door closed behind him, his expression hard. "What are you playing at?"

Panic pulsed through her, at the thought that somehow someone had figured out what she was doing. "I don't understand," she whispered.

"Last week's package was one hundred pills short."

"What? No. That's a mistake."

"No shit it's a mistake," Dex said. "What the fuck, Eva? Are you trying to get yourself killed?"

She shook her head, desperate to make Dex understand, desperate to get him out of her house before Liz showed up. "I'm tired," she said. "I'm not sleeping. I must have miscounted." She couldn't explain the bone-deep exhaustion that accompanied trying to be two completely different people simultaneously.

"You need to fix this."

"I will."

"Today," he insisted.

Next door, she could hear Liz's footsteps descend the stairs, and Eva closed her eyes momentarily. "I can't today."

Dex looked incredulous. "Do you have something more important to do?"

She looked down at the coat, still gripped in her hand. "My neighbor and I are shopping for a Christmas tree."

Dex looked up at the ceiling, as if he couldn't believe what she was telling him, and swiped his hand across his jaw. "Jesus Christ," he said. Then he looked at her, his gray eyes piercing through her. "Do you realize how hard I had to work to convince Fish to let me handle this? How close he came to sending someone who wouldn't ask questions or give a shit about a fucking Christmas tree?" His voice was growing louder, and Eva worried that it would travel through the wall. Or onto the front porch, where Liz would be any minute.

As if on cue, she heard Liz close her front door and lock it.

"You need to go, Dex. I'll take care of it. I promise."

He looked at her, as if he were trying to see beneath the surface, to glean whether something bigger was going on. "By tomorrow," he said.

"Tomorrow," she agreed.

He pulled open the door and came face-to-face with Liz, startled, her hand raised to knock.

"Hello," she said, her gaze traveling between Dex and Eva, curious.

Dex's expression shifted into an easy smile. "I hear you two are shopping for a tree. Have fun." He gave them a wink, ever the performer playing his part, before bounding down the stairs and striding away.

"Who was that?" Liz asked. "He's handsome."

Eva tried to gather her wits, to lighten her expression to match Dex's friendly tone. The last thing she wanted to do now was shop for a tree, but if she backed out, Liz would have a hundred questions. "That was Dex," she said.

"Are you two...?" she said, trailing off.

Eva pulled her door closed and locked it. "It's complicated," she said. "Let's go."

As they drove north toward Santa Rosa, Eva let the miles put distance between herself and what happened, compartmentalizing it into a tiny ball, where it sat, like a pebble in her shoe. She was furious with herself for being so careless. For working herself so thin she'd made a mistake like that. She couldn't risk any kind of targeted attention, and yet she'd invited it in.

By the time they reached the tree farm, she'd worked out a plan. After they returned to Berkeley, she'd work all night. Again. She redoubled her efforts to focus on Liz, who was describing the tree they'd buy, a special one they'd plant in front of the house instead of propping it in a stand of water for a few weeks.

"You won't believe how beautiful it will be," Liz told her as they walked between rows and rows of tall, majestic pines. She examined each tree, checking to see whether it was full all the way around, before moving on to the next one. She spoke softly, carried somewhere else by memory. "My dad and I used to do this when I was a girl. Every place we lived—and there were many—the two of us would look for a new tree to join our family." She reached her hand out as they walked, brushing the pine needles with her fingertips. "He made Christmas magical."

When Eva was little, when she thought there was still a chance they'd come back for her, she used to fantasize what Christmas would be like if she'd grown up with her birth family. If her mother hadn't been an addict but instead the kind of parent who would insist Santa was real, staying up late assembling toys and filling stockings. And when Eva woke, she'd race to the tree and tear off wrapping paper, each present bigger and better than the last, always exactly what she wanted. Maybe her grand-parents and extended family would come over. Perhaps there would be cousins, other children to round out the image of her perfect family. But now that picture had shifted, carrying with it the knowledge that those Christmases would have been heavy with her mother's absence.

"Will your daughter be coming for the holidays?" Eva asked, unsure how she'd feel about meeting Ellie, of being displaced by the daughter of Liz's heart.

"She's working," she said. The finality of her tone made it clear that she didn't want to discuss it more.

Liz slipped between two trees and into another row. "This one," she called, her words muted by the thick pine needles surrounding them and underfoot.

Eva followed the sound of her voice and found her in front of a tree, nearly eight feet tall and perfect in shape. "How are we going to get it home?" Eva pictured the two of them driving down the highway with this massive tree strapped to their roof, its roots dangling behind them.

"They'll deliver it," Liz said, walking around the tree slowly, looking at it from all angles. "We'll string it with lights that will sparkle. We can bundle up, make some hot chocolate, and sit on the porch and admire it. The best part is that the tree will be here, year in and year out. No more dead trees by the curb at New Year's," she said.

As if Eva had ever dragged a dead Christmas tree to the curb. "What if it rains?"

Liz shrugged. "Outdoor lights. Glass and ceramic ornaments. I have boxes of them at home in New Jersey. But I couldn't stand the idea of a treeless Christmas so I packed some of my favorites and brought them with me."

Liz took the tag that they'd been handed upon entering and hung it on the tree, claiming it as theirs, and removed a different one that they would take with them to the front of the tree farm to pay.

The daylight was melting into evening as they pulled out of the lot and headed south toward home. Eva leaned back in the seat and stared out the window as the warm glow of the afternoon began to fade, thinking of the long night ahead of her.

------

Their tree was delivered two days later, its roots wrapped in a burlap bag. It came on an enormous truck that also carried equipment to dig a hole deep enough to plant it. Liz supervised the entire thing, choosing a spot in front of Eva's side of the porch. After the tree had been planted and the workmen paid and tipped, Liz opened her front door and carried out a box labeled *Christmas*.

With Liz's stereo blasting carols, the two of them got to work. First they strung the white twinkle lights, and then came the ornaments. Liz had a story for nearly every one of them. Gifts from colleagues and former grad students, whom she remembered with vivid detail and fondness. Handmade ceramic ones from when her daughter, Ellie, had been a little girl. "I'm probably the only visiting professor who ever packed a box of Christmas ornaments for a six-month post," she said. "But I've never had a single Christmas without a tree." She set aside a clumpy wreath constructed out of dough, the name *Ellie* written on the back, a quiet sadness on her face that Eva pretended not to notice.

As they worked, Eva found herself wanting to slow things down, to draw the evening out. She thought ahead to this time next year, when everything would be resolved, one way or another. She'd either be somewhere far away or dead. And Liz would be long gone, her short time in Berkeley a distant memory, Eva just another name on a holiday card list.

When the last of the decorations had been hung, Liz disappeared inside and returned carrying something wrapped in tissue paper. As she handed it to Eva, she said, "I wanted to be the one to give you your first

Christmas ornament. I hope that from now on, wherever you are, wherever you go, you will think of me when you look at it."

Eva unwrapped the layers of tissue paper, revealing a handblown glass bluebird.

"The bluebird is the harbinger of happiness," Liz said. "That's my Christmas wish for you."

Eva ran her finger over the smooth glass. The detail on it was amazing, with deep swirling blues and purples, fading into almost ice white in some places. "Liz," she whispered. "It's incredible. Thank you." She reached down and hugged Liz.

Liz pulled her tight, embracing Eva in a way she'd always imagined her mother might, and she nearly broke, so strong was her desire to be known. To be seen, instead of constantly protecting herself, measuring her words and actions against discovery. It all felt like too much to carry alone, and Liz was the sort of person who might help Eva out from under it. The words rested right behind her lips, trembling, waiting to break free, but Eva swallowed them down. "I didn't get anything for you."

"Your friendship is gift enough," Liz said. "Let's turn on these lights and have a cup of hot chocolate."

They carried chairs from Liz's dining room onto the porch and sat with their feet propped up on the railing. The tree lit up the dark night, its lights glowing as if from within, cloaking everything else in shadows.

"I found out my mother is dead," Eva said, her voice just a whisper in the dark. She couldn't give Liz the truth about her life, but she could give her this. "She died when I was eight."

Liz turned sideways in her chair and looked at her. "I'm so sorry," she said.

Eva shrugged, trying to steel herself from the pain she still felt at the discovery. "I'm trying to tell myself this is better. Simpler. At least she had a good reason for not finding me."

"That's one way to look at it," Liz said, turning back toward the tree. "Will you try to find your grandparents?"

Eva thought about how the discovery of her mother's death had crushed her, and she wasn't sure she had it in her to be disappointed all over again. "I don't think so," she said. "It's easier not to know."

"It's easier until it's not," Liz said. "Which is kind of how life goes. When you feel ready, maybe you'll look again."

With every conversation, with every confidence Eva shared, she was drawing Liz closer to her, to the truth of who she was. She wanted to both push Liz away and inhale her at the same time. It settled something inside of her, to set some of her secrets down. To know that even after she disappeared into a new life, someone would hold the pieces of her old one and remember who she'd been.

In the distance, the Campanile bells chimed the hour. When they were done, Liz said, "That man from the other day. Tell me more."

Eva hesitated, so tired of lying. "It's nothing," she finally said. "He's just a friend."

Liz sat with her explanation for a few moments before asking, "Are you safe?"

Eva shot her a look. "Of course. Why?"

Liz shrugged. "I thought I heard yelling. And his face, for a split second…" She trailed off. "My ex-husband used to do that. Be angry one second, then the next it was as if a mask had slipped over his true self." She shook her head. "It just triggered something in me, that's all."

Eva considered telling Liz a version of the truth. That Dex was a colleague. That she'd made a mistake at work and put him in a bad position with their boss. But that was the tricky thing with half-truths. They led so quickly toward bigger revelations, like sliding down a hill, gaining momentum with every one.

Liz turned in her seat again so that she was facing Eva, watching her, waiting for her to explain.

"We had plans to meet for lunch," she finally said. "I forgot. He was mad. But it's fine. I'm fine."

Liz stared at her, as if weighing Eva's story, waiting for the rest of it. But Eva remained silent, and next to her, she felt Liz's curiosity and worry morph into hurt. Disappointment that Eva didn't trust her with the truth. "I'm glad to hear it," Liz finally said.

As Eva looked at the tree, something shifted inside of her, something shiny and vulnerable and dangerous rising close to the surface, breaking through her hard exterior. And Eva knew, without a doubt, that being loved by Liz was more terrifying than anything she'd ever done, because she knew she wouldn't always have her.

---

Long after Liz had gone to bed, Eva sat there, watching the houses along the street go dark, one by one, unwilling to turn the lights on the tree off and go inside. *Not yet*, a tiny voice inside her whispered. She felt invisible, as if she were the ghost of who she used to be, come to visit this life and lead herself somewhere better.

From beyond the tree's illumination, Eva heard the sound of quiet footsteps. She sat up, her senses sharpening, thoughts leaping immediately to Dex, or to Fish, and the fact that she wouldn't even know it was him until it was too late.

A man appeared on the front walk, cast in a dark shadow from the bright lights of the tree, and she squinted into the black night as he approached and made his way toward her. Agent Castro stepped into the circle of light created by the tree and leaned against the porch rail.

Eva remained seated and waited. All these weeks preparing. Organizing. Planning. And now the moment had arrived.

She glanced at Liz's dark windows and said, "How long have you been waiting?"

"A long time," he said. "Years."

Eva took in his face, fatigue etching shadows beneath his cheekbones, and realized they were not so different. Both of them weary from trying to maintain a facade that had grown unwieldy.

In a quiet voice, he said, "What can you tell me about a man named Felix Argyros?"

Eva kept her eyes on the tree. "I've never heard of him." That much was true.

"You might know him as Fish."

She didn't answer. As long as she didn't say anything, she could stay inside this neutral space where she'd neither betray Fish or have to lie to a federal agent.

He continued. "You are not my target, Eva. If you help me, I can protect you."

Eva gave a short, mirthless laugh. If Fish knew Castro was here right now, Eva wouldn't see the end of the week.

"You're going to have to make a choice," he said.

"I thought the task force was disbanded." If Castro was surprised she knew this, he didn't let on.

"Let's just say we scaled back. You've turned into quite a sports fan."

Eva kept her eyes on the tree, although all her attention was on Castro, marking his posture, watching his body language. She knew he didn't have anything on her, or he would have arrested her, not crept up to her porch late at night, asking questions. "I'm just a server who likes football and basketball," she said.

"Want to know what I think?" he asked.

"Not particularly."

"I think you want out." His voice was soft, but his words cut through her anyways, how clearly he saw her. How much of her mind he already knew.

She shot him a quick glance, and he smiled, as if something had just been confirmed. "Time's running out," he said, pushing off the railing and standing upright. "I can either keep this conversation a secret or let slip to someone inside the department that we've talked. How do you think that might go over with Fish?" He shook his head slightly and said, "Even if you were to tell him about it first, he'd have doubts. And in my experience, doubts always cause problems."

Eva stared at him, her options narrowing down to just one. "Why me?" she asked.

Castro locked his eyes onto hers and said, "Because you're the one I want to help."

He slid his card onto the railing and walked down the front path, disappearing as quietly as he'd appeared.

# CLAIRE

On the ride home from the A's event, Kelly and I are silent, my mind leaping forward and backward, trying to rewrite what I've just done. I know what those people will do with the videos and photos they took. They'll show up online first, then eventually migrate to television. The question is how soon, and will anyone recognize me?

I relish the quiet of the car and stare out the window, looking at the darkened apartments that back up against the freeway. As we head up the on-ramp, Kelly says, "What happened back there?"

I keep my face averted, wondering what she'd say if I unloaded everything from the past few days. I imagine her eyes growing wide as I speak, the horror of what I've done to save myself edging out any friendliness that used to live there. "What do you mean?" I ask.

"The way you jumped in between Donny and his girlfriend when he lost his temper. What did you leave behind?"

The road is nearly empty this late at night, and the car glides over several lanes, settling in the middle. "It's better if you don't know."

Kelly keeps her eyes on the road, occasional headlights from the opposite direction briefly illuminating her face, before it's covered in darkness again. "Did your husband hit you?"

I let the question hang in the air, wondering if I have the nerve to answer it. Finally I whisper, "Many times."

"And now you're worried he might see the video and find you."

"I don't know how I could have been so stupid," I say.

We drift off the freeway into downtown Berkeley, and in almost no time, we're approaching Eva's house. When she pulls up in front, Kelly turns to me. "Let me help," she says.

I know better than anyone how secrets can fester, cutting you off from the rest of the world. I never had any true friends in New York, other than Petra, because I had too much to hide. So much to conceal. And now that I've escaped, nothing's changed. I have to hold Kelly at the same distance in order to protect my secrets. They're just different secrets.

I offer a weak smile, wishing more than anything Kelly and I could be friends.

"Thanks," I say. "But it might be too late for that."

---

Upstairs at my computer, I type in the web address for *TMZ*. Right at the top is a link showing Donny and Cressida's fight, posted just forty-five minutes ago. The headline says "Fight Between Baseball Star Donny Rodriguez and Girlfriend Turns Physical." I click on it, and the video pops up. There's no sound, just the footage, but the resolution is incredible. It shows Donny and Cressida fighting, the way he grabbed her arm and yanked her toward him, and me, stepping into the middle of all of it.

There are already over two hundred comments, and about halfway down, I see it.

> NYpundit: Hey, does anyone think that woman in the background looks a little bit like Rory Cook's dead wife?

"No," I breathe into the empty room and think about the Google alert this mention has activated. To Danielle's email. To Rory himself.

I quickly navigate to his inbox and open his alerts folder. The email sits at the top of a long list of unread notifications, and my first instinct is to delete it. But that will only delay the inevitable. Danielle will still see the alert, read it, and click on the link. She will watch the video, perhaps several times, before taking it to Bruce. Together, they'll figure out the best way to approach Rory, to show him that the wife who was about to leave him, the one who supposedly died, is alive and well and working for a caterer in Oakland.

I check the box next to the message, along with several others for good measure, and hit Delete, and then toggle over to the trash and empty it. I'm screwed either way.

---

By Sunday morning, over a hundred thousand people have viewed the video, and I scroll through at least one hundred replies to the comment from last night. Most of them are chastising NYpundit for being blind, stupid, or simply a callous conspiracy theorist.

> People like you are what's wrong with this country. You hide behind your computer and throw out baseless theories in the hopes of becoming famous.

But NYpundit isn't giving up. He posted a screenshot of my face from the video, and next to it, the same image from the *Stars Like Us* magazine article. You tell me, he says.

They do look similar, another commenter concedes. If you swap out the hair, maybe.

I know that despite my short blond hair, Rory will recognize me right away. The way I move, the expression on my face as I step between Donny and Cressida is unmistakable. It's only a matter of time until Rory sees the video and tracks me down—through Tom, or Kelly—and I need to be far away from Berkeley when that happens.

But so far this morning, the Doc remains empty of the words I expect to materialize there at any moment.

Did you watch the video? Do you think it's really her?

_____

But when text finally appears, it's not about the video.

**Bruce Corcoran:**
Charlie sent me a draft email of a press release and a sworn deposition.

_____

**Rory Cook:**
What's in it?

_____

**Bruce Corcoran:**
Everything.

_____

The word sits there, and I can feel the weight of it, whatever *it* is.

Bruce continues typing, and I can practically hear his appeasing tone.

**Bruce Corcoran:**
Obviously, we aren't going to let this happen. We have people looking into Charlie's background. All the way back to college. We'll find something that will put an end to this.

**Rory Cook:**
There's a lot there. Keep me posted.

**Bruce Corcoran:**
Will do.

A knock on the door downstairs startles me. I creep down and peek through the window and see Kelly standing on the porch, holding two cups of coffee from the coffee shop. I'm tempted not to answer, to get back upstairs to find out what *everything* means and what exactly a senior accountant from the foundation knows about Maggie Moretti's last weekend with Rory.

But she's seen me. "I thought you might need some caffeine this morning," she calls through the closed door. "I wanted to thank you for helping the girls yesterday. They finished last night and it's pretty good."

We settle on the couch, the low table between us. Kelly sips from her cup, and I hold mine, the heat radiating through my hands.

"There's a video of me on *TMZ*," I tell her.

"I saw," she says. "But it's only online. Nothing on TV. So unless your ex likes to troll celebrity gossip sites, you'll probably be fine."

If she looked at the comments at all, it's unlikely she read far enough to catch NYpundit's. I rotate the cup in my hands, wishing I could explain that it isn't so simple. That this isn't going to go away so easily.

"Thanks for checking in with me, and for this." I hold up my coffee. "But I need to get packing. I'm leaving this afternoon." I look around the space that's been my refuge for the past few days. My coat, thrown across the back of the chair, the stack of newspapers on the floor next to the couch, how quickly this house has begun to feel like a home.

"There's still a chance he won't see the video."

I place my coffee on the table between us, untouched. "It's more complicated than you might think."

"Then explain it to me," she says. "If you need money, I can loan it to you. If you need a different place to say, I have a friend who can find one for you."

In this moment, I'm reminded of my mother, who never hesitated to reach out to someone in need and offer help, even when she couldn't afford to give it. I want more than anything to let Kelly help me. But I can't risk pulling her—or her family—into something bigger than any sane person would be willing to carry.

"Thank you," I say. "I appreciate everything you've done, more than you will ever know."

"Let me at least help you earn a little more money before you go. Tom's got a party this afternoon. No media, I promise. Just a straight-up event at a house in the hills with killer views. I can pick you up at two and have you home by nine." She gives me a sad smile. "Early enough so you can still technically leave today."

On the other side of the living room wall, tucked away in the dark garage, is Eva's car, and I feel an urgency to go now. Not to waste another minute. To toss my coffee into the trash, clear out the debris of the last few days, throw my things into her car, and take off.

But caution pulls me up short. I can't afford to be impulsive, to make another mistake. I need to have a plan. Figure out where I'll go next, gather the relevant documents I might need from Eva's office, and pack. Even if Rory sees the video right this second, the earliest he might appear in town is tomorrow. I can still leave tonight, with another two hundred dollars in my pocket. I can't afford to say no.

"I'll see you at two."

After Kelly leaves, I head back upstairs to my computer, hoping to see more of the discussion about Charlie. But the Doc is empty again, and I feel the silence, like a whispered threat only I can hear.

---

I start with Eva's desk, locating the most recent bank statement and setting it aside. From the box in the corner, I pull the title and registration to her car, her social security card and birth certificate, and take a second unsuccessful look for a passport. I see myself somewhere far away, a big city like Sacramento or Portland. Maybe Seattle. Finding a cheap motel or hostel, and then a job, filling in Eva's information on the W-2, the momentum of possibility growing inside of me.

I grab a pay stub from DuPree's, the restaurant where Eva worked, and add it to my pile. Maybe I can use them as a reference. I reach up and touch my short blond hair. To anyone outside of Berkeley, I *am* Eva James. I can prove it with a driver's license. A bank account. A social security card and tax returns. Like a funhouse mirror, I'm no longer sure where I end and she begins. I imagine a restaurant manager somewhere, calling DuPree's, asking about me. *Eva James? Yeah, she worked here.*

I turn back toward my computer. Where should I go? The possibilities bubble up inside of me. Heading north seems to be the best choice, with so many large cities and miles between here and Canada. Maybe I can circle back and settle in Chicago or Indianapolis. I begin my search, using Craigslist to look for jobs and inexpensive places to live, calculating how long my money will last.

After an hour, I click back over to the Doc, which is still empty, a blank white square offering nothing but stress and fear. It's the only thing anchoring me to my old life, and I'm tempted to cut my losses, log out, and leave it all behind. I have to find my own path forward, think about my own next steps, not some hypothetical Maggie Moretti scandal that might not even be true. Maggie is dead. And if I don't keep my wits about me, I could end up that way too.

Because once Rory sees the video, I'm certain he'll come. He'll fly to Oakland and track down Tom, demanding answers. All Tom will be able to tell him is Eva's first name. He has no W-2. No employee records to even indicate where Eva lived.

But Kelly knows.

I can see Rory, giving her that smile, the one that knocks even the most hard-hearted donors into writing a check. I know what he'll say about me—that I'm troubled. Unbalanced. Prone to exaggeration and lies. I'd like to think Kelly could withstand that, but the truth is, I don't know her well enough to be certain of anything. Which is why by tonight, I need to be gone.

———————

The party is up a winding road, perched high in the Berkeley Hills. Kelly and I arrive shortly after two. A quick check-in with Tom has us starting with tablecloths of crisp white linen that snap open and float onto each table in a large room with 360-degree views of the bay.

"Where do you think you'll go?" Kelly asks in a low voice. The bartender Tom hired, a twentysomething graduate student, bounces around behind the bar, earbuds in, setting up bottles, polishing glasses.

I smooth my hands across the tablecloth and look out the plate glass windows, the harsh afternoon sun making the view look washed-out and dirty. "Maybe Phoenix," I lie. "Or Las Vegas. East, I think."

I've decided to head north, bypassing Sacramento in favor of Portland. Save as much of my cash as possible by using Eva's debit card and zip code to fill up at the pump, going as far as I can until her money runs out. I've packed a small bag, simple things, enough to get me through at least a week on the road until I can get settled somewhere more permanent.

Kelly leans closer. "You won't want to do casino work. They fingerprint."

I take a step back, wondering what she knows, what I must have inadvertently revealed.

She catches the look of panic on my face and says, "Hey. I don't mean anything by that, other than you might want to avoid it if your husband is working with the police to find you."

Tom emerges from the kitchen wearing a white chef's coat and calls us in for the debrief. Kelly and I drop what we're doing to step up for our final instructions before the party starts. As he finishes, the hostess joins us. She's young—about my age—and doesn't pay us much attention as we stand to the side, letting Tom explain how service will work. Her eyes slide over us, as if we're furniture, before she says, "That sounds perfect. Please make sure to keep the appetizers circulating."

---

Soon, Kelly and I are moving among the crowd with our heavy trays. The glass windows have been opened so that guests can pass between indoors and a small grassy yard overlooking Berkeley and the bay beyond. The sun has moved across the sky, and the view that seemed harsh earlier is now cast in rich greens and golds. There's a chill that might make me shiver if I wasn't working so hard. As promised, the party is private, no sign of anyone interested in photographing the guests.

At a table near the edge of the yard, I set my tray down to gather dirty glasses and empty plates, and let my eyes linger on the horizon.

San Francisco is shaded in deep blues and purples as the sun begins to set, the lights on the Bay Bridge becoming more vibrant against the darkening sky, a stream of cars traveling into the city, their red taillights a bright necklace. Behind me, the party goes on, voices mixed in with pockets of laughter, the clink of glasses and cutlery, and beneath it all, low classical music smoothing out the edges.

I heft my tray back onto my shoulder and make my way carefully toward the house. As I cross the threshold, one voice lifts up above the others. A woman's, bright with surprise and joy. "Oh my god, Claire! Is it really you?"

Heat zips up my spine, spreading outward, growing into a white-hot panic as the party swirls around me. My eyes dart toward the exits—front and back—measuring which one might be closer, but people press in on me with no clear path of escape.

I should have left when I had the chance. And now it's too late.

# EVA

Cold January wind and a resolution—one way or another, she was done. Either Agent Castro was going to help her escape or she'd do it herself. They were meeting in a deserted beach parking lot in Santa Cruz, an hour and a half south of San Francisco. Eva hoped Fish's reach didn't extend so far. She'd driven slowly, watching her rearview mirror for anyone following her. The road that wound through the low hills separating the 101 freeway with the coast was only two lanes. Several times she pulled over and let cars behind her pass. No one appeared to notice her. No cars doubled back. By the time she pulled in next to Agent Castro's car, she felt confident they were alone.

They walked down the stairs that led to the beach without speaking. Wind blew her hair around her face, and the pounding waves seemed to vibrate through her. She wondered what they looked like to outsiders, walking on the beach in the middle of winter. Would people think they were a couple, hashing out an argument? Or perhaps siblings, come to scatter the remains of a loved one? She was almost certain they would never guess drug dealer and DEA agent.

"You're making the right decision," he said.

Eva stared out at the ocean, salt spray misting her face. She resented the word *decision*, as if she were choosing between a sofa and a chair, deliberating between options, weighing the pros and cons.

She felt time slow down, forcing her to notice the moment that separated before and after. The last time something had split her life so cleanly, the consequences had bled far into the future, staining everything. "I haven't decided anything. But I'm willing to listen to what you have to say," she said finally.

Agent Castro shoved his hands in his pocket, his eyes squinting against the wind. "Felix Argyros is someone we've been tracking for a long time. As I'm sure you're aware, his reach in the Bay Area is extensive and deep. And he's dangerous. We have at least three active murder investigations that we think are connected to him."

Eva gave him a sharp look. "You're wasting your time trying to scare me. I know what he can do to me, which is why I won't agree to anything until you can offer me protection."

Agent Castro's brown eyes studied her face, and she held his gaze, digging deep to hold it, to show him she was determined to do this her way. She had what he wanted, and if he wanted it bad enough, he would agree to her terms.

"Of course we'll offer you protection. We'll be with you twenty-four hours a day until after you testify, and I've been authorized to offer full immunity."

Eva laughed and looked down the beach, where in the distance, a lone woman threw a stick for a golden retriever into the ocean. "'Immunity' is a meaningless word. I'm talking about witness protection. Giving me a new identity, setting me up somewhere else."

Agent Castro blew out hard, thinking. "I can ask," he said finally. "But I can't make any promises. It's not as common as you might think, and we don't usually do that for people of Fish's caliber."

Eva knew he had to say that, to try to direct her to what was simpler and cheaper for his bosses. But she wouldn't be deterred. "I know how hard it is to make a conviction stick on a guy like Fish. I know how likely it is he'll get off on a technicality. And if he does, what do you think will happen to me? Your immunity won't help me then."

"I understand," Agent Castro said. "All I can do is assure you we know what we're doing."

"Like you knew what you were doing getting Brittany involved?"

"Brittany was a mistake," he conceded. "But it wasn't a complete disaster, since she led us to you." He turned his back on the ocean to face Eva, and his coat billowed out like a parachute. "You have to trust us."

Eva nearly laughed out loud. Trusting others had never turned out well for her, and this would be no different. "If you can't offer me witness protection, I don't think I can help you."

Castro's eyes softened, and she noticed the laugh lines that framed them. Someone, somewhere, must know what he looked like when he was happy, and she found herself wondering who that was, what it was like to love a man who spent his days chasing shadows.

"Look," he said. "I've been doing this a long time, and I've seen a lot. Of all the people I know in this business, you're the one who doesn't fit."

Eva looked beyond him, out across the churning waves and white-caps to the horizon line, knowing that it was just an illusion, that it would always be out of reach no matter how far you traveled, how hard you tried to get there. "You don't know anything about me," she said.

"I know you grew up in a group home. I know what happened to

210

you at Berkeley, and I know you shouldn't have been the only one punished."

She bit back a response, angry at him for knowing her secrets. She'd needed someone to say that years ago, when it could have actually helped her. Now? They were just empty words.

He continued. "I think you're a good person who was forced to make an impossible choice. Help me help you."

Eva stared at him, trying to make him believe she was still considering it, letting the silence spool out between them. She knew enough about life to know that the minute you agreed to something—whether it was making drugs for a football player or a drug dealer, or turning evidence over to the feds—they stopped trying to take care of you as soon as you said yes.

Agent Castro continued. "If you don't cooperate, we will prosecute you. Immunity will disappear, and I won't be able to do anything for you once that happens. You'll go to jail, for a very long time."

Eva thought she had enough for Castro, but the minute she handed it over, he wouldn't have to promise her anything. "If you can give me what I'm asking for, we might be able to come to an agreement," she said.

"I'll do my best."

Eva hugged her arms tight against her body and said, "I assume you'll keep following me. I have to ask that you not make things difficult. You seem to think Fish is a midrange dealer, but if he finds out we talked, he'll kill me, and then you'll have nothing."

---

She barely registered the return drive to Berkeley, her mind taking over, sifting through her options and next steps. Regardless of what Castro might be able to do for her, she needed to be ready to walk away from all of it—Berkeley, her house, her job. And Liz.

Eva arrived home after dark, the lights in Liz's apartment warm and inviting. She paused to touch the soft branches of their tree, empty of decorations now, waiting for another Christmas that would never arrive. Would Liz imagine Eva here, decorating it alone? Would she try to call Eva and wonder why she never answered her phone? Come back to visit friends and find Eva gone, her apartment abandoned? Eva knew what that was like, to feel the ragged strands of unanswered questions, tickling the back of your mind, tormenting your quietest moments with *why*.

As if she'd conjured her, Liz appeared, opening her door and peering out at Eva, still standing next to the tree. "What are you doing out there?"

Eva looked at her, framed by the bright rectangle of light, and didn't answer.

Liz took a step out onto the porch, her smile fading as she caught Eva's expression. "Are you okay?" she asked. "You look upset."

"No, just tired."

Liz looked as if she wanted to say something, but hesitated. Finally, she said, "When are you going to tell me what's really going on with you? Whenever I ask, you give me nonanswers. Or tell me you're tired. But that's not it. Why won't you talk to me?"

"I talk to you. All the time."

Liz shook her head. "No. You tell me things that have already happened. That are already over. But I know almost nothing about your days. Nothing about what you struggle with. What worries you. Why you're not sleeping. Out of nowhere, a man appears, fighting with you. Then I never hear of him or see him again." She took a deep breath. "No, Eva. You don't talk to me. You don't even trust me."

"You're reading too much into things," Eva said, hating how she sounded. Patronizing. Dismissive. When what she wanted, more than anything, was to throw herself at Liz's feet and beg her to fix it. To help her.

Liz's voice was low as she stepped all the way onto the porch and crossed her arms over her chest. "I thought we were friends. But you lie to me. All the time. About where you go. What you do. Who you spend time with. I'm not stupid. I pay attention. I hear you at night, on the phone sometimes. Arguing. With that guy?" Liz gave a thin laugh and said, "Don't bother answering. I already know you won't tell me the truth."

Eva was tempted to throw the truth in her face. To spit the words at her, like bullets, piercing Liz's belief that she could carry what Eva was hiding. She imagined rolling back the shelves in her kitchen and leading Liz down into her basement lab. *This is where I make the drugs*, she'd tell her. *I cook them up on that camping stove over there and give half to an incredibly scary man who might have me killed if I stop.*

Eva thought of Castro's words from earlier. *Of all the people I know in this business, you're the one who doesn't fit.* "I live in a world where I don't belong," she finally said.

Liz stepped toward her, but Eva backed away, needing to maintain the space between them. "Why would you say that?" Liz asked. "Look at what you've done. What you've accomplished, despite all the odds against you."

"And there it is," Eva said under her breath. What she'd been running from her entire life. Eventually, everyone—even Liz—viewed her successes and failures through the lens of pity they felt for her.

A pressure began to build up inside of Eva, all the things she wanted to say but couldn't. She pressed her fingers to her temples and stepped toward her door, needing to get out from under Liz's gaze, needing to escape inside where she could think clearly, where she wouldn't have to hide and obfuscate. "I can't do this. I'm sorry."

Liz reached out, closing the distance between them, and laid a hand on Eva's arm. "You can't run from what's hurting you. You can't bury it and hope it will go away. You have to face it. Look at it. Talk about it."

Eva yanked her arm away. "Please stop. You can't fix this with a fucking pep talk about honesty and self-reflection."

Liz recoiled, but her gaze was fiery, her voice rising to meet Eva's. "Then tell me. Whatever it is. Just say it."

Again, Eva fell silent, the words simply too big to speak. She looked through Liz's window and into her living room, remembering the first time she sat there, terrified that her entire world was about to crumble because of Castro. Not understanding that Liz would be the one to pull it all apart. To dismantle Eva's walls enough to shine light into her darkest corners. To make her yearn again for something more. To force her to want to be someone better.

When it became clear Eva wasn't going to say more, Liz pulled away, letting Eva unlock her door and step inside. But as she closed and locked it, Liz's voice floated in from the porch. "When you're ready to talk, I'll be here."

Eva made her way to the couch where she curled up in a ball, wishing she was already gone. That this part was already over.

# CLAIRE

## Sunday, February 27

I'm frozen, waiting for the owner of that voice to find me, grab my arm, and look into my face. To call me out and snatch what little bit of freedom I have left.

From across the room, Kelly's watching me and mouths the words *Are you okay?* I nod and force myself to keep moving. I slide between guests until I'm out of the center of the room, keeping my tray elevated near my chin, high enough to partially obscure my face, or to tip it forward onto someone else if I have to.

Our hostess enters, arm in arm with a woman I don't recognize. The two of them talk, their heads bent toward one another, when someone else from across the room calls, "Claire, over here. Paula wants to tell you about our trip to Belize."

And I realize our hostess's name is Claire. My hands begin to tremble—shake, really—my arms and legs suddenly turned to jelly, unable to support me. I make my way over to Kelly and hand her my tray. "I need to use the restroom," I whisper.

"You look like shit," she says. "What happened?"

I shake my head, brushing off her concern. "I'm okay. I didn't eat enough before work, and I'm a little woozy. I just need a minute."

"Hurry," she says, though I can tell she doesn't believe me.

In a small downstairs powder room, I splash cold water on my face and stare at myself in the mirror. I can change my appearance. Use someone else's name. Go to another city. But the truth will always follow me. No matter how careful I am, how guarded, I will always be one mistake away from discovery.

I dry my hands and slip back to the party, picking up a new tray on my way. I give Kelly a nod and plaster a smile on my face. Around me, conversation swirls, and I'm back to being invisible again. But my ears catch on the name Claire several times over the evening, and even though I know they're not talking to me, I still flinch. By the end of the evening, I'm battered and jittery, ready to leap into Eva's car and go.

———————————

On the ride back to Eva's, I give in to the exhaustion, the flush of adrenaline still seeping out of me. The wad of bills Tom gave me pokes a sharp corner through my pocket. Two hundred dollars, which brings my savings up to nearly eight hundred dollars. With the help of Eva's car and her debit card, that can carry me a long way from here.

"You ready to go?" Kelly says, breaking the silence. We're only a few blocks from Eva's, one light and a couple stop signs between now and goodbye.

"Yeah," I say.

She passes me a scrap of paper. "My number. Call me if you need anything. If you're comfortable doing so, let me know where you land."

"I will," I say as she pulls up to the house and stops.

She gives me a sad smile. "You won't. But that's okay."

I hesitate before reaching across to give her a tight hug. "Thank you for being my friend. For helping me."

She looks into my eyes and holds my gaze, her brown ones steady on mine. "You're welcome."

---

Inside, I go upstairs, needing a shower to wake me up for the long drive ahead. I let the steam fill me up, remembering the last time I prepared to leave a place, gearing myself up for a very different kind of departure. I emerge and dress quickly, tidying up the bedroom as best I can, making sure whatever or whoever Eva was running from won't find a trace of me when they finally show up. I hesitate in front of Eva's dresser, the note I'd found still tucked into the mirror. *Everything you ever wanted is on the other side of fear.* I have no way of knowing what this meant to Eva, or why she might have thrown it away. But I feel the need to take something of her with me. Not the legal paperwork that outlines the space she filled in the world, not the clothes she wore, but something from her heart. I slip it out of the mirror and tuck it into my pocket.

I enter her office, picking up the stack of papers I'd collected and sliding them into my purse. I check the Doc, the time stamp at the top showing no activity since that morning's exchange. What a waste of time this has been, a useless distraction. Rory and Bruce are almost never apart. Anything they have to say to each other can be whispered across a quiet room. Whatever Charlie Flanagan knows about the weekend Maggie died…it doesn't have anything to do with me.

I want to let go. Disconnect. But a tiny voice inside my head warns me that this isn't over. That with the video out there and the search and recovery still active, I need to use every resource available until I'm certain the danger has passed.

"And when will that be?" I say into the empty room. I wait, as if I might get an answer. With a sigh, I close my computer and slide it into my bag, then click the light off, plunging the room into darkness, trying not to think about how flimsy my plan feels. Paper-thin and already ripping along the edges.

Downstairs, I set my bag by the couch and go into the kitchen to put away the last of the dishes I'd washed that afternoon. Inside the refrigerator, a lone can of Diet Coke sits on the top shelf, and I grab it, popping it open, eager to get as much caffeine into me as I can.

The window over the sink is a black square, reflecting the room back at me, so I tug the curtains closed and take a long swallow, the bubbles reigniting my energy. Behind me, Eva's phone buzzes with a call.

I pick it up, the screen flashing *Private Number*. That woman again. Still worried. Still hoping Eva will call her. I wonder how many more times she'll try before she gives up and assumes Eva doesn't want to talk, that the friendship must not have been what she thought it was. I feel sorry for her, whoever she is. Tossing her worry into the void, never knowing that it's landing in the wrong place.

After a few seconds, the screen lights up with a new message. I'm tempted to ignore it, to delete it without listening, but curiosity pushes me forward. A part of me wants to hear her voice again, to pretend the worry she feels is for me. That there's someone out there hoping I'm safe. Happy. I press Play.

But it's not the woman looking for Eva. It's a voice I recognize, one I've heard hundreds of times, speaking directly into my ear.

*Mrs. Cook. It's Danielle. I know you didn't get on that flight. You need to call me.*

A loud rushing fills my head, my heart slamming against my chest in a rhythm that seems to say *They know. They know. They know.* The Diet Coke can slips from my fingers and crashes to the floor.

I stare at the phone, unable to breathe. How many messages have I listened to that began exactly like this? It shoots me straight back in time, tension and fear twisting me into a hard knot.

*It's Danielle.*

With questions about my failures, or things I forgot to do.

*It's Danielle.*

Always pressing me, watching me.

*It's Danielle.*

And she's found me. Which means it won't be long until Rory is on his way. Below me, the can lays on its side, dark-brown liquid pooling out, a growing puddle that resembles blood.

# EVA

The day Liz moved, Eva stayed hidden inside her house, watching from her upstairs office as Liz's rental furniture got loaded onto the company's truck. Liz had slipped a note through her mail slot a few days after their argument, just a piece of paper, her neat script slanted, as if from another era. *Everything you ever wanted is on the other side of fear.* Eva had crumpled it up and tossed it in the trash can by her desk.

She knew that when Liz's apartment was empty and the truck was ready to leave, Liz was going to want to say goodbye. Eva tried to imagine facing Liz on the porch after two weeks of near silence, searching to find the words to apologize, to tell Liz that their friendship had mattered to her, despite the way she'd behaved.

She distracted herself by getting her own affairs in order. She checked her bank account in Singapore. She organized the evidence on Fish she'd been able to gather so far. She'd had all of it notarized the other day, just in case. The bored notary public had cracked her gum—thumbprint here, sign there—not even looking at what Eva had typed up.

But something tugged on her subconscious now, some piece of unfinished business that wouldn't let go until she looked at it, one last time. Soon, she'd be gone, with a new name and a new life. And once she was, she could never return. The opportunity to see her birth family, maybe even speak to them, would be closed forever.

She entered her grandparents' names into a Google search and clicked on one of the people-finder websites, quickly entering her credit card information to access the premium options that would give her a phone number and a street address.

It wasn't hard. All this time, the information had been there, waiting for her to find it. Nancy and Ervin James, and an address just a few miles away in Richmond.

When Liz went to buy sandwiches for the movers, Eva slipped away. She wasn't cut out for prolonged goodbyes. And there was too much she'd left unsaid to pretend otherwise.

———————

She drove north, marveling at how close they'd been all this time, and wondered if they ever thought of her. If they ever looked for her. Perhaps they didn't pay for access to her address like Eva had, but maybe they'd done their own web search. *Eva James.* And there she'd be, on a list of people who shared her name. *Age 32, Berkeley, California.*

She exited the freeway and navigated the last few blocks, finally driving down a wide, barren street filled with run-down houses. The yards were filled with junk, dead grass and weeds leaching all the color out of the environment. This was nothing like what she'd imagined, and she was tempted to keep driving, to hang on to the illusion she'd built for herself over the years.

She pulled up outside a faded green house with a broken window in the garage door. Someone had taped a piece of cardboard over it, though the tape looked old and brittle, the cardboard warped from water damage and edged with mold. Across the street, a dog chained in the yard split the silence with its barks.

As she walked up the cracked cement path, her eyes scanned the brown lawn and tattered shrubbery and tried to see herself playing there, but none of it matched what she'd spent so many years picturing. Where were the flower beds she'd imagined her grandmother tending? The well-maintained car in the driveway? Where were the ironed curtains in the windows, the driveway her grandfather power-washed once a year? What she saw was so unexpected, like an out-of-tune piano hitting all the wrong notes, loud and jarring.

Eva stood on the shady porch, trying to breathe through her mouth, the stench of cigarette smoke seeping through the closed door. She knocked, and inside, the sound of footsteps approached, causing her to want to turn around and walk away. She no longer wanted to see what was behind that door.

But before she could move, it was pulled open. An older man stood in loose-fitting jeans and an old T-shirt, his ropy arms covered in tattoos. "Help you?" he asked, looking past her, toward her car parked at the curb. She was struck immediately by his eyes. They were hers. Same shape, same shade, and for a moment, she felt a breathless recognition, like the center piece of a puzzle snapping into place, completing the picture.

"Who is it?" a voice called from inside.

Over the man's shoulder, Eva could just make out a large, lumpy figure in a chair. The smell of cigarette smoke was overwhelming, and underneath it something else—unwashed bodies and overcooked food.

"Sorry," Eva said, backing down the steps. "I have the wrong house."

The man stared at her, and she held her breath, waiting for a flash of recognition in his eyes, to see something shake loose—perhaps he'd see the ghost of her mother—his dead sister—standing before him. But he just shrugged, said "Suit yourself," and swung the door closed.

She turned and walked down the walkway, her legs and arms uncoordinated and jerking, lurching her from the front path to the sidewalk and into her car. As she started the engine, she chastised herself for ever thinking they might be more than this, angry that she'd believed anything but the lowest possible denominator.

And yet, as she navigated the streets back to the freeway and headed south toward Berkeley, she realized she'd spent her whole life wishing for something she never would have had. All these years, she'd believed that if only they had loved her enough to raise her, she somehow could have avoided what happened to her at Berkeley. She could have finished her degree and built a legitimate life for herself. But now she knew that had she grown up there, she never would have made it to Berkeley in the first place.

*Information is power.*

Eva could walk away with no regrets, knowing for certain the past held nothing of value for her. That sometimes, the death of a dream can finally set you free.

———————

When she arrived home, the moving truck was gone, Liz's apartment empty. The windows were uncovered, revealing bare rooms, the red accent wall almost glowing, and a cold and heavy sadness settled over her.

She stepped onto the porch and unlocked her door, keeping her eyes trained forward, trying not to notice that Liz had left the flowerpots she'd tended so carefully. She glanced to her right, to the tree they'd planted together, the only thing left of their friendship, where it would continue to stand, a quiet sentinel, keeping her secrets.

# EVA

Jeremy's text came fifteen minutes before Eva was to leave to meet Dex at a basketball game.

> I'm failing my classes. I have a paper due on Tuesday
> and I need something to help me get an A on it. Please.

Of all her clients, Jeremy had been the most persistent, badgering her for weeks to sell him something. She'd managed to put him off, offered to connect him with someone else, but he'd refused. He wanted her. He trusted her. In the past, she would have rolled her eyes at his loyalty, but now she knew he was smart to be cautious.

She texted back.

Going to men's basketball game at Haas. Meet me at
entrance to section ten at halftime.

She would hand off with Dex in the club room and then find Jeremy. She pulled four from her discards—pills that had an odd shape or were broken—and slid them into a plain white envelope. They weren't pretty, but they'd get the job done.

Two days earlier, Castro had slid up next to her in the frozen-food aisle at the supermarket. He'd only been there for a second, just long enough to give a location and a time, and say that she'd soon have her answer. Eva felt the hours, the minutes, slipping away, carrying her forward to an unknown outcome. She looked around her house and wondered if she'd miss it. Her gaze trailed across the familiar walls of the living room—her favorite chair she'd sat in millions of times, to watch TV or read. The prints on the wall, chosen because she wanted to infuse her dark and lonely life with splashes of color. Her old textbooks, the only reminder of who she'd hoped to become. And yet, the pieces didn't add up to a life. Eva felt a clarity as she stood there, as if she'd already left, and realized none of it mattered. Nothing would be missed. The only person she'd ever cared about was already gone.

She grabbed her coat, tucking the package of pills in an inner pocket—the envelope for Jeremy in another one—and her voice recorder into her purse for another night of what would probably be useless chitchat, and slipped out the door, trying to ignore Liz's empty windows, the sound of her footsteps on the porch louder, echoing that emptiness back to her.

She walked the few short blocks to campus, cutting across the wide lawn that led down toward the library, and followed a dark and winding path that let out by Sather Gate. A stream of students and fans headed toward Haas Pavilion, and she pushed through the crowd, entering the arena and going straight to her seat.

She gave a tight smile to the people who sat around her, familiar faces now that she was attending all the home games. But she didn't talk to anyone. Instead she stared down at the court where the team was warming up and let the sounds of the arena fold over her as she realized how far off course she'd drifted, like a boat pulled by the tide. She was a world away from where she started. Lost at sea, with no hope of navigating back to familiar land.

---

Dex didn't show up until the middle of the first half. "Sorry I'm late," he said as he slid into his seat. "Did I miss anything good?"

Eva ignored his joke and looked down toward the student section, standing room only, where they moved and jumped as one, jeering the opposing team. "I never went to a single basketball game as an undergrad," she said. "All I did was study and go to class. Except for at the end. With Wade."

Dex nodded but didn't say anything.

"I always thought I'd stay in Berkeley. Maybe to teach, or to work in one of the labs. This was the only place that felt like home to me." Below them, a player had grabbed a rebound and executed a fast break toward the basket at the other end, and the crowd around them went wild. But Eva continued. "I'm living an upside down and backward version of the life I wanted. I'm here in Berkeley. I have money and a home. I have everything I thought I wanted, and yet it's all wrong."

Dex shifted in his seat so that he could look at her. "You think anyone else has it any better?" Dex gestured toward an older man at the end of their row, whose sweatshirt looked frayed at the cuffs, whose eyes had bags under them. "Look at that guy. I'll bet he's some kind of an accountant in the city. Taking the BART at the crack of dawn, shoving himself into the smallest space on the train. Eating his breakfast at his desk. Kissing his boss's ass and taking his two weeks in the summer, barely making enough to pay for his basketball season tickets. You want that life instead? What we have is better."

She wanted to throttle him. *Better?* Hiding and scheming and constantly watching her back? How many people in the seats around them had the constant fear of either being arrested or being killed for their mistakes?

She was edgy, rattling around in a life that was slowly emptying. But the longer this took, the less certain she was Castro would be able to get her out. She wanted to have a backup plan, a way to disappear on her own if she had to.

As the noise level in the arena rose, Eva leaned closer to Dex and lowered her voice so her recorder wouldn't pick it up. "I've got an undergrad client who wants to buy a fake ID," she said, hoping Dex wouldn't hear the waver in her voice. "She's nineteen. Wants to get into San Francisco clubs. Do you know anyone who can make her one?"

If Dex thought she was lying, he showed no sign of it. He leaned his elbows on his knees and angled his face so he was looking at her. "I used to know someone in Oakland who did that. But it was years ago, back when you could slide one photo out and another one in." He shook his head. "Now? Her best bet would be to find someone who looks like her willing to give her theirs. Pay them for their real driver's license and let them report it stolen. It happens all the time."

She looked toward the court, pretending to be interested in the game so that he couldn't see the defeat in her eyes. "That's what I told her," she said. "But you know what college kids are like. Two years seems like an eternity at nineteen."

A whistle sounded, signaling a time out, and loud music blared over the sound system.

Her voice grew louder again. "What ended up happening to that friend of yours, the one who referred Brittany?"

Dex stared at the cheerleaders dancing on the court below them and said, "He's been dealt with. Wasn't my call, but I can't say I'm sorry about it."

"Do you know for sure he was a part of the investigation?"

Dex shook his head. "It doesn't matter."

"Seems kind of dangerous," she said, "to get rid of the guy who was Brittany's contact. Won't that draw the attention of the police again?"

Dex gave a tight smile that didn't reach his eyes. "They'll never find him."

Eva felt a hollowness directly beneath her ribs and waited for him to continue.

"Fish has a warehouse in Oakland. Some kind of import/export bullshit. There's an incinerator in the basement."

She swallowed hard, fighting to keep her gaze steady on his, and nodded, hoping her recorder was picking this up and not just the jumped-up music of Daft Punk. Below them, the cheerleaders twirled and spun, their hair flying out, arms and legs pumping faster and faster as the music accelerated.

Claustrophobia began to overwhelm her, the heat of the arena, the people crammed into narrow seats that spiked upward toward the roof, giving her the sense that they were all pressing in on her. Eva checked the time on the scoreboard. "Let's get a head start," she said. "Beat the crowds. I'm starting to get a headache, and I think I want to go home."

"You don't have to ask me twice." Dex pushed himself out of his seat and slid past the people in their row, Eva following behind him.

———

They were first in line at the bathroom, and the drop took less than thirty seconds. "See you next week?" Dex asked, pulling his coat tight around him.

Eva looked out the window of the clubhouse, down to the baseball diamond below them, thinking ahead a few months to spring when the players would be down there, running bases and spitting sunflower seeds into the grass. Hopefully, she'd be gone by then, one way or another.

She looked at him, taking in the profile that had become as familiar as her own. This was a hard life, and he'd done his best to teach her everything he knew. And she'd learned well. For a long time, she'd been happy enough. But those days felt far behind her, like faded snapshots of a person she used to know. "Sure," she said. "Stay safe."

"Always," he said, giving her a wink.

Back on the crowded concourse, she glanced at the time. She had five more minutes to get across the arena and meet Jeremy. She wasn't lying about the headache, which was creeping around her temples, and she knew it would be a full-blown migraine by the end of the night. She pulled her phone out of her pocket and texted Jeremy again.

**Meet me at the entrance to section two instead.**

She pushed through the doors of the clubhouse and maneuvered her way back into the crowd.

People squeezed past her on their way back to their seats, and she searched for a small corner to claim while she waited. She looked across the court, to section ten, trying to see if Jeremy was over there waiting for her, when someone caught her eye.

At first, she saw just the back of him—short brown hair. A sport coat large enough to conceal a holster. As if in slow motion, she watched him glance at his phone, read something, and push off the wall, heading in her direction.

She glanced at her own phone, as if seeing it for the first time, realization creeping over her, blurring her vision around the edges. She thought back to every text she'd sent over the past few weeks. To Dex. And to Jeremy, telling him exactly where to meet her, and when. And there was Castro, where Jeremy was supposed to be.

In a flash, she saw it all again. A piece of white paper being handed through an open car window. *Brittany*. Who had her number and was able to pass it on. The Whispr app was useless if someone was reading her texts at the same time she was.

She pushed through the crowd, a lone figure against the tide of people making their way back to their seats, keeping her head down. Afraid to look anyone in the eye, certain Castro's hand would grab her any moment, yanking her backward, asking her to empty her pockets. Explain why she was still selling drugs. Telling her their deal was off.

She burst out of a side exit and into the cold night air, sprinting down the stairs, her compromised phone still gripped in her hand. As she passed an overflowing trash can, she fought the urge to bury it under old food wrappers and empty cups. To get rid of it as soon as possible. But she held on to it, knowing that she had to keep using it, that Castro needed to believe nothing had changed.

She walked briskly toward Sproul Plaza, pulling up her last text to Jeremy and hitting Reply.

> By the way, I ran into your mom today. She looks
> great!

That was the code she set up with all her clients, the one that let them know it wasn't safe to meet. Hopefully, Jeremy would go back to his spot in the student section and forget about her.

Eva walked up Bancroft and dropped the plain envelope containing Jeremy's pills into a trash can outside the student union, and turned toward home.

# CLAIRE

*Mrs. Cook, it's Danielle. I know you didn't get on that plane. You need to call me.*

A deep, thumping fear passes through me as I set the phone down and back away from it, as if Danielle might be able to reach through it and grab me, pulling me back to New York, where Rory waits.

My mind swirls, cloudy with panic. How did she find me so fast? The video has been up for less than twenty-four hours. And then, a terrible realization. Could all of this have been a setup? How else would Danielle know how to reach me—on a burner phone belonging to a stranger all the way across the country? My breathing comes out sharp and rasping, and I fight the urge to vomit.

If Rory and Eva were connected… I try to grab on to the second half of that idea. Of how they might have met, how they could have hatched a plan to send me to Puerto Rico, swapping tickets at the last minute and leading me somewhere with no friends. No resources, isolated and alone. A perfect target. Because if something happened to me here, no one would know.

But I can't fit it together. The plane wasn't supposed to crash. And I never intended to end up at Eva's. I was going to call Petra. Slip into and out of Eva's life within a few hours. Rory couldn't have known I would end up here. He certainly couldn't have orchestrated it.

I let the silence of the house wash over me, willing myself to calm down and look at events as they really happened, not through the lens of an abused woman, paranoid and seeing threats where there are none. My mind works backward. Somewhere, somehow, there's a link. I pick up the phone again, tracing the edges with my fingers, staring at the black screen, my faint shadow reflected back at me.

*Me.* Bruce told Rory he was looking into the number I'd called the day of the crash. I think back to the evening I unlocked Eva's phone and dialed Petra's number again, hoping somehow the call would connect. If they can access the records for Petra's number, it's possible they can also see who else tried to call her.

I'm the one who led Danielle here. If they know the number, what else do they know? Could they somehow use the phone to track me? I look toward the kitchen window, the back door, tempted to open it and toss the phone into the bushes.

"Think, Claire." My voice sounds scratchy in the empty room. This isn't television or a bad movie. Rory has a lot of money, and Bruce has connections that might give him some information, but I don't think they'd have the capabilities to track the phone. To follow me the way law enforcement could.

I take a deep breath and let it out slowly. I do it again, and then once more, allowing the most important question to surface.

Why is Danielle calling and not Rory? It doesn't fit with how Rory likes to operate. And if they knew where I was, they wouldn't have called at all. Rory would have just shown up, slipping up next to me when I least expected it. *Hello, Claire.*

With shaking fingers, I listen to the message again, Danielle's voice still sending a jolt of fear through me, even though I'm expecting it. *I know you didn't get on that plane. You need to call me.* This time, I notice her voice, low and urgent, as if she's delivering a warning, not a threat.

One thing is certain—I need to go. The oven clock reads just past ten. Late enough that I can ease out of town without anyone noticing, but early enough that I won't be the only one on the road. I leave my bags by the door and grab Eva's key ring, heading toward the garage. Time to see if Eva's car works.

———————

The garage is locked with a padlock. I strain my eyes in the dark, flipping through the keys until I find the right one, and pop the lock open, praying the car will start. That it has gas. That it's in enough working order to get me out of here.

The door lifts easily on well-oiled springs, and I enter the even darker space, letting my eyes adjust, making out the edges of dusty shelves with paint cans, a cobwebbed ladder leaning against a wall. But no car. Just the shadow of tire marks to show where it should be, a large tray in the center, spattered with dried oil. I feel the loss like a blow, crushing what little hope I had. No matter which way I turn, opportunities and openings slam closed again, forcing me into a tighter and tighter corner.

I walk all the way to the back, my gaze scanning the bare walls, as if I might find a clue if I just look hard enough. When I turn around to face the darkened street beyond, my mind fights to rearrange my plans into a new configuration. One more night at Eva's. An early morning BART train to San Francisco. Precious money spent on a bus ticket north. Gone before the sun comes up.

I relock the garage and start to head back inside. But when I step around the tree and into view of the front porch, I pull up short, nearly dropping Eva's keys. Peering into the uncovered windows of the apartment next door is the man who bumped into me the other day. The one who seemed to be watching me through the window of the coffee shop.

I shrink back into the shadows, glancing over my shoulder and down the street, wondering if I should slip away. But I've left Eva's door unlocked, with my bag, computer, and purse sitting just inside.

I take a deep breath and approach. "Can I help you?"

He turns and gives me a warm smile, as if we're old friends. "Hello again." The light coming from my living room window illuminates his face enough for me to see his eyes—a startling gray color that looks like a stormy ocean. "Can you tell me who I might call to inquire about renting this apartment?"

I take a few more steps onto the porch and put myself between him and Eva's unlocked front door and say, "Seems a little late to be apartment hunting."

He opens his hands wide. "I was just passing by and I wondered about the empty unit."

"I wouldn't know. I'm just staying here while my friend travels."

"Ah. When will she return?" He holds perfectly still, his face a mask revealing nothing. But I feel a shift as he waits for my answer, as if whatever I tell him is of the utmost importance.

*When will she return.*

"She's out of the country," I finally say, wanting to put as much space as possible between Eva and this man.

He nods as if this explains something, a smirk curling the corners of his mouth. He steps closer to me, reaching out to pluck something from my shoulder. "Spiderweb," he says. But he maintains his proximity, and I feel the heat of him, the smell of cigarettes and cologne enveloping me, and I shrink back toward Eva's door, wondering suddenly if he might follow me inside.

He gestures toward Eva's front door and says, "I know this looks like a good neighborhood, but you really shouldn't leave that unlocked for any length of time, especially at this time of night. Berkeley isn't as safe as it seems."

I feel as if he's punched me, my chest constricting into a tight ball that makes it hard to breathe. Without responding, I grab the knob and twist, slipping inside, locking the door behind me.

I hear him say, "Thank you for your help," before descending the stairs again. I scour the room, searching for any hint that he's been inside.

But everything is as I left it. My bags, undisturbed by the wall, nothing amiss. I sniff the air, but there's no trace of his cologne. He couldn't have been inside. I was in the garage for less than five minutes. I press my fingers against my eyes, trying to hold myself together, trying to think rationally amidst the panic racing through me.

I enter the kitchen and nearly step in the puddle of Diet Coke, which has spread out from the tipped-over can, traveling all the way toward the shelves and under it. My eyes follow the path, catching on the cast wheels of the shelving unit. I bend farther down, being careful not to kneel in the brown liquid, and peer underneath, where the Coke has pooled up against the bottom edge of a doorframe.

I circle around to the end of the unit, pushing it forward until I'm looking at a door with a padlock looped through a steel hinge. "What the hell, Eva," I mutter.

I grab her keys again and find the one that pops the lock, and when the door opens, I feel around on the wall for a light switch, turning it on. A fan below me begins to whir, and I creep down a small set of stairs that leads into a tiny basement that might have been a laundry room at one point.

But it's not a laundry room anymore. Counters and shelves line the walls, with a small sink and portable dishwasher in the corner. Ingredients are arranged on the shelves—large containers of calcium chloride, at least thirty bottles of various cold and cough medicines. A camping stove sits in the corner, several silicone pill molds upturned next to the sink, as if to dry. High above me in the wall is a boarded up window, the fan centered in it, spinning.

To the left of the stairs is a counter strewn with papers and a voice recorder next to them. I lean over, reluctant to touch anything, and begin reading what appears to be a notarized letter to someone named Agent Castro.

*My name is Eva James and this is a sworn statement of events beginning twelve years ago all the way through the present, January 15 of this calendar year.* I read quickly, the pages turning faster, the story of a college student who just wanted to fit in. Who took the only option she believed was available at the time, latching on to a man named Dex, who promised her things he had no intention of ever giving her. A life. Happiness. Freedom. It's the story of a woman who was tired of the corner she'd been forced into, a woman ready to burn it all down on her way out.

Eva wasn't a con artist or an identity thief. She was a woman like me, for whom the world will never bend, trying to set her path straight.

I pick up the voice recorder and press Play. The sound of a sports arena fills the small space, chants and cheers, an announcer's voice, a marching band of some kind.

"Seems kind of dangerous to get rid of the guy who was Brittany's contact." Eva's voice, just as I remember it. "Won't that draw the attention of the police again?"

A familiar voice, one I heard not ten minutes ago on the porch, warning me not to leave my front door unlocked, answers her. "They'll never find him. Fish has a warehouse in Oakland. Some kind of import/export bullshit. There's an incinerator in the basement."

I stop the recording, unable to listen to any more. Like scenes flipping, faster and faster, images appear in my mind. The cash purchase of her home. Eva's desperation at the airport. The way she shoved her purse into my arms, without even looking through it to see if there was something she wanted to keep. The phone she had with her, and the black one she left behind. No wonder Eva didn't tell me the truth. This is why she couldn't return to Berkeley.

And why I need to get out of here. Now.

I leave the lab untouched, but I gather the paperwork and the voice recorder, pressing them close to my chest as I sprint up the stairs.

# EVA

Eva was meeting Agent Castro at the Round House, a diner that sat at the entrance to the Golden Gate Bridge on the San Francisco side. She parked down by Crissy Field and walked up, checking over her shoulder several times as she made her way along the shaded paths of the Presidio. She'd taken the long way into the city, through San Rafael and Mill Valley, instead of crossing over on the Bay Bridge, hoping she wasn't followed.

A letter had arrived from Liz the day before. Eva touched the folded edges of it, like a talisman, pulling it from her pocket again to read.

*Eva,*

*I'm so sorry we didn't get a chance to say goodbye. I had really hoped we could talk one more time before I left. I feel like I owe you an apology. I made some assumptions that I shouldn't have, so I'm going to spell it out for you, just so we're clear. There are no conditions on my friendship. I don't expect you to be anyone other than who you are. Whatever your past is, I accept it. Whoever you want to be, I will still love you.*

*When you share your problems with someone else, your load gets lighter. And so, I'm here, whenever you're willing to share what's troubling you. Just because I'm no longer next door doesn't mean I won't be there when you need me. Call me anytime.*

And then she'd scribbled a phone number at the bottom. Eva tucked the note back into her pocket where she'd been carrying it since its arrival, wishing she'd met Liz all those years ago instead of Dex, wondering how different her life would have been if all she'd had to confess was one bad mistake in the chemistry lab. She could see how that might have been something Liz could forgive. Eva had been young and stupid. She certainly wasn't the first person to do something dumb for a guy.

But it was too late now. Liz was gone, and soon, Eva would be too. Maybe it was better this way.

----

She found Castro sitting in the back, near the kitchen, away from the giant windows that overlooked the bridge. "I ordered you a burger and fries," he said by way of a greeting.

She dropped her bag on the seat and slid across from him. The red vinyl booths were filled with tourists taking selfies with their cell phones. In the parking lot outside, a tour bus unloaded and a crowd of people made their way toward the walking side of the bridge.

Nerves slipped through her, like long ribbons twirling and twisting into a tangle as she imagined leaving from there. Exiting the restaurant and climbing into an anonymous sedan and disappearing. Her fingers tapped the table, her leg jiggling beneath her. "Thanks," she said. "But I'm not really interested in a meal and small talk, if that's okay with you."

Agent Castro nodded. "My supervisor denied the request for witness protection," he said.

Eva felt the air rush out of her, the sounds around them growing sharper. The clatter of plates and cutlery, the steady drone of conversations. All of her plans dissolved and vanished, as if they'd never existed. "Why?" she managed to ask. "You told me yourself you'd been after Fish for years."

Agent Castro took a packet of sugar from the small cup at the edge of their table and traced the edges of it with his fingers, unable to meet her eyes. "I happen to agree with you. But like I said, witness protection is expensive, and we don't do it very often."

"When *do* you do it, then?"

He looked up at her, and she saw genuine regret in his eyes. "We use it mostly for big targets. Organized crime. Major networks. I know Fish feels like a big target to you. And he certainly is for me. I've been close to him more times than I care to admit. And every time, he slips away. My contact goes dark, and I'm back at square one."

"All the more reason to make this happen," she said, working hard to keep her voice low. To not let the desperation she felt break through.

"I can offer you twenty-four-hour protection at an undisclosed location. All the way through the trial. I promise you'll be safe. If you have an attorney, now would be the time to call them."

Eva sat with his words. Let them assemble into a picture. Her, alone in a hotel room, two guards at the door. An armed escort to and from the trial that would surely result in a not-guilty verdict. Or a mistrial. And then what? She'd be free to go back home? To unlock her front door and

240

do what? Wherever she went, Fish's people would find her. Dex would probably do the job himself. After a betrayal like this one, he wouldn't rest until he'd found her.

When she was a child, the girls in the group home would go to Sister Bernadette for advice with a problem—a friendship gone bad, an unfair teacher, a foster home that hadn't worked out. Eva never had, but she'd listened all the same, sliding herself along the edges of their conversations, absorbing whatever wisdom Sister Bernadette had to offer. She would often tell them *The only way out is through*, that no matter the situation, one step would lead to the next, and the next one after that. And so Eva leaned into this new development. Wrapped her mind around it and got to work thinking through to the other side. She found it ironic that both Sister Bernadette and Dex offered her such similar advice. *Play through.*

"Then I guess we move forward and hope for the best," she said. "What do you need?"

Castro tucked the sugar back into its cup as the server brought their food, the smell of the burger and fries turning her stomach sour. "Ideally, we'd like to put a wire on you and have you meet with Fish."

"That's impossible," she said. "I've never met him. It would be a huge red flag if I asked to now."

Castro's eyes narrowed. "This whole deal goes away if you start lying to me." Gone was the apologetic tone, the regret he felt at not being able to do more for her.

"I'm not lying to you," she said. "That's not how things work. I've been trying to find out more—how the drugs are moved, about Fish himself. But I don't know much more than my small corner of it."

Castro sat back in his seat, both hands flat on the table. Finally, he said, "We have proof, Eva. Photographs of the two of you together."

Eva shook her head, confused. "That's not possible," she said. "I swear I've never met him."

Castro reached into his coat for his phone and flipped through photos until he found what he was looking for. Then he held it up so she could see the screen.

It had been taken at Haas, the night she was supposed to meet Jeremy. She recognized the people around them, the sad accountant in his frayed sweatshirt at the end of the row. And there, in the middle of the frame, were Eva and Dex, their heads bent toward each other, deep in conversation. The quality was incredible—the shot must have been taken with a high-powered lens.

She shook her head again, unable to process what she was seeing. "That's not Fish, that's Dex."

Castro pulled the phone back and stared at her, squinting as if he didn't quite believe her. "I don't know who Dex is. But that man is Felix Argyros. Fish."

# CLAIRE

Sunday, February 27

I sprint up the stairs and through the kitchen, my shoes tracking Diet Coke into the living room, stuffing Eva's sworn deposition and voice recorder into my bag. I don't know what compelled me to take them, what instinct warned me that leaving them behind would be a mistake. My mind flashes back to the man on the porch, how close he stepped, the scent of cigarette smoke still tickling the back of my throat, and I know without a doubt these papers, this recorder, are what he's after. Then I think of Eva's cell phone, sitting on the kitchen table, Danielle's message still on it. I scurry back to grab it, powering it off before shoving it into my pocket.

Outside a car drives by, the radio a faint thump as it passes, and I peek through the curtains, thinking about who might be out there, watching from the shadows. I have to force myself to open the door and step onto the porch, my instincts in disarray, unsure whether I risk more by leaving or staying. But in my mind, I see the basement drug lab, a notarized letter to a federal investigator, and a man who is most certainly not a DEA agent, leaning in too close, a silent promise that he'll be back.

I cross the lawn quickly, keeping my head down as I walk toward campus, bracing myself for a voice or a hand on my shoulder to stop me. In the distance, a cat yowls, long and low, then rises into a scream that sounds almost human.

---

I find a small motor court motel on a busy street, about a mile from campus. My shoulders ache, my feet hurt, and I'm freezing. A light burns in the small office, revealing an older woman smoking a cigarette and staring at a television mounted on the wall. When I enter, she turns to face me, her eyes squinting through a cloud of smoke.

"I'd like a room please."

"It's eighty-five dollars a night plus tax," she tells me.

"That's fine," I say, although I wobble a little as I do the math.

She gives me a once-over and says, "I'll need your name, your driver's license, and a credit card."

"I'd like to pay cash."

"Doesn't matter. We have to enter the card into our system. We won't run it until you check out, and if you want to pay by cash then, we won't run it at all."

I consider arguing with her, but I don't want to solidify myself in her memory. I hand over Eva's driver's license and her credit card, anxious as I watch her enter them into her computer, waiting for the tiniest hesitation—perhaps just her eyes, a slight widening, then flicking back up to my face. But she taps in the number, her expression bored, before handing everything back.

"How many nights?" she asks.

I can't think past this moment, the days stretching ahead of me, blank, with no idea what I'll do next. "I don't know. One? Two?" At eighty-five dollars a night, my money will run out quickly.

"I'll put you down for two," the woman says, handing me a key. "Room five, just out the door and to your left. Checkout is at eleven. If you're here past that, we charge you for another night."

The room is small, with cheap carpeting and a polyester bedspread on the double bed that faces a television on a small bureau. A tiny desk and lamp are in the corner next to the bathroom. I sit on the bed and try to let the last few hours drain out of me.

The clock on the nightstand reads eleven thirty, and my head is heavy with fatigue. The party in the Berkeley Hills feels like it happened a month ago instead of just a few hours. I lean forward, covering my face with my hands, and choke down a sob. I have no name, no plan, and not nearly enough money.

My eyes are gritty with exhaustion. It's been two days since I've had any real sleep, and I fall back on the bed, fully dressed, hoping tomorrow brings a solution.

------------

I wake early, having slept so deeply I didn't even dream. As I look around the room in the early morning light, I let my mind adjust to this new reality. My entire life exists within these walls. Outside, I'm either a dead woman or a drug dealer on the run.

I sit up, my muscles screaming from two nights in a row of heavy catering work, and think of Kelly, already working her shift in the coffee shop, imagining me driving toward the heat of the desert. I wish I were there with her, sitting in one of the deep chairs while she makes idle conversation from behind the counter. I ache for the simplicity of it, to have a place in the world where I belong.

My stomach growls, so I grab my NYU hat and some cash and dart down to the corner mart with ten dollars I can't afford to spend, and return with an enormous cup of coffee and a package of stale cinnamon buns. My only option—weak as it is—is to find something on the thumb drive I can use against Rory to trade for my freedom. A secret he cares more about keeping than he does about punishing me.

I turn the TV on for company and slowly set up my computer, plugging in the thumb drive and looking through the desk for the Wi-Fi directions. When I'm logged in, a quick check of Rory's email shows nothing new, but when I click over to the Doc, a jolt like a lightning bolt shoots through me.

They're talking about me.

**Rory Cook:**
How the fuck did she do it?

---

**Bruce Corcoran:**
I don't know. The airline said she was scanned onto the flight. No one disputed that.

---

**Rory Cook:**
They said her seat was empty. Do you think they know?

---

**Bruce Corcoran:**
I think they would have contacted you immediately if they thought there was any chance she wasn't on the plane. Do you want me to tell them?

---

Rory's words come fast, his anger nearly leaping off the screen.

**Rory Cook:**

Absolutely not. I'm going to handle this quietly. Let
the NTSB keep thinking she's dead. I've scheduled the
plane for Oakland tonight.

---

Just as quickly as the words appeared, they disappear again, line by
line, until I'm looking at a blank doc, the top reading *Last edit made
by Bruce Corcoran.* Bruce's icon vanishes, leaving only Rory's behind.
I know what Rory means when he says *I'm going to handle this quietly.*
It means he's going to make a problem disappear, out of view of the
public. And I've given Rory the perfect cover to do whatever he wants
to me, because the whole world already thinks I'm dead.

I feel the walls closing in, Danielle, Rory, and Bruce tracking my
every move, forcing me into a smaller and smaller box until I'm trapped
with only one way out.

A banging on a door across the courtyard startles me, causing my
elbow to slip forward, knocking my coffee toward the keyboard. I
jump, trying to grab it before it tips, a small amount spilling on the
surface of the desk. But in my haste to save the coffee, I accidentally
press a few keys. "Shit," I say, hurrying to delete what I typed, my eyes
leaping again to the top right corner, hoping Rory logged off when
Bruce did.

I stare at the screen for what feels like an hour, but must have only
been a few minutes. No new text appears. But at the top of the page, it
now reads *Last edit made by Rory Cook 2 minutes ago,* and I pray neither
of them will remember who wiped the Doc clean.

In the bathroom, I splash cold water on my face, the cheap fluores-
cent lighting making my skin look haggard and washed out. I brace my
arms on the counter and try to regroup. Deep breath in, deep breath out,
five, eight, ten times. I bring my attention to the way the faucet drips

around a rust-edged drain, the repeating swirl of fake granite, before forcing myself back to work.

Seated in front of my computer again, the weight of futility settles across my shoulders. I'm unsure of what to look for or where to start. Should I look for more about Charlie? Or maybe I could find some kind of financial or tax fraud. The problem is, I don't know enough about finance to recognize anything that might be useful. I'm about to double-click on the thumb drive when my eye catches again on the alert at the top of the Doc. *Last edit made by Rory Cook two minutes ago.* A quick check of the time tells me it's been at least ten.

I hit refresh, expecting to see the time update, but instead I'm redirected back to the Gmail log-in page. "No," I whisper into the room.

I retrieve the crumpled Post-it Note with Rory's password from Eva's wallet and enter it again, but it fails. I try once more, slower this time, but again it tells me the password is incorrect.

I picture Rory, seated at his desk, having just watched the video of me stepping between Donny and Cressida, my poorly executed cut and dye job barely a disguise at all. And then, unbidden, text appearing on his screen with his own name attached. I can see him calling Bruce, demanding to know how someone might have accessed his account. And then I see his horror when he realizes the only person who would have had the opportunity to steal the password—and a vested interest in watching him—is me.

I stand and press my fists against my eyes, tears seeping through the creases. "I can't do this," I whisper into the empty room. "I can't. I can't." I open my eyes and grab the wallet, the nearest thing to me, and hurl it against the wall. The change purse pops open, a cascade of pennies and dimes falling down and burying themselves somewhere behind the dresser while the wallet itself lands with a thump on the surface.

But something inside of me loosens, the sudden action releasing just enough anxiety, like a pressure valve, yanking me back to center, the dingy room coming back into focus. I don't have the luxury of falling apart. Rory knows I've been watching him. Listening in on conversations he believed were private, watching his panic over what Charlie knows about Maggie Moretti. There has to be some way I can use that.

Behind me, Kate Lane's voice catches my attention.

"A little less than a week ago, Flight 477 crashed into the waters off of Florida. Ninety-six people perished in the crash, and investigators are one step closer to figuring out what happened with the recovery of the black box." The screen cuts to old footage, the same bobbing coast guard boats, the same pieces of floating wreckage they showed last week. "Vista Airlines officials declined to comment on rumors that flight attendants failed to confirm the total number of passengers with a head count. But anonymous sources inside Vista Airlines report that this is not unusual when flights are delayed. Airline officials say they have confidence that the manifest was accurate, that the number of passengers matched all flight records."

I freeze, absorbing this information, thinking back to the thread I'd read, the commenter who was so certain a person couldn't get scanned onto a flight without actually getting on it, because of the head count.

But now, I see that Eva might have done it. A laugh, incredulous and tickling, tumbles around inside of me, and I sit back in my chair, trying to imagine her out there in some anonymous hotel room, watching this same report, having somehow slipped off the plane and vanished.

I think about the risks Eva took to gather the notes and the recordings—things that implicated her alongside whoever that man was on her porch. And I wonder what went wrong, why she didn't turn it over. Whatever it was, it had her running, unable to return home.

And I wonder what she'd want me to do with it.

I stare at the wall, though I'm looking beyond what's in front of me to the image of Eva, laughing and running away from me, backlit and growing smaller the farther away she gets. I watch her until she's just a dot. Just a nothing. Almost gone.

I trace the edge of the thumb drive with my finger, certain there are secrets there Rory wants to keep hidden. I just don't know what they are.

But Rory doesn't have to know that.

As if Eva were whispering in my ear, an idea begins to unfurl, outrageous and bold. But it will require me to come out of hiding and confront him. To pick up a phone and dial his number, telling him what I have, embellishing and fabricating across the blank spots, weaving just enough of a story to make him believe I know more. Not just about Charlie, but the contents of the hard drive, wrapped up and ready to deliver to the media and authorities. Unless he gives me what I want.

And yet, the idea of calling him, of hearing his voice on the other end of the line, like a hook drawing him toward me, makes me shudder. Because if I'm wrong and this doesn't work, it will make everything worse.

I pick up Eva's cell phone, glad I brought it with me, a way to contact him without revealing my exact location. But I hesitate before turning it on, my instincts still snagging on how Danielle managed to track down the number, and what else they might already know. Whether she's out there waiting for me to make another mistake. I take a deep breath and let it out slowly, then power it on.

Immediately, another voice message pops up, along with a text. My finger hesitates, unsure which to click on first, before deciding on the voicemail.

*Mrs. Cook, it's Danielle again. I don't blame you for not trusting me, but you have to believe I'm trying to help you. Mr. Cook is on his way to California, and I'm fairly certain it's because he knows you're there. I'm texting you a recording from yesterday. Use it. I'll back you up.*

I stare at the phone, my mind traveling in twenty different directions, picking through her words, trying to see the trick. What she really wants me to do. Because after all the times she'd looked away, stayed silent when she could have spoken up, I have a hard time believing she wants to help me now.

I open the text, which is a voice memo file titled *Recording 1*. I grab the remote and mute the TV, then press Play.

Muffled voices fill my motel room—arguing—and I realize it's Rory and Bruce, though I can't make out their words. Then there's a knock on a door and Rory's voice calling, "Come in."

Danielle's voice, closer, says, "Sorry to bother you, but I need your signatures on these forms."

"Of course," Rory says. "Thank you, Danielle, for handling all of the details with the NTSB. I know how much you loved and respected Mrs. Cook."

"There's so much I wish I could have done differently," Danielle says.

I hear the rustle of papers, then Rory's voice again. "That should do it. Please close the door on your way out."

Danielle's voice sounds farther away as she says, "No problem, Mr. Cook. Thank you." Then an opening and closing door.

I expect the recording to end there, but it doesn't. Rory's voice speaks again, a shade colder. "What have you found out?"

Bruce finally speaks. "In 1996," he says, as if reading from a file, "Charlie Price—or rather, Charlotte, as she prefers to be called now—was arrested for possession with the intent to sell. They couldn't make it stick, and the charges were dropped." I hear a page turn. "She moved to Chicago, where she worked as a server. Seemed to stay out of trouble. She still lives there."

Charlotte? *She?* Charlie's a woman?

"Anything else?" Rory asks.

"Not really. No husband, boyfriend, or girlfriend. No kids. Family seems to be either dead or estranged. Nothing we can use as motivation." Bruce's voice grows softer. "Nothing we've said so far has swayed her. Not money, not threats. She insists on telling the truth."

Rory's voice is low and dangerous, sending a chill rippling through me. "And what does she claim to be the truth?"

"That you and Charlie were having an affair behind Maggie's back. That you were there when Maggie died, and you timed the fire to start after your departure. That you showed up at Charlie's apartment, frantic and shaking like a leaf." A pause. When Bruce continues, I can barely hear him. "She doesn't care about the NDA she signed. She doesn't care about anything we've offered."

"That's not acceptable!" Rory yells, and I recoil, as if he were in the room yelling at me. "This will derail everything. You have two days to make this problem disappear."

I hear Bruce gathering things, collecting papers, the snap of a briefcase latch. "Understood," he says.

Footsteps, the sound of a door opening and closing. Then silence. I'm about to stop the recording when I hear another knock on the door.

"Enter," Rory says.

Danielle again. "I'm so sorry to bother you. I think I dropped my phone somewhere. May I come and look?"

A grunt from Rory.

"Here it is. It must have fallen—"

And the recording ends.

I sit on the bed, stunned. *There's so much I wish I could have done differently*, Danielle had said, the words spinning a different meaning, now that I know she was saying them to me. Offering an acknowledgement, and perhaps also an apology.

That Danielle would risk so much to get this for me is astonishing. All those years of scrambling behind me, of meticulously keeping me on schedule. I thought she was just another arm of Rory, controlling me. Perhaps, if I'd bothered to turn around and really look at her, I'd have seen something else. Not someone intent on bringing me down, but a woman desperately trying to prop me up.

I listen again to Danielle's message, to the urgency in her voice, the way it cracks, the whispered edges of fear. *Use it. I'll back you up.*

On the silent television screen, two political commentators are talking, their lips moving soundlessly. Across from them, Kate Lane says something to the camera, then smiles. I turn up the volume in time to hear the familiar tune for *Politics Today* fading into commercial.

It's unreal that just a week earlier, I was making the final preparations for my Detroit trip, imagining a life as Amanda Burns, living peacefully in Canada. And how quickly things went wrong, landing me here instead, pressed between the secrets Eva was keeping, forced to dance between landmines I can't even see.

I'm not going to call Rory. Threats will never work on him. If they did, I would have used them long ago. What Danielle has sent me is so much better. Rory's voice, Rory's anger, packaged into the perfect sound bite.

I Google the email address for Kate Lane, then go to the Gmail homepage and set up a new email account and draft my email, the words coming effortlessly. When I'm done, I hesitate. The minute I send it, everything will be set into motion. There will be no way for me to go back. But this is the only trick left in my bag.

I reread the email one final time.

> Dear Ms. Lane, My name is Claire Cook, and I am Rory Cook's wife. I did not die on Flight 477, as has been previously reported. I am in California, and I have recently received evidence that implicates my husband in the death and cover-up of Maggie Moretti. I would like to speak with you about it at your earliest convenience.

And then I hit Send.

# EVA

Dex was Fish.

Fish was Dex.

Eva felt her reality shift, pieces sliding into place in a different order, a different picture, as panic and confusion pounded through her. What had she missed?

"Didn't you wonder why you'd never met Fish, why Dex was your only contact?" Castro asked.

"I was told that's how it worked. I didn't question it." Eva shook her head. "But why would Dex lie?" she whispered.

"By allowing the people who worked for him to believe he was just carrying out orders from above, it gave him a measure of deniability. It allowed you to trust him in a way you wouldn't have if you'd known he was the guy at the top."

"Is this common?" she asked. "Don't people work really hard to earn that spot? Don't they want everyone to know what kind of power they have?"

Agent Castro shrugged. "Sometimes," he said. "But to be honest, those types of dealers are pretty easy to catch. They're in it for their ego. They want everyone to know how important they are, and to be afraid of them. But Fish"—Castro tipped his head toward her—"or rather, Dex, is what we call a long-term operator. Someone who cares more about longevity than anything else. More than power, more than fear. They're smarter and harder to pin down." Castro took a sip of his coffee and continued. "I've only seen this once before. A woman up in El Cerrito who pretended she had a husband who was calling the shots. She had her finger in a lot of things, mostly because people trusted her to keep them safe from a man who never even existed."

Eva thought about how Dex had put himself between her and Fish. How he protected her and warned her. Led her to believe he was on her side, that they were working together. She thought back to how rattled he was at the football game last fall. How scared he'd been of angering Fish. All of it an elaborate act.

And then her mind flew back to that early morning when he'd shown her the body, and events rearranged in her imagination as she saw Dex executing the man and then calmly walking to Eva's door, knocking, and leading her back again, to show her what he'd done.

She felt sick at how naive she'd been.

"So now what?" she asked.

"It's time for you to get an attorney and make a deal. We'll put a wire on you and see what we can get."

Eva thought of all she'd gathered and tucked that knowledge close, her final card to play. There was no way she was going to wear a wire. "And what do I get in exchange?" she asked. "Since witness protection is not an option."

"You get to not go to jail when this is all over."

On the table, Eva's phone buzzed with a text, and her gaze flew to Castro's phone, wondering whether it, too, would light up. But it remained dark.

"You'd better answer that," he said.

It was from Dex.

**Are we set for six? Where do you want to meet?**

She showed it to Agent Castro. "Stick to public places where my people can blend in," he advised. "From now on, I don't want you to be alone with him, or anywhere we can't get to you quickly. No more sports arenas, no more deserted parks. My team will stay on you until we can get the wire set up. One, two days, tops."

Eva took her phone back and, with trembling fingers, typed: O'Brien's? I'm starving.

She imagined driving back to Berkeley and sitting across the table from Dex, forcing herself to act normal while she waited for Castro to line up his fucking wire guy.

Castro must have sensed her rising panic because he said, "You're going to be okay. Just stick to your routine and do everything you normally would. Make the drugs, meet with Dex. Don't give him any reason to be alarmed."

Through the window, Eva could see fog rolling in, the bright orange of the bridge fading before her eyes, and she worried that would happen to her. She'd grow so faint, she would disappear from the page and no one would know she'd been there at all.

The restaurant hummed with conversation, the sound of cutlery against dishes filling her ears, the whole world moving around her while she stood still. "I don't have a choice, do I?"

Castro's eyes softened with sympathy. "You really don't."

———————

Eva was halfway across the Bay Bridge when she began to hyperventilate, cars on all sides, inching forward, funneling her toward an inevitable outcome. No fucking way could she do this.

She imagined herself driving north—passing the off-ramp to Berkeley, past Sacramento, Portland, and Seattle. She looked in her rearview mirror and studied the people in the cars behind her. Which ones were Castro's? Whoever was keeping an eye on her would never let her get that far.

_____

At home, she packed quickly, only taking the essentials, leaving the house as it was. If anyone came looking for her, she wanted it to appear as if she'd just stepped out. That she'd be back any minute. She thought of her lab downstairs, the tools and ingredients, the evidence she'd gathered for Castro, and decided to leave it. Eventually, he'd show up looking for her, and he was welcome to all of it. She was no longer going to play by anyone else's rules.

Eva's plan was to park near O'Brien's. Appear to be on her way to meet Dex, and then slip down into the BART station and catch the first train that came. To make her way back into San Francisco, pay cash for a bus ticket to Sacramento, and then figure out how to keep going. North, and then further north still, until she reached the border.

But the sight of Liz's glass bluebird ornament on her dresser caused her to pull up short. She picked it up, running her finger over the swirls of blue, the delicate beak, the edges of the wings. The only thing that was ever given to her out of love. From the only person who ever truly cared about her.

Eva thought about Wade, who had promised to take the blame. Dex, who pretended to be someone he wasn't so he could better manipulate her. And Castro, who expected her to do the impossible, but giving her nothing she needed in return. Men who made promises they never intended to keep. People like Eva were always going to be collateral damage.

And then there was Liz, who saw the very best version of herself. She felt the outline of Liz's letter still in her pocket. *When you share your problems with someone else, your load gets lighter.* Like a rat in a maze, Eva's path was narrowing, leading her toward the only person she could trust.

Eva grabbed her emergency cash—five thousand dollars—and packed her computer, leaving her compromised cell phone on the counter. Then she slipped out of the house, still gripping the glass bluebird in her fist.

---

The first train that arrived was crowded. She waited until the doors were closing before jumping on, looking toward the platform for any sign someone was following her. She imagined Castro's agents above her, moving out in an ever-widening circle with her car at the center, parked at a meter on Shattuck, wondering where she went. What happened to her.

Eva scanned the faces of the people around her, silently discarding a man sleeping in a corner and a couple huddled over an iPad, deep in conversation. But there was a woman directly across from her that Eva caught glancing at her as the train hurled south, toward Oakland. She had a magazine open, but as Eva studied the ads above the woman's head, waiting for her to turn the page of her magazine, the woman remained motionless.

At the next stop, Eva waited until the last second to slip off the train, and watched the woman, still reading, slide past her and into the dark tunnel. She huddled in a corner of the station, her bag slung over her shoulder, watching commuters board and exit trains before picking another one, this time heading toward San Francisco. For the next hour, she transferred and backtracked until she was certain she was alone.

At the airport, she paid cash for a red-eye ticket to Newark.

"One-way or round-trip?" the ticket agent asked.

Eva hesitated. Had Castro put her on some kind of list? Again his words—*midlevel target*—flashed in her mind. "One-way," she answered. The finality of it sent a shudder through her. If she was wrong, a one-way ticket would sound the alarm.

---

She didn't relax until well after takeoff. As the passengers around her slept or read, Eva stared out the window, thinking of an evening just after Halloween, when she'd found Liz sitting on the back steps, looking out at their yard in the deepening twilight. "What are you doing back here?" she'd asked.

Liz had looked up from where she sat and smiled. "I love the smell of the evening, when the sun has disappeared and everything starts to cool down. No matter how much life changes, this never does." She closed her eyes. "My ex-husband and I used to do this, when we were first married. Sit outside and watch the sky change from day to night."

Eva sat on her own step, looking at Liz through the iron bars of the railing. "Where is he now?"

Liz shrugged and brushed her fingers along the edge of the concrete step. "Last I heard, he moved to Nashville. But that was twenty years ago. I have no idea if he's still there."

Eva wondered how she could be so calm about the man who'd abandoned her with a young child and never looked back. "Does Ellie ever hear from him?"

"I don't know—we don't really talk about him. But I don't think so. He sent cards for her birthday for a few years, but those stopped when she was still young." Liz looked across the yard, to the back fence and the trees beyond. In a quiet voice, she said, "For a while, Ellie blamed me for that. As if I could make that man care about her. But now that she's grown, she can see him for who he really is, and understand her childhood was probably better without him in it."

Eva marveled at her calm tone. "How can you not hate him?"

Liz gave a soft chuckle. "Hate can eat you up inside. I could devote hours a day to despising him. But it wouldn't matter. He's out there, somewhere, living his life, and if he thinks about us at all, it's probably only in passing. I decided a long time ago to forgive him, which is a lot easier than hating him."

Eva thought about the strength that must have taken, to raise her daughter on her own while still following her own dreams. To set the betrayal aside and choose to be happy.

"Have you always been this way? Able to see beyond the worst in people?"

Liz laughed. "It takes a long time to learn how to see the world as a place where people aren't doing things *to* you. My husband didn't set out to break my heart, or Ellie's. He was just acting on his own desires, living his own story. I hope I've become someone who doesn't get angry when others are just trying to get by. I hope I can be the kind of person who looks toward forgiveness first."

Eva stared across the yard toward the bushes by the back gate, their shadows quickly disappearing in the fading light. "I'm not very good at forgiveness."

Liz nodded. "Not many people are. But what I've learned in life is that in order for true forgiveness to occur, something has to die first. Your expectations, or your circumstances. Maybe your heart. And that can be painful. But it's also incredibly liberating."

"Is this your roundabout way of telling me I need to forgive my birth family?"

Liz had looked at her, surprised. "I think you need to figure out how to forgive yourself. For whatever it is that still chases after you."

As Eva flew east, the window next to her a black square, she wondered if this was the death Liz was talking about. Her entire life, abandoned in Berkeley, just a hollow shell that no longer fit the person she was becoming. It didn't make sense, even to her, why she needed to see Liz one more time. But somehow she understood that this was how she'd forgive herself.

# CLAIRE

While I wait for a reply from Kate Lane, I flip through the notes I took from Eva's lab, sinking again into the story of a chemistry prodigy, an outcast, and a drug dealer. When I'm done, I stare at the curtained window, the sound of distant traffic just beyond the door, and picture her out there, moving silently through crowds of students, shoulders hunched, hands shoved into the pockets of her green coat, head tucked into her chest. Invisible. Her solitary life always holding her apart. Never safe, never known.

And I know why she decided to do what she did.

I drink the rest of my cold coffee and eat the last cinnamon bun, wishing I could check the Doc. I imagine Rory, packing a bag and assembling a small team. Coordinating with Bruce. A short trip to California for personal business, Danielle quiet and watchful, taking notes. Waiting for another opening to tell me what she knows.

Just then, my email pings with a response from Kate Lane's production assistant.

> Ms. Lane is definitely interested in this story. We will need to verify your claim before moving forward. Please send a number where we can reach you so we can confirm you are who you say you are.

I toggle over to the settings on Eva's phone, find her number, then type it directly into my email reply. Ten minutes later, the cell phone rings and I leap for it. "Hello?"

"Mrs. Cook, it's Kate Lane."

The sound of my own name sounds odd to my ear, making me feel exposed. "Thank you for talking with me," I say.

"Well, you tell an interesting story. But I first need you to explain how it is you aren't dead, when the NTSB says you got on that plane."

The years of silence pile up in me, the secrets I've guarded for so long, the belief that no one would want to know the truth. I start slowly, describing Rory's abuse and how desperate I was to leave him, how my plans to disappear in Detroit fell apart, and how Rory had discovered them. "And then I met a woman at JFK. Her name was Eva James, and she agreed to trade flights with me," I say. "When I landed, I found out the Puerto Rico flight had crashed. I've been stuck here, with no money and no way to disappear, so I took a job with a catering company." I tell her about the *TMZ* video and how Rory was now on his way to California because of it.

"So Eva James died in the crash instead?"

I close my eyes, knowing I need to be careful. The best way I can protect Eva is to let the people who are after her believe she's dead. "She did."

"Jesus," Kate breathes out. Then she seems to regroup. "I guess we'd better move on to Maggie Moretti."

"I have a recording of my husband and his assistant, Bruce Corcoran. In it, they're discussing a woman named Charlotte Price, who has direct knowledge of my husband's involvement in Maggie Moretti's death."

There's a pause as Kate Lane absorbs this information. "When was this recording made?"

"I'm not sure," I admit. "In the last few days. My assistant made it and sent it to me sometime last night. She's willing to verify its legitimacy."

Kate seems to think about this. "Before we do anything, I'll need to listen to it. Can you text it to my producer?" She rattles off a number, and I send it off.

Soon, I hear it playing across the phone line. The knocking, Danielle's voice, then Rory and Bruce's. When it's done, Kate lets out a sigh, her voice gentle. "Mrs. Cook, I'm sorry. But I don't think we can put that on the air."

"What do you mean?" This was my last shot. I'd laid everything on the table—revealed where I was and what I'd done—and the outcome is still the same. "He all but admits he was responsible."

"It's not enough," Kate says. "His assistant outlines the accusation, and while your husband doesn't deny it, it's not an admission."

"He's on his way to California," I tell her. "He knows what I've done. This is the only thing that might stop him."

"I want to help you," she says. "What you've told me is huge in its own right. An abused wife, a man about to run for Senate, two women meeting in an airport and switching tickets. Let me put you on the air to tell that story."

I swipe a hand across my eyes and say, "And like all the other women who have come out against powerful men, I'll be the one ostracized, while he sails on to Congress."

"Your concern is valid," she says. "But this might buy you time. While you tell your story, others can be working on the link between your husband and Maggie Moretti. Have your assistant send the recording to the New York district attorney. We'll look for Charlotte Price and see if she wants to go on the record. If there's anything there, we'll find it." I hear her shuffling more papers in the background, and the sound of someone's muffled voice. "Let's get you over to our San Francisco studio while we work the phones on this end. Tell me where you are, and I'll have a car sent over."

I tell her the name of the motel, feeling unsettled and agitated. Coming forward to talk about what Rory did to me was exactly what I wanted to avoid.

"I'll be in touch if anything comes up," Kate says. "The car should be there in about an hour. Be ready."

"I will. Thank you."

I begin packing my things, shoving them into my bag haphazardly. By this time tomorrow, I'll be Claire Cook again, shouldering all the baggage that comes along with it, facing the circus my accusations will create. I think about Eva, out there somewhere, and hope that at least this might set her free.

A knock on the door startles me, and I worry that Rory might have bumped his trip up, slipped out of New York without Danielle knowing, and somehow located me here. That by the time the CNN car arrives, there will be nothing but an empty room.

I peek through the curtains and see a man, his arms folded across his chest, revealing a brief glimpse of a gun holster under his coat.

I call through the door. "Can I help you?"

He smiles and flashes a badge. "My name is Agent Castro," he says. "And I'd like to talk to you about Eva James."

# EVA

New Jersey
February
**One Day before the Crash**

The plane bumped down at two o'clock in Newark, after flying all night and an interminable layover in Chicago. After taxiing to the gate, Eva hurried up the Jetway, stopping only to buy a new prepaid phone at a kiosk, tossing the packaging in the trash, and dialing the number Liz had written at the bottom of her letter. "It's Eva," she said, relieved to find Liz at home. "I'm actually in New Jersey. Is it possible I can stop by?"

"You're here? How? Why?" Liz's surprised voice floated through the line.

"It's a long story," Eva said, passing through baggage claim and out into the frigid February air. "Can I tell you in person?"

———————

Just a little over fifty miles from Manhattan, Liz's New Jersey street looked like it belonged in the Midwest, with small, well-cared-for houses, a mix of brick and painted stucco. When Liz opened her door, she pulled Eva into a tight hug. "This is such a surprise," she said. "Come in."

She followed Liz through the house to a large room off the kitchen that overlooked a snowy backyard. An afternoon talk show was on the TV in the corner, and Liz switched it off, gesturing for Eva to sit on the couch. Liz perched next to her and said, "I've missed you. Tell me everything."

Eva froze. The whole flight, she'd rehearsed in the dark while people slept around her. Tried to find the right place to begin unraveling it all. But now that she was looking into Liz's questioning eyes, waiting for Eva to say something, she couldn't make her mouth work at all.

Her gaze traveled around the room, to the bookshelves crammed with books, a messy desk covered in papers, and a couple half-emptied packing boxes in the corner.

She took a deep breath and gave Liz a wobbly smile. "I don't know where to start," she told her.

Liz took Eva's hands, warm and dry against Eva's sweaty ones, and she felt a little calmer, Liz's energy passing through her, making her heart rate slow. "Just pick a place and begin."

"I'm in trouble," Eva said, her voice low and tentative. And then she began. She told Liz about Wade. How he made her feel special. Eva looked into her lap and shrugged. "It was the first time anyone had made me feel that way. Interesting. Attractive. Like a normal person living a normal life."

She described the meeting in the dean's office, how no one showed up for her, and how she'd felt she had to accept their terms. "They had all the power. All the leverage. I was just a kid. It was easy for them to kick me out and pretend none of it happened."

"Didn't the university appoint an advocate for you?"

Eva had never even considered such a thing. She shook her head, and Liz looked disgusted. "You could have appealed. There are procedures that should have been followed." But then Liz seemed to catch herself, because she said, "You couldn't have known, and that doesn't help you now. Go on."

Eva thought about what came next, a decision so significant, her entire life cleaved in two. She let out a slow breath, dragging out the moment, knowing she'd have to step forward and tell the rest, but not wanting to. Terrified Liz wouldn't understand. That what she'd said in her letter, about accepting Eva as she was, wouldn't apply to what she was about to confess.

Eva was tempted to end the story there. Tell Liz she was on her way to Europe, had a layover, and wanted to stop by and say hi. But she knew Liz wouldn't buy it. And eventually, Castro would show up at Liz's door and tell her the truth. Eva needed to be the one to tell Liz. To make sure Liz understood why she'd done what she did. She prayed some of Liz's forgiveness would come her way.

"That guy you saw me arguing with is named Dex. Or at least, that's the name I know him by. Apparently, he has others." Eva told her about Dex's offer, about how she had no money. Nowhere to go, and how it seemed like a lifeline at the time.

As she spoke, Liz's eyes grew wider, her expression more and more shocked. Eva knew what Liz expected to hear. Typical problems such as a lost job. An unwanted pregnancy. Maybe stolen money or property. But Eva could tell Liz didn't expect this. She couldn't bear the weight of Liz's eyes, and she leaned forward, resting her head in her hands, covering her face, elbows on her knees.

Next to her, she felt Liz rise from the couch and move away from her. Eva held her breath, waiting for the sound of Liz opening her front door, a quiet voice asking Eva to leave. Or the sound of her picking up the phone to call the police. But instead she heard Liz move into the kitchen and open the refrigerator, the sound of ice, and she returned with a bottle of vodka and two glasses. She poured generously and took a drink. "Continue," she said.

Eva sipped her vodka and told her the rest. Brittany. Agent Castro. The evidence she'd assembled, Castro's news that she didn't qualify for witness protection. And finally, that Dex was Fish. "I'm sure he knows by now that something is up. I was supposed to meet him yesterday, but I never showed."

"You have to cooperate," Liz said when Eva had finished telling her everything. "It's the only thing you *can* do." She finished her vodka and poured another glass, topping off Eva's as well. "My God, Eva."

"I can't."

"You have to," Liz insisted. "This is how you get your life back."

Eva tried not to lose her temper. "It doesn't work like it does on TV. Even if Dex goes to jail, I'm still at risk. No matter where I go, his people will find me. I tried to make Agent Castro understand this, but he said his hands were tied." Eva began to cry, great hiccupping sobs, and Liz wrapped her arms around her, holding her tight.

"You have to stop running," she said into the top of Eva's head. "Stop covering up lies with more lies."

"It's not that simple," Eva said, pulling back and wiping her eyes. "Castro thinks I can testify and then somehow go back to my regular life. As if Dex would ever let me get that far. The only thing I can do is leave. Disappear and let Castro figure it out without me."

She waited for Liz to argue with her, to threaten to turn her in. But Liz just said, "Okay. Let's follow this line of thinking. Where will you go?"

Eva shrugged. "I'll stay in New York for a while. Find a way to get a fake passport. I have money."

Liz nodded. "A fake passport. And then you'll leave the country?"

Eva knew what Liz was doing. She'd had a professor at Berkeley use this kind of Socratic method to help students reason out an argument. But she went along with it. "Yes."

Liz rolled her glass between her hands, the ice settling toward the bottom. "You'll be someone new. Someone without a past. What will you do with your time? Will you work? Buy some property? Rent? How will you explain yourself to others?"

"I'll figure it out. Make something up."

"And constantly be afraid, looking over your shoulder, waiting for someone to discover the truth." Liz's quiet voice landed hard in Eva's ears. "You need to make a deal, and you need to do it now." Liz set her glass down and put her finger under Eva's chin, forcing Eva to look at her. "What happened to you was shitty and unfair. But you have to go back and own your part of it. Either Dex is going to jail for a long time, or you are. Who's it going to be?"

"And what if Dex's people get to me first? He has to know by now." Panic began to swirl around inside of Eva, and she started to cry again.

Liz handed her a tissue and said, "You have to fly back before Castro knows you've left. Call him the minute you land, and wait for him at the airport. Do not leave until he comes in to get you. Understand?"

"Why can't I just disappear?" Eva whispered. "Pretend I've never been here?"

Liz's eyes softened. "You know they'll come here eventually and ask me questions. I can't lie for you."

Maybe this was why Eva came. To be forced to do the right thing. To be held accountable by someone who loved her enough to not let her make any more mistakes. For Liz to be the mother she'd never had.

Relief melted through her, to be able to set everything down and let someone else—someone who cared about her—tell her what to do. "Okay," she said.

They sat together, with only the faint ticking of a clock somewhere deep inside the house, the silence between them heavy with all that Eva still wanted to say.

All her life, she'd craved connection. Family. Friendship. Then Liz came along and gave it to her, without asking for anything in return. Eva wanted to ask *Why me?* But she wouldn't, because there could never be enough words to fill the hole Eva had inside of her, the deepest part of the heart, where the most precious love and the truest friendships are stored.

She knew that walking out the door tomorrow would require an act of courage Eva wasn't sure she possessed. To turn her back and leave this life, with all its sharp edges and hard knots, and trust that there would be something on the other side for her.

"Do you remember the day we met?" Liz's voice was the same low tenor Eva remembered from their first meeting, and it passed through her like warm honey. "I was crumpled in a heap on the ground, and you walked over and lifted me up." Eva started to speak, but Liz silenced her with an upheld hand. "Do not ever forget who you are and what you mean to me. In a world crowded with noise and selfishness, you are a brilliant flash of kindness." Liz turned Eva so she was facing her and held her by the shoulders. "No matter where you go, no matter what happens, know I will be out here, loving you."

Eva let her tears fall, the last of her walls crumbling beneath Liz's words. Every regret, every disappointment, every heartache that Eva had ever endured seeped out of her, a slow leak of sadness, until she was empty.

---

After she'd booked her flight back to Oakland, they sat together on the couch, Eva trying to soak up every last moment with Liz, knowing it would never be enough. From the front of the house came the sound of a key in the lock, then the door opening and closing. "Mom?" a voice called. "Are you home?"

"Back here, honey."

A young woman came through the kitchen, tossing her keys on the counter and dropping her heavy bag on the floor. She stopped suddenly when she saw Eva and Liz on the couch. "Sorry," she said. "I didn't know you had company."

"Eva, this is my daughter, Ellie."

Ellie rolled her eyes and stepped forward to shake Eva's hand. "I go by Danielle now. It's nice to finally meet you."

# CLAIRE

## Monday, February 28

I stare at Agent Castro, feeling as if the careful stitches holding my secrets together have been pulled apart. "I don't know who that is."

He flips his sunglasses on top of his head and says, "I think you do. You just finished a call on her phone." My eyes dart toward Eva's cell phone, sitting on the dresser, wondering how he'd know that. He continues. "So let's try this a different way. Good afternoon, Mrs. Cook. It's wonderful to see you looking so well. My name is Agent Castro, and I'm a federal DEA officer. I have some questions I'd like to ask you." Beyond him in the parking lot is an anonymous sedan with government plates. "Maybe we should go inside and chat," he suggests. His tone is friendly but firm, and I nod, opening the door wider to let him enter.

We sit at the small table by the window, two chairs facing each other. He pulls the curtains open, flooding the tiny room with light. "I'd like you to tell me how you know Eva James."

"I don't, really."

"And yet, up until yesterday, you were staying in her house." He gestures toward Eva's green coat, tossed over a chair. "And wearing her clothes." Then he holds up his own phone. "Mrs. Cook, we've had Ms. James under surveillance for several months. That includes having her phone cloned."

"Cloned?" I ask. "What does that mean?"

He leans back and studies me, the weight of his gaze making me uncomfortable. Finally, he says, "It means that anything you do with that phone, we know about it. We get copies of all texts and emails. When that phone rings, we know it. Whatever is said on it, we hear it."

My mind jumps back to the conversation I just had with Kate Lane. To Danielle's messages and the voice recording. And I know now why Eva left the phone behind. "Did she know?"

He shakes his head. "She was working with us on an active investigation, and we couldn't risk her changing her patterns with the people she worked with. But we began to worry when Eva failed to show up at a prearranged meeting last week. And then you arrived."

I look down at my hands, resting in my lap. I think about the car Kate Lane is sending for me, and whether Agent Castro will let me get in it, or whether I'm going to be stuck here, answering his questions until the moment Rory arrives.

"Why don't we start with how you met Eva," he repeats.

"If you've been listening in on my phone conversations, then you already know."

"Fair enough. Then tell me more about what happened at the airport. Whose idea was it to switch places?"

I'm unsure how to describe my role. Am I a victim? A co-conspirator? I was neither, just a woman desperate for a solution. Any solution. "Eva approached me," I finally say.

Castro nods. "How did she seem to you?"

"That's an impossible question to answer, since nothing she told me was true." I think of the way she stared into her drink, as if the weight of the world rested on her shoulders, and know that beneath her lies, the fear was real. "She was scared," I finally say.

"She had a good reason to be. Did anyone come to the house looking for her?"

I tell him about the man who showed up on the porch, about what he said and what he didn't say.

"Describe him," Agent Castro says.

"About my age. Maybe a little bit older. Dark hair. Olive skin. Long coat, and these crazy gray eyes. Not quite blue."

"While you were staying at Eva's house, did you see any drugs?"

"No." I think about that basement lab. Of the hours Eva must have spent working underground, and what it had cost her up above. And I think about the notarized letter and recordings, carefully gathered and documented, and weigh the benefits of handing them over now. If I do, Castro will have what he needs, or as much as Eva is able to give him, which might be enough to fulfill whatever promises she made.

I retrieve the envelope and voice recorder and slide them across the table to him. "I found these yesterday when I discovered her basement."

He sets the recorder aside and flips through the pages of Eva's statement, then jots the notary information into a small notebook.

"I had no idea what she was running from. She told me she had just lost her husband to cancer. That she'd helped him die and that she might be in trouble because of it." As I recount the story, it sounds even crazier than it did at the time. "You have to understand, I was desperate enough to want to believe pretty much anything. And I think she knew that."

"Eva has had years of practice deceiving people. She's very good at what she does. She had to be, to have done it for so long." He leans forward, resting his elbows on the table. "I need you to understand that my job is to investigate drug crimes," he says. "Not fraud. Not identity theft. And you are not under investigation by me." His voice softens, now that his questions have been answered and I get a peek at the man beneath the surface, someone who genuinely wants to help me. "I understand you're hiding from your husband?"

"I am."

"I'm not here to get you into trouble, Mrs. Cook. But Eva was helping me, and I need to know what happened to her. What she told you."

"Nothing true," I say. "None of it was real."

He looks out the window as a black town car glides into the spot next to his sedan. "I think your ride is here."

We stand and I open the door.

"Claire Cook?" the driver asks. He's large, in his midtwenties, squeezed into a dark suit with sleeves that just barely cover a tattoo circling up his right wrist. In his ears are those giant circles, stretching enormous holes in his earlobes.

*Berkeley. Where everyone is just a little bit weirder than you are.*

As he loads my bag into the trunk, I notice his gaze land on Agent Castro's gun beneath his coat. He looks away and slams the trunk closed, stepping away from the rest of our conversation.

Agent Castro turns to me. "Good luck," he says, shaking my hand. "If possible, I'd like to touch base again before you leave town. Assuming you go back to New York."

"Sure," I say, looking toward the busy street, cars and buses blowing past the motel. "Though what happens next depends on the next few hours. How much trouble I'll be in for what I did, and whether anyone will believe what I have to say."

"If your husband was involved in what happened to Maggie Moretti, it won't matter if they believe you or not. The evidence will back you up."

I tear my eyes away from the street and look at him. "You don't know the Cook family very well if you think they won't fight. The rules are different for people like them."

276

I wait for Agent Castro to tell me I'm wrong, but he doesn't. Even he knows that the power of money can make all kinds of problems disappear.

Finally, he says, "A little advice? Get on the air as soon as possible. Your husband can't touch you if the whole world knows you're alive."

———————

Traffic into the city is horrible. We progress slowly through the toll booth and up onto the Bay Bridge, walled in on all sides by cars. Alone in the back seat, I stare out the window, my gaze traveling across the water and landing on Alcatraz, small and squat in the middle of the bay, the slate-gray water surrounding it.

The driver adjusts the rearview mirror so he can see me better, his sleeve riding up even higher, and I catch another glimpse of his tattooed arm. "Okay if I turn on the radio?" he asks.

"Sure," I tell him.

He flips around until he lands on some quiet jazz. I pull Eva's phone out of my purse to check the time, and see that I have a missed text from Danielle.

> I just found out that Mr. Cook's already got a guy on the ground in Berkeley looking for you. A local, some-one who can better blend in with the people there. But I'm told he's big, with a tattoo sleeve on his right arm. Be careful.

# EVA

New Jersey
February
**One Day before the Crash**

Ellie—or rather, Danielle—did not look as Eva had expected Liz's daughter to look. Instead of the eclectic woman she'd imagined, a woman who wore long flowing skirts and worked for a hardscrabble nonprofit, Danielle had her dark hair pulled back into a conservative bun at the base of her neck. She wore pearls and a tailored suit with low heels. But the resemblance between mother and daughter was immediate. Danielle had the small stature of her mother, the planes of her face an almost mirror image of the friend Eva had grown to love. But where Liz was calm and centered, Danielle seemed agitated.

Liz stood to give her daughter a kiss. "Are you just getting home from work? It's late."

Ignoring her mother's question, Danielle said to Eva, "I didn't know you were coming to town."

The way Danielle said it, like an accusation, rumbled low inside of Eva, warning her to be careful. "A last-minute trip," she said. "In and out."

"Because?" Danielle's gaze held Eva's.

"Because she wanted to," Liz interjected, throwing a warning glare at her daughter.

"A quick visit to see some friends," Eva said, hoping to defuse some of the tension. "I have to head back tomorrow."

Danielle waited a moment, as if to see if Eva would offer more details. When she didn't, Danielle said, "Mom, can I see you in the other room?"

Apologetic, Liz turned to Eva. "Make yourself comfortable. I'll be back in a minute."

The two women huddled in the living room, the sound of their whispered conversation floating back to Eva in snatches. She rose from the couch and wandered into the kitchen under the pretense of looking at the pictures on the refrigerator.

"What is the matter with you?" Liz hissed.

"I'm sorry. I'm exhausted and stressed, and I've still got to pack for a trip to Detroit tomorrow," Danielle said. "I wasn't expecting a houseguest."

"What's happening in Detroit?"

"The foundation has an event there tomorrow. I was supposed to accompany Mrs. Cook, but I just found out Mr. Cook is sending her to Puerto Rico instead. He wants to do the Detroit trip himself." Danielle sighed. "I'm sorry to be so snappy with you. But this last-minute itinerary change is making me edgy. Something feels off."

"In what way?"

"Mrs. Cook has been singularly focused on this trip for months, in a way that's unusual for her."

"I think you're working too hard. Worrying about things that aren't there." Liz's voice sounded soothing, and Eva imagined her taking Danielle's hand and squeezing it.

"I don't think so, Mom. There's been other weird stuff. Her driver told me last month she took the car—alone—to Long Island. The GPS tracked her all the way to the eastern tip. She doesn't know anyone who lives out there. And I've had to cover for her a few times with financial discrepancies. Withdrawals. Receipts that don't match." Eva could hear the worry in Danielle's voice, the tension of watching and waiting for something to happen. "I think she's going to leave him."

"Good. Finally."

"Yeah, but I don't think the Puerto Rico trip is a part of that. And I'm worried the Detroit trip was."

"Do you think Mr. Cook knows?"

"No, but if this messes her up somehow..." She trailed off. "I don't like the idea of her traveling alone, or with people only loyal to *the incredible Rory Cook*. And now I've got to go to Detroit and act as if I'm one of them when I can barely stand to look at the man, knowing how he terrorizes her."

"If she's smart, she'll go to Puerto Rico and never come back."

Eva had stopped pretending to look at the pictures and was now entirely focused on listening to this story unfold, piecing together the bare bones of an idea.

In two steps, she was across the kitchen and over to the couch, grabbing her laptop and setting it up on the counter so she could still listen in. As the two women continued to talk, Eva Googled *Rory Cook, wife*, and studied the image that appeared. A beautiful woman, her dark hair framing her face, wearing high-end, trendy clothes, walking down a New York sidewalk. The caption read *Rory Cook's wife, Claire, visits the new restaurant, Entourage, located on the Upper West Side.*

In the next room, Danielle said, "Somehow I don't think staying in Puerto Rico is an option for her. I feel terrible that she has to go, that she's going to wake up and Bruce is going to be the one to tell her of the change, that he'll be the one to take her to JFK." With an impatient sigh, she continued. "Anyways, I'm sorry I was rude to Eva. I'm sure she's lovely. What's the real story? Why is she really in town?"

Eva held her breath, staring at the details of Claire Cook's face, but not seeing them anymore. Instead, she waited to hear whether Liz would keep her secrets or reveal them all, dishing them up to her daughter like a late-night snack.

"Eva's hit a rough patch," Liz said. "But she's going to be fine. She's a survivor."

Eva let out a quiet sigh of relief.

"Look," Danielle was saying. "I need to pack since we're leaving at the crack of dawn. Do you know where my black wool coat is?"

"Upstairs in the spare bedroom closet, I think. Let me see if I can find it."

"Thanks, Mom."

Such a simple sentence, probably uttered hundreds of thousands of times. And yet, the power of it nearly brought Eva to tears. What it must be like to have someone always in your corner. She thought she'd had that with Liz, but seeing her together with her daughter, the way they trusted and confided in each other, Eva knew what she and Liz shared was nothing more than a close friendship. And she felt stupid for ever thinking it was more. What would Liz advise her daughter to do if she found herself in Eva's position? Would she also encourage Danielle to turn herself in to the authorities? Or would she help her daughter escape?

On the screen in front of her, she imagined what Claire Cook would think tomorrow when she woke to discover her husband had changed her itinerary. That she'd be flying out of JFK to a tropical paradise instead of into the freezing Detroit temperatures. Perhaps she wouldn't care. Perhaps Danielle's instincts about the importance of this trip were wrong. But if they were right, if Claire was planning to run, she'd find herself desperate for a solution. Another way out.

And Eva might have just the solution in mind.

"What are you doing?"

Eva whipped around to find Danielle in the doorway, holding the bag she'd dropped there earlier. Eva closed the lid of the computer, hoping Danielle hadn't seen too much, and gave her a blank smile. "Nothing."

She held Danielle's gaze until Danielle finally turned away, up the stairs to pack for her trip.

Eva opened the laptop again and toggled away from the photograph of Claire Cook, and over to the airline website. She clicked on *Change my reservation*, and in the drop-down menu, she switched out *Newark* for *JFK*, Liz's words echoing in her mind. *She's a survivor.*

Eva was determined to make that true.

# CLAIRE

## Monday, February 28

I press my back into the seat, my gaze leaping from Danielle's text to the driver's right hand, resting casually on the steering wheel. *A tattoo sleeve on his right arm.*

My mind flies back to the motel lot, and I realize he hadn't said anything about CNN. He'd said *Claire Cook,* and like an idiot, I got in the car.

Vehicles press in on us, all the way to the edge of the bridge. Steel cables rise into the sky above a small strip of sidewalk, and then a two-hundred-foot drop to the cold water below.

Castro's advice, to get to the studio as soon as possible, taunts me now. This man will take me somewhere else—a deserted beach perhaps, or north to somewhere even more remote, and finish this.

A green Jetta slides up next to us, with a woman behind the wheel, her lips moving in silent conversation with someone I can't see. I'm no more than three feet away from her, so close I can see her pink nail polish and the delicate silver hoops in her ears. I fight back tears, trying to think. If I screamed, would she hear me?

Our car moves several feet forward before stopping again, and now I'm looking at a white panel van with no windows. My eyes trace the tiny openings between the cars, an ever-shifting maze as vehicles inch forward. I'm going to have to jump out and run.

The lane next to us begins to move, and again I'm looking at the woman in the green Jetta. She throws her head back and laughs, unaware that I'm watching her from behind tinted glass.

About thirty yards ahead, a dark tunnel looms with signs for Treasure Island. The driver's eyes find mine again in the rearview mirror. "Traffic will clear up once we get through the tunnel," he says.

If I'm going to get out, a dark tunnel might be a good place to do it.

I rest my arm on the windowsill, my palms sweaty and slick against the door, and carefully lift the lock, watching him in the mirror, making sure his eyes remain on the road.

I'm only going to get one chance.

Jazz music swirls around the back seat, the rhythm fast and erratic, matching my pulse, and I hug my purse close, making sure it's secure over my shoulder. I have one hand resting on the latch of my seat belt and my other hand lowering to the door handle, ready to yank it open and leap out. If I scream for help, surely someone will step up.

I regulate my breathing, counting down the feet until the car is plunged into the darkness of the tunnel.

*Twenty feet.*

*Ten.*

*Five.*

The driver looks at me again in the mirror. "You okay?" he asks. "You look a little pale. I have some water up here if you need it. The CNN studio is just a few blocks once we get off the bridge. Not much farther now."

I feel the air rush out of me and collapse against the seat, clasping my shaking hands in my lap. *CNN. Not Rory.* Dizzy relief floods through me, and I squeeze my eyes shut, trying not to fall apart.

This is the price of abuse. It has twisted my thinking into such a tangle I can't tell what's real and what's not. Logically, I can see how impossible it would have been for them to find me so easily. And yet, years of being under Rory's influence has made it so that I've given him nearly super-human power. To see where I'm hiding, to know my every thought and fear, and to then exploit them.

Finally, the car picks up speed, and we enter the tunnel. The darkness is a brief blink, and then we're out the other side. As if by magic, the entire city rises up before us, bright white buildings shining in the early afternoon sun.

"Mrs. Cook?" he asks again, holding up a small bottle of water.

"I'm okay," I tell him, as much for myself as for him.

---

*Breaking news: We interrupt our regularly scheduled program to bring you Kate Lane, live from Washington, DC, with a story that is just emerging from California. Kate?*

The voices talk in my ear, though I sit alone on a stool placed in front of a green screen. Several producers and assistants are clustered around the single camera, zoomed in on me, but the red light indicating that I'm on-air remains dark. Next to it, a television screen shows Kate Lane in her DC studio, the feed piped directly into my earpiece. My head is still fuzzy from the adrenaline, but the freezing temperature of the studio clears it a little. On the far wall of the studio is a large digital clock with a bright-blue background that reads 1:22, and I watch the seconds tick down, trying to align my heart rate with them.

Shortly after I'd arrived at the CNN studio, weak and shaking, a producer had handed me an iPad with Kate Lane calling via video chat. They'd been able to talk with Danielle, who had agreed to send the recording to the New York State Attorney General. Kate's sources inside the department told her they should have some news about next steps very soon. Charlotte Price had also been located and was willing to go on the record as soon as her attorney could file to void the NDA she'd signed so long ago.

"So now it's up to you to tell your story," Kate had said. "Paint a picture of your marriage for us. Tell us what your husband was like, and what you were running from." Her expression softened. "I have to prepare you for what will likely happen once you come forward. People are going to dig into your life. Your past. Say hateful things about you and to you, in a very public way. It won't matter whose side people are on—yours or your husband's—your life will be put under a microscope regardless. Every choice you ever made. Every person you ever talked to. Your family. Your friends. I have an obligation to make sure you're clear, before we proceed."

Hearing Kate spell out exactly what I'd feared for so many years made me hesitate, and I considered stepping back. Letting Danielle and Charlie's evidence do all the work. No one needed to hear the details of my abuse in order to lay Maggie Moretti's death at Rory's feet.

And yet, I knew that if I didn't, I'd be destined to live and relive moments like the one on the bridge. I would never be truly free if I scurried away to hide under another rock. I'd be complicit in Rory's abuse as long as I continued to protect him. The world didn't need to hear my story, but I needed to tell it. "I understand," I told her.

"Live in five seconds," someone says.

"Good evening." Kate's voice fills my earpiece, as if she's sitting right next to me. "In the last hour, attorneys for Rory Cook, head of the Cook Family Foundation and son of the late Senator Marjorie Cook, have been fielding requests for questioning related to the death of Maggie Moretti, who died twenty-seven years ago on a Cook family property. But even more extraordinary is the fact that authorities received this information via Mr. Cook's wife, previously believed to have perished on Flight 477. CNN has discovered that she is alive and living in California. We have her here now, via satellite, to discuss the accusations against her husband and why she felt she had to hide. Mrs. Cook, so good to see you."

The light on the camera in front of me illuminates, and the director points at me. I fight the urge to reach up and touch my hair, aware of how different I look. "Thank you, Kate. It's good to be here." My voice sounds lonely in the empty space, and I try to stay focused on the television monitor that shows a background of the San Francisco skyline behind me.

"Mrs. Cook, tell us what happened and how you came to be here today."

Now that I'm here, I can see that it was always going to come to this. For too long, I believed my voice alone wouldn't be enough. That nobody would want to hear the truth and step in to help. But when I needed it most, three women showed up. First Eva, then Danielle, and finally, Charlie. If we don't tell our own stories, we'll never take control of the narrative.

I square my shoulders and look directly into the camera, feeling the terror of the last hour, the stress of the past week, and the fear of the past ten years slipping off me, now nothing more than the faint whisper of a shadow.

"As you know, my husband comes from a very powerful family, with unlimited resources. But what you don't know is that our marriage was a difficult one. For the cameras, he was charming and dynamic, but behind closed doors, he became violent, triggered without warning. The world saw us as a happy and committed team, but beneath the veneer, I was in crisis. Guarding my secrets. Trying to do better, to be better. Desperate to live up to the impossible standards my husband set for me, terrified when I couldn't.

"Like many women in this situation, I was stuck in a cycle of abuse for years. Afraid to anger him, afraid to speak up, afraid that if I did, no one would believe me. Living like that breaks a person down, one tiny piece at a time, until you can't see the truth in anything or anyone. He'd isolated me from anyone I might have gone to for help. I'd tried before to leave him. To tell the truth of my marriage. But powerful men make powerful enemies, and no one wanted Rory Cook as an enemy. The only way out that I could see, that didn't involve public scandal or a prolonged court battle, was to simply disappear."

"But a plane crash?"

"That was a tragic coincidence. I wasn't supposed to be on that plane to Puerto Rico. I planned to disappear in Canada. A last-minute scheduling change derailed everything. But then I met a woman at the airport willing to trade tickets with me." I think about the people still looking for Eva and deliver my line. "Unfortunately, she perished instead of me, and I will forever be grateful to her, for giving me the chance to escape."

"Tell us what you were escaping from."

I imagine Rory somewhere, called to the television to watch the resurrection of his dead wife, rage pounding through him as he stands, helpless, while I snatch his precious reputation and tear it to shreds. "Almost from the beginning," I say, "he would berate me for laughing too loud, for eating too much, or too little. For missing his calls. For spending too long talking to one person at an event, or not enough time talking to another. If I was lucky, that's all it would be. Yelling and insults, followed by days of silence and icy glares. But about two years into the marriage, the yelling progressed to shoving. And shortly after that, to hitting."

A photograph fills the screen behind me, an image of Rory and me walking on the beach in the Hamptons. It had first appeared in *People* magazine, then quickly became one of several stock images news outlets used when reporting on Rory's private life. "This picture was taken last summer. You can only see what's in the frame—a couple walking on the beach, holding hands. What you can't see is everything beneath it. How angry my husband was with me, how tightly he gripped my hand, so hard my ring cut the inside of the finger next to it. My long sleeves hide bruises from the night before, after I'd forgotten the first name of an old friend of Rory's. You can't see the lump on the back of my head from where it slammed into the wall, or the pounding headache I had. You can't see how lost I felt. How alone."

I look down at my hands, the fear and desperation I felt in that one captured moment cascading over me once again. And how much I didn't want to do this, to have to recount every blow, every indignity, as a way to justify myself.

Kate's voice is quiet in my ear. "Why come forward now? You'd gotten away. You were set up in California. You were free."

"I was never free. First of all, I had no identity, and no way of getting one. I had no money. No job. I was able to get temporary work with a catering company, which led to my image being posted on *TMZ*, forcing me to come forward."

I look into the camera, keeping my gaze steady, and imagine I'm speaking directly to Eva. For a short time, we inhabited the same skin. The same life. I know things about her no one else will know, and that binds you to a person, a gossamer-thin thread crossing time and space. Wherever I am, she will be too. And wherever she is...I hope it's far from here.

"But I also felt that I needed to honor the woman who died in my stead," I say. "There are people out there who loved her. Who might want to know what happened to her. They deserve to have closure as well." I pause for a moment, thinking about the scrap of paper I found at Eva's, still shoved in my pocket. "I'm ready to step beyond the fear," I tell Kate. "I want my life back. *Mine.* The one that belongs to me. My husband has stolen a lot from me. He's stolen my confidence. He's stolen my self-worth. And I don't think he deserves to steal any more. From anyone."

Across the studio, the digital clock flips from 1:59 to 2:00.

*Zero hours left.*

*I'm free.*

# CLAIRE

New York City
**One Month after the Crash**

I've never been in the townhouse on Fifth Avenue when it was this empty. There was always someone here, cooking or cleaning, scheduling appointments, standing guard outside Rory's office. But in the wake of my CNN interview and the subsequent grand jury investigation into Rory's involvement in Maggie's death, everyone has been dismissed. The rooms are silent, and I feel like a ghost, walking the same route I used to take in my middle-of-the-night wanderings. Perhaps I am one, returning to haunt the life I left behind, and finding everything changed.

At first the story was slow to take shape, while Rory's attorneys battled to uphold the nondisclosure agreement. But once he lost, a crash of information flooded the media, with something new released almost every day—the fight Rory and Maggie had the night she died, how it had ended with her unconscious at the bottom of the stairs and Rory scrambling to save himself from what he believed he'd done. How Rory had driven straight to Charlie's apartment, only a few blocks away from his on the West Side. At the time, she'd tried to help him. She believed the story he'd told, a deer in the road on his way back to the city, the car on the verge of going into a ditch, a close call that had him severely rattled. Until news of Maggie's death started to emerge. Charlie, who was young and in love with Rory, and had once hoped Rory would leave Maggie for her, began to grow alarmed. When she started asking questions, Rory's father paid her to keep quiet and then slammed her with a nondisclosure agreement so steep it guaranteed she'd stay that way.

For years, she'd tried to leave it behind her, until the rumors of Rory's run for Senate surfaced. Charlie was no longer a scared twenty-year-old. Like many, she'd grown tired of watching powerful men never being held accountable, *boys will be boys* evolving into an impenetrable armor, shielding them from blame.

The media had a field day. Revisiting the summer Maggie Moretti died, reprinting old articles with updated information, interviewing her friends again, this time adding in Charlie and her relationship with Rory, which overlapped the one he had with Maggie by several months. Everyone wanting to know more about the love triangle, to look into every corner and see something new. To be the outlet that got the newest morsel to dish out via Twitter.

I've tried to stay out of the spotlight, but Kate Lane was right. My first week back, I'd made the cover of *People*, my face turned in three-quarter profile, my hair returned to its original shade, and the headline "Resurrected."

While most people were sympathetic, having harbored doubts about Rory's involvement in Maggie's death for years, there were others who attacked me viciously, questioning my character, calling me a gold digger, a vindictive wife bent on destroying all the Cook family had built. Blaming me for the fact that the Cook Family Foundation was now under investigation by the New York Attorney General for allegations of misuse of charitable assets and improper self-dealing.

Through the LLC documents, my attorneys have been able to shield me from legal jeopardy, and I'm free to leave the state. New York isn't home anymore. I can't wait to get back to California and away from this circus.

I enter my office, where stacks of boxes line the walls. Armed with a very specific list and a limited window of time fiercely negotiated by my attorneys, I'm here to get what belongs to me. My clothes. My jewelry. My personal items. My gaze falls on the photograph of my mother and Violet on the wall, and this time I lift it off its hook and place it with the other things I'm taking with me. I let my eyes linger on my sister's smile, the way the dimple creases her left cheek, the way the sun shines through her hair as it blows in the wind, making it look like spun gold. The memories feel sweet when they come, instead of the sharp ache I've been running from for so many years.

I pick up a small statue, six inches tall, an original Rodin that Rory bought last year, and think of how much money I could get if I sold it. But it's not on my list. Aside from my own things, all our joint assets are locked down, though really there's very little I want or need in my new life in Berkeley.

Kelly had helped me find an apartment. I'd called her a few days after my CNN interview, after I'd met with my attorneys and begun the long process of unraveling everything I'd done.

By that time, I was leading the news on every network and cable news show. "Holy shit, Eva," she'd said, and then caught herself. "Sorry. I guess I should call you Claire."

I smiled and sat down on the bed in the hotel room my attorneys were paying for, exhausted from hours of depositions. We were only going to be there for a few more days, and then I'd have to return to New York to finish up. I imagined her on campus somewhere, her backpack heavy with books, pausing on one of the shady paths that crisscrossed campus to take my call. "I'm sorry I misled you."

"No, I'm sorry the job I got you started this mess."

"It would have happened eventually, one way or another. The life I was trying to live would have been unsustainable." I cleared my throat. "Listen, you mentioned you could help me find a place to live? After all of this is finished, I'd really like to stay in Berkeley."

"Let me make a few phone calls and get back to you," she said.

The apartment was located on a narrow street that wound up the hill behind the football stadium, the top floor of a narrow wooden structure nestled in between the towering trees of Strawberry Canyon. The landlady, Mrs. Crespi, was a friend of Kelly's mother and was more than happy to rent it to me. She warned us that parking could be troublesome on game days and that the sound of the cannon they fired after touchdowns could be startling at first. It had about forty wooden stairs, and when we reached the top, Mrs. Crespi opened the door and stepped aside so I could enter first. Not even eight hundred square feet, it was like a tree house. Kelly huffed next to me and said, "You might want to think about grocery delivery. I can't imagine carrying anything heavier than a purse all the way up here."

"I have three tenants, professional women like yourself," Mrs. Crespi said. "I charge fifteen hundred dollars a month, but that includes all utilities. If you decide to take it, I'll need first and last for security deposit. And the furniture can stay since it's difficult to move things in and out of here. I can have it professionally cleaned if you like."

My attorneys had negotiated a monthly stipend, although it wasn't much. I'd have to sell all my jewelry and find a job, but I was looking forward to the chance to be on my own. To earn my own way. "That should work," I said, stepping into the living room and kitchen space.

Even though I knew it was going to be small, the fact that nearly the entire west side of the room was glass made the apartment seem bigger.

A sage-green couch faced the window, with a small TV mounted on a stand next to the front door. Behind us, a tiny kitchen with a patch of counter space for food prep, a stove, and a refrigerator took up the back of the room. Beyond that was a short hallway leading toward a bathroom and tiny bedroom.

I walked to the window. A blanket of green treetops swooped down the hill, with the university buildings tucked in between them, glowing like half-buried treasures in the late afternoon light. Beyond that, San Francisco Bay shimmered, the sun casting the city skyline and bridge in the distance as a silhouette. "I love it," I said, turning to face Kelly and Mrs. Crespi.

A smile illuminated Mrs. Crespi's wrinkled face. "I'm so glad." She opened the file she was holding and handed me a lease agreement. "You can move in whenever you're ready."

I took the paperwork from her and grinned. "I'm ready now," I said, and turned back to the view again.

---

"Do you want me to pack up everything in the bathroom, or do you want to go through the drawers yourself?" Petra stands in the doorway to my office, and I turn from the box I've been sorting through to face her. When I'd returned to New York, she had been the one to pick me up from the airport. She'd waited until we were safely in the back of the town car she'd hired before falling apart.

"This feels like a dream," she said through her tears. "When I saw that the plane had crashed..." She trailed off and pressed her fingers to her eyes, taking a deep breath. "And then you show up on CNN and eviscerate that motherfucker."

It turned out, I hadn't copied her phone number down wrong. "I had it disconnected," Petra had explained when I'd asked why it didn't work.

"After I talked to you at the airport, I worried Rory might do some kind of reverse directory assistance and figure out who it belonged to. So I got a new one. But then the news…" She'd shrugged, unable to continue, tears tumbling down her cheeks again.

I close the lid on one box and slide another one toward me. "Pack it all," I tell her now. "The lotions and makeup are expensive. It'd be stupid to throw them away."

"I still think you should stay here," Petra says. "This is your home and you're entitled to it. Maybe not all the contents." She glances at the Rodin statue. "But you should fight for what's yours."

"I don't want it," I say, turning back to the box and sealing it closed. "I don't need all this space."

"It's not about the space," Petra argues. "It's about what belongs to you."

"Then we'll sell it and I'll get half."

"I want you to stay in New York."

I walk toward her and give her a hug. "I know," I say, pulling back. "But you know why I can't. I need to start over somewhere new. You should come to California. The light, the air…they're different there. You'd love it."

Petra looks skeptical. "I'd better finish that bathroom. We're almost out of time."

She leaves and I open the last box, sorting through it quickly, discarding most of it. The money from my jewelry will allow me time to explore my options in California. Maybe I'll keep working events with Kelly. Or I'll go back to school. I imagine myself taking the BART into San Francisco, perhaps working at the museum there, going out to dinner with the friends I hope to finally make.

After I'd finished the CNN interview, Agent Castro had taken me back to Eva's house to walk him through my time there. I wasn't sure what more I could tell him that he didn't already know. They'd submitted

Eva's DNA to the NTSB and were waiting to see if it matched any of the remains they'd recovered so far.

"It's possible we'll never know," he says. "They tell me there are any number of reasons why she might not have been in your seat. Maybe she traded with someone, or perhaps the impact of the crash caused her to get thrown from the wreckage and carried away with the current. If that's the case, we may never recover her body." He shrugged and looked out the window, as if the answer to what happened to Eva might be out there somewhere, visible only to him.

"What about the drug dealer?"

"Dex," Agent Castro said. "Also known as Felix Argyros, or Fish. We have a lead on him up in Sacramento."

An agent passed through the living room, carrying Eva's camping stove bagged in a clear plastic evidence bag. "She must have been so desperate, to have chosen a life like this."

"I think Eva would argue that this life chose her." Agent Castro sighed. "She was a hard person to know. I'm not really sure I ever had a good handle on her. But even though she ran, she still tried to do the right thing. What she left behind will be critical in indicting Fish."

"She sounds complicated," I said.

"She was. But I liked her. I wish I could have done more for her."

I didn't say what I was thinking, that Eva didn't need anyone. She'd done just fine on her own.

---

I pick up a pile of clothes and carry it into the living room, setting it alongside the rest of the things I'll be taking with me. I check the time. We only have about thirty more minutes. I hear Petra closing drawers in the bathroom upstairs, muttering something to herself, and I smile.

My work mostly done, I walk down the hallway that leads to Rory's office and peek inside. It's been completely cleared out. His desk, Bruce's, even the books on the shelves are gone, all of it confiscated by the attorney general. I cross over to the empty bookshelves, reaching up and engaging the button, and the drawer below opens. As I suspected, it's empty.

I hear someone unlocking the front door, and I straighten up, feeling guilty because I'm not supposed to be in here. But it's only Danielle. She stops in the doorway when she sees me. "Looking for ghosts?" she asks.

I smile. "Something like that."

Danielle had been waiting for me when I first returned to the town-house. She'd led me into the kitchen and made me a cup of tea. When we'd settled across from each other at the center island, I finally asked the question that had been nagging at me since her first message. "How did you know where to find me?"

She gave a small, sad smile. "Eva was a friend of my mom's." She took a tentative sip of her tea and told me a story of an unlikely friend-ship between two women—one who'd believed she didn't deserve to be loved, and the other who'd tried so hard to love her anyways. "Although I only met her briefly, there was something furtive about her. She had an edge that felt dangerous." Danielle set her cup down on the island and traced a swirl of marble with her finger. "But my mother was devoted to her. Swore that Eva was a good person who needed to know someone believed in her." Danielle shrugged.

"But that still doesn't explain how you knew to call me on her phone."

"She was at my mother's house in New Jersey the night before the Detroit trip. She must have eavesdropped on a conversation I had with my mom, because afterward, I caught her Googling photos of you. I was worried she'd try to target you somehow." Danielle shook her head, as though the thought embarrassed her.

"How's your mom doing?"

Danielle looked toward the living room, where the sun streamed through the tall windows, laying patches of light on the hardwood floor. "Not well," she said. "It's been hard for her to reconcile that Eva's really gone. That if Eva had just followed the plan they'd agreed upon and returned to Berkeley, she'd still be alive."

I took a sip of hot chamomile tea, letting the flavor bloom in my mouth, knowing I could never tell Danielle or her mother about what I believed really happened to Eva. I would leave it up to Eva to reach out, if and when she ever wanted to. "Eva Googling me couldn't have been enough for you to know where to look."

"It was the video," she said. "There you were, in Eva's hometown, with hair similar to Eva's and..." She trailed off. "I took a chance. Looked up Eva's number on my mom's phone and hoped you'd answer when I called." Danielle bent her head down, turning her cup slowly in her hands. When she looked up again, her eyes were wet with tears. "I had to do something, after all those years of staying silent. I'm so, so sorry I didn't do more to help you." She let out a shuddering breath. "I thought that by keeping you on task, on schedule, I could protect you. If I worked hard enough, maybe he wouldn't have a reason to be angry."

I reached across the island and put my hand on top of hers. "You helped me when it mattered most. More than I ever could have hoped for."

She squeezed my hand, a silent apology. Late, but not too late.

————————

The faint sound of a siren travels through the thick glass of Rory's office window. I look around the room, trying to picture the afternoon of Danielle's recording and where she might have dropped her phone in order to catch it. "One last question," I say. "How did you know to record that particular conversation? Did you know what they'd be talking about?"

Danielle steps into the room and runs her fingers across the back of one of the chairs. "I'd just seen the video of you at the A's event, and even though Mr. Cook never said anything to me about it, his sudden trip to Oakland made me believe he had seen it too. I was hoping to record a conversation about their plans to find you, to give you an idea of where and how they'd be looking. I had no idea I'd end up with something so much better."

"It was an incredibly brave and stupid thing to do."

Danielle grins. "That's exactly what my mom said." She checks her watch. "We'd better finish. Time's almost up."

I close the drawer with a quiet click and follow Danielle into the living room, where we pack the last of my things.

Petra enters the room just as I'm zipping my bag closed. "Ready?" she asks us.

I give the room one last look. The thick rugs, the expensive furniture, all of it meaningless to me now, and I smile at them both. "Ready," I say.

# EPILOGUE

John F. Kennedy Airport, New York
Tuesday, February 22
**The Day of the Crash**

*I hunch down on the ground next to the Jetway, picking up the scattered items from Claire's purse, my only view the shoes of the people in line around me, and shove it all back inside, save my prepaid phone. That I hold up to my ear.*

*My plan is simple. First, I'll ease sideways, as if I need to lean against the wall for balance. Then, I'll turn away from the straggling line of travelers, obedient and forward-facing. After that, it will be a simple matter of walking with purpose in a new direction.*

*I'm just about to speak into the silent phone, to launch into another fake conversation—maybe something urgent, requiring a little space, a little privacy, when someone says, "Ma'am, are you okay?"*

*The voice comes from above me, behind the crowd of travelers that block my view. Another gate agent materializes, and I slowly rise to a stand, my knees popping. "I dropped my purse," I explain, pulling it back onto my shoulder, feeling the slight tremor of a closing door. A missed opportunity.*

*"Since you're scanned onto the flight, I'm going to need you to stay in line," the gate agent says.*

*I reclaim my spot in front of the women who were complaining about the wait, the slope of the Jetway pulling me forward. Somewhere, Claire is already in the air, flying toward California, and I feel a stab of guilt. Not for the lies I told, but perhaps I should have at least warned her to be careful.*

*As the line to board the plane inches forward, I wonder if I'd met Claire under different circumstances whether we might have been friends. It feels wrong to be the last person to speak to her before she disappears, to be the only person in the world who knows what happened to her and still not know anything of substance about her. Who she loves. What matters to her, or what she believes in when she needs to believe in something. The specifics of the circumstances that have narrowed down to this single, outrageous option.*

*We have one thing in common. Each of us is desperate enough to take the risk. To turn our backs on who the world demands we be. It isn't just what has been done to each of us—by Dex, by Claire's husband—it's a system that tells women we are unreliable, and then expendable. That our truths don't matter when set side by side with a man's.*

*I try to clear my mind. To focus on what will come next for me. Liz will worry when I don't call as promised, but it has to be this way. When Castro arrives on her doorstep, Liz needs to be able to say with confidence that I returned to do the right thing.*

*Perhaps a few months from now, Liz might get a small package in the mail. A Christmas ornament—with no card, no return address—from the ripe vineyards of Italy or the crowded streets of Mumbai. And she'll know that I'm sorry. That I'm happy. That I've finally forgiven myself.*

*As soon as I board, I'm going to ask to have my aisle seat changed to a* window. I want to view the world—its wide vista expanding in a graceful arc below me—and imagine myself in it. My true self, the person Liz showed me I can be.

I hope that when the plane takes off, we'll fly straight into the sun, the light so bright it will burn away the last vestiges of everything and everyone I'm leaving behind. That it will carry me forward, higher than I've ever been, above the fear and the lies, tearing away a page filled with mistakes, the fragments scattering behind me like confetti.

And in its place, I'll create a new life built from the scraps of memory—some true, some the wished-for imaginings of a little girl who never found her place—constructed with luck and wide beams of gratitude holding it all together.

Maybe someday I'll dream of my life in Berkeley. Not the one I lived, with its dark corners and deceitful shadows, but the one I conjured up years ago, in a narrow bed above a dusty church in San Francisco. I'll visit again the light-dappled trails of Strawberry Canyon, high above the old stadium, with its view of a city skyline that seems to rise straight out of the bay. In my mind I'll walk along campus paths that wind among the redwoods, smell the damp bark and moss soft beneath my feet, listen to the stream tumble and jump across the rocks.

Ahead of me, the line starts moving again, space opening up between people, allowing me to breathe easier. Whatever was wrong has been fixed, and I can feel everyone around me relax, anticipating the vacation that waits for them on the other side of the four-hour flight south.

As I make my way down the Jetway, I feel as if I'm shedding my old self, piece by piece, growing lighter the closer I get to the plane. Pretty soon, I might not weigh anything at all. A laugh bubbles up, light and crisp, carrying none of the debris it usually does. In this moment, I have all I ever wanted. And for the first time, for the only time, it's enough. I hitch Claire's purse tighter over my shoulder and touch the outside of the airplane as I step over the threshold, for luck, and don't look back.

# READING GROUP GUIDE

1. What do Claire and Eva have in common? In what ways are they different?

2. How do you feel about Eva's decision to manipulate Claire?

3. Put yourself in Claire's shoes. How would it feel knowing that you've traded your life for someone else's? Would you feel guilty or fortunate? Why?

4. Describe the obstacles Claire faces once she escapes from Rory. Were there any difficulties that surprised you?

5. Compare Claire's relationships with other women in the book like Eva, Danielle, Petra, and Kelly. Are any of these women similar? In what way?

6. Discuss Eva's childhood. How does it affect how she behaves as an adult?

7. Identify some of the triggers Claire faces as a result of Rory's abuse. How do you think she can overcome them?

8. Claire makes the difficult decision to go public with her story, knowing full well that she may be met with criticism and disbelief. Why did she make this decision? Would you have handled the situation differently?

9. Liz is the only person Eva allows to get close to her. Describe their friendship. Why is it important to Eva? What does it mean to her?

10. Eva faces several huge difficulties in her life. Do you think her drug dealing is justified, given her circumstances?

11. Characterize Eva's relationship with Dex. Why does she feel betrayed when she learns the truth about him?

12. How did you feel after reading Eva's final chapter? Do you think there was anything different she could have done?

13. What do you think Claire will do next with her life? Will she be happy?

# A CONVERSATION WITH THE AUTHOR

**What inspired you to write *The Flight*?**

I've been intrigued by the idea of whether someone could disappear from their life for a long time, and have often played out the various ways they could do it in my imagination. The things they'd need. How they'd get them. Where they might go, and what they'd do when they got there. What they'd have to be leaving behind. I knew early on that I wanted it to be a woman, and I wanted her to have an inner strength, even if her current situation didn't allow her to use it. What might be the tiny ways she'd fight back, fight for room for herself?

**Which of the two women—Eva or Claire—did you enjoy writing more? Did you find either of them more challenging?**

I love both of my characters for different reasons. I love how scrappy Claire is, how she can look at a situation and figure out how to make it work for her. And I love Eva because she's so flawed yet lovable. I enjoyed writing them both. I would say writing Claire was more challenging, because I was pushing her forward in time, having her act and react to things she didn't know yet. Eva felt more natural to me, living in the past, filling in the blanks. With Claire, the tension had to be immediate, the pacing had to be tight. With Eva, I was allowed to sink more into emotion, to flesh out her backstory and how she ended up where she did.

**We're in an era where women are finally starting to feel safe sharing their stories. How does this book relate to the #MeToo movement?**

I wanted to acknowledge how hard it still is for women to come forward with their stories. Even in this era of #MeToo, the cost remains high both personally and professionally. Just because we have a name for it doesn't mean it's fixed.

**Can you talk a little bit about the systemic forces of oppression that both Claire and Eva face? What made you choose to write about these topics?**

As an educator, I feel like it's my obligation to shine a light on what still isn't working in our society. The way a woman's truth is sometimes held to a higher level of scrutiny than a man's. The benefit of the doubt that so often goes the other way. I've known people like Claire, and I've known people like Eva, for whom things don't always turn out okay. In the United States, we like to talk a lot about progress; however, change—not just for women but for all marginalized groups—is slow. Too slow.

**What does your writing process look like?**

I wake up early in the morning to write. During the workweek, I'm up at 3:45 and write until 6:00. Then I teach a full day of school and shuttle my kids here and there after school, making dinner, supervising homework. Early mornings—with a large pot of coffee—is my most productive writing time. My process is somewhat old school. I favor drafting with paper and pen, especially if I'm having trouble. It slows my brain, it allows me to put down words that "don't count," and it allows me to get warmed up before committing words to my computer. I draft pretty fast—I think I had a first draft of *The Flight* done in about three or four months. Then I like to spend a year or more revising and rewriting.

**As a genre, suspense is huge right now. How do you think this story sets itself apart from other books in the space?**

I feel like this book has the commercial appeal of the suspense genre, with the emotion often found in upmarket women's fiction. But what really sets this book apart from the others on the shelves is the fact that I wanted both of my protagonists to be strong, savvy women. There's nothing crazy or unstable about Claire or Eva. It's important that the stories we tell reflect the strong women in the world today.

**How did you map out all the twists and turns that happen throughout the story?**

With lots and lots of note cards! It was really challenging to be writing a dual timeline and then weave it all together. It helped to have a clear vision for how the book would end, and I knew the ending pretty early on. From there, I mapped out Claire's and Eva's story arcs—what I wanted each of them to overcome, what I wanted each of them to learn.

**What is the importance of female friendship in a narrative like this one? Have you found friendship with women to be just as important in your life as it is in Eva's and Claire's?**

Female friendship is incredibly important in this story. We can all think about that one friend who showed up right when we needed her, giving us exactly what we needed to push us forward. I have been lucky enough to have some amazing female friendships. And as a single mother, it's especially important to have those touchstones. My friends keep me sane. They make me laugh. They listen to what I'm struggling with and step in to help in innumerable ways. Humans are, by nature, social animals. And while I'm a dedicated introvert, I rely on my friends every day.

**Why did you decide to set a thriller in Berkeley?**

After college, I landed a job in the Cal Athletic Department. I worked in fundraising, so I spent a lot of time at Memorial Stadium, as well as Harmon Gym (which would later become Haas Pavilion). It was the best job for a just-graduated-from-college person who wasn't entirely sure she was ready to have a "real job" yet. I loved my years in Berkeley, made many great friends there, and often dream of moving back someday. I decided to set *The Flight* in Berkeley so I could revisit it in my imagination. Go Bears!

**What are you hoping readers gain from *The Flight*?**

I want readers to be inspired by the courage of both Claire and Eva, who did what felt impossible to each of them. No matter the circumstances, there's a way out. As Claire's mother put it: *If you pay attention, solutions always appear. But you have to be brave enough to see them.*

# ACKNOWLEDGMENTS

My deepest gratitude first goes to the entire Sourcebooks family: publisher and chief book champion Dominique Raccah; my brilliant and supportive editor, Shana Drehs; the marketing and promotions teams (including Tiffany Schultz and Heather Moore); the talented art and production departments (Heather Hall, Holli Roach, Ashley Holstrom, Kelly Lawler, and Sarah Cardillo); and the formidable sales team. It's been a joy to have met so many of you: Cristina Arreola, Liz Kelsch, Kay Birkner, Todd Stocke, Margaret Coffee, Valerie Pierce, and Michael Leali. Thank you for taking *The Flight* into your capable hands and building buzz around the book. It is true that books change lives, but you do too.

A heartfelt thank-you to my beloved agent, Mollie Glick, who stood behind me as I wrestled this book into existence, who believed in it, and in me. And a thank-you to her many assistants (Sam, Emily, Julie, Lola...) who also read and offered feedback and support.

Thank you to my foreign rights team, who have enthusiastically introduced *The Flight* to the wider world. And to my film agents, Jiah Shin and Berni Barta, thank you for championing this project in Hollywood. Deepest appreciation also goes to my publicist, Gretchen Koss of Tandem Literary, not only for her brilliance in marketing and promotions, but also for her expert hand-holding. There is nothing better than getting an email from Gretchen that reads "Don't worry about a thing. I've got this."

*The Flight* wouldn't be what it is today without the support of my writing partners, Aimee and Liz. You both read multiple versions of this book and saw right from the start what I was trying to accomplish. I adore you both. And a special shout-out to the brilliant freelance editor Nancy Rawlinson who helped push *The Flight* that final mile to completion.

Thank you to my beta readers and friends: Amy Mason Doan, Helen Hoang, Julie Carrick Dalton, Lara Lillibridge, Robinne Lee, Jennifer Caloyeras. All of whom said, "You have something here. Keep going."

Thanks to my lifelong friend Todd Kusserow for talking me through federal drug investigations, burner phones, and explaining how a person might obtain a flawless forged identification package. I love our conversations, our text exchanges, and I adore you. Thank you to John Ziegler, who helped me think through all things airport and air travel. This whole book is based on the possibility that two people could swap tickets at the gate, and John helped me nail that down. And a shout-out to Gloria Nevarez, commissioner of the West Coast Conference and long-time laughing buddy, for chiming in last minute with some very important details about NCAA basketball. It made me painfully aware of how long ago our time together in Berkeley was that I couldn't remember these details myself.

Thank you to the talented and engaging Instagram book reviewer Kate Lane for letting me use her name in the book and for her continued support of *The Flight*. I hope I've portrayed someone as smart and as lovely as she is. Make sure to follow her at @katelynreadsbooks_ because she has the best book recommendations. And my heartfelt gratitude to all the online book champions—the Facebook groups and Bookstagrammers devoted to reading and supporting authors. You make our job promoting our books so much easier and more fun.

Thank you to my parents, whose support and schedule shuffling has given me the time and space to write and publish a second book. And to my kids, Alex and Ben, who both continue to inspire and amaze me. I love you.

And finally, thank you to the University of California, Berkley, a place I hold close to my heart, and the friends I made there (I'm looking at you, Joan Herriges and Ben Turman). I loved revisiting my time at Cal and portraying what I love best about it on the page. Go Bears!

# ABOUT THE AUTHOR

Born and raised in Santa Monica, California, Julie Clark grew up reading books on the beach while everyone else surfed. After attending college at University of the Pacific, she returned home to Santa Monica to teach. She now lives there with her two young sons and a goldendoodle with poor impulse control. Her debut novel *The Ones We Choose* was published in 2018 and has been optioned for television by Lionsgate. Visit her online at facebook.com/julieclarkbooks, Twitter @jclarkab, and Instagram @julieclarkauthor.